Dancers in the Dark

Dancers in the Dark

Howard Dando

Writers Club Press
San Jose New York Lincoln Shanghai

Dancers in the Dark

Writers Club Press
an imprint of iUniverse.com, Inc.

For information address:
iUniverse.com, Inc.
5220 S 16th, Ste. 200
Lincoln, NE 68512
www.iuniverse.com

ISBN: 0-595-17861-8

Printed in the United States of America

Dedicated to Debra, Judy, Georgeann and Bob, and my family and friends for their faith and support.

"O body swayed to music, O brightening glance,
How can we know the dancer from the dance?"
W.B. Yeats

CHAPTER I

The senior class of Grand Chenier High circled the Prom King and Queen, clapping to the beat of pounding hip-hop music. Billy whirled Temple, faster and faster around the dance floor until a pint of whiskey stirred in his brain. He grabbed Temple's shoulder, but the dance hall suddenly swirled in a vortex of spinning red and yellow lights. Billy slipped and splayed on the floor. The crowd hooted. They had seen it before. Billy LaVoi, the star quarterback, had led the school to an undefeated season, and at every victory party he was the first to pass out.

Johnny Muskoke, a three hundred pound Catawba Indian, hoisted his teammate up and carried Billy out of the dance hall and down to the dock. Johnny propped Billy at the front of the boat and Temple wrapped a white shawl around Billy's broad shoulders.

Johnny took Temple's thin, white hand into his huge bear claw. "He's broken up about you leaving."

"You're still looking out for him."

"That's what linesmen do for their Quarterback." Johnny stepped out of the boat. "Be careful out there, kid."

"Johnny, you know I've run the backwaters all my life."

"I mean up there." Johnny waved vaguely to the north. "And don't forget where you came from."

Temple Drake watched Johnny depart and vanish into the dance hall. In the distance she heard the sweet, lush melody of *This Magic Moment*, one of her favorites. When the song ended, she pushed an oar against the dock, and headed in the direction of a yellow moon that sat on the black swamp. Temple breathed in the seductive scents of Jasmine that grew wild along the marshy riverbank of the Bayou.

When she came to the Grand Chenier channel she pulled in the oars and let the current drift her home. The music had faded, and the only sound was water gently lapping the boat. A mist was rolling in from the sea, curling clouds over the water. Surrounded by blackness with only stars above, Temple felt aloft on a celestial raft in a diamond sky.

She slid her hands softly down her scarlet satin gown, cool to the touch, yet soft and silky against her legs. She had made the dress herself, it took nearly a month, but it was worth it, even if only for a few hours. Nobody had ever seen her in anything other than blue jeans. The low cut dress surprised those who thought she had no breasts, since she habitually wore oversized T-shirts and jackets. She had cheated a little, sewing some extra padding underneath the cups of the bodice. It worked like magic. Boys on the dance floor positioned themselves for a peek at her pert breasts. She arranged her loose blond curls on the sides of her face to frame her clear green eyes and transform herself into a bewitching Southern Belle.

A sultry June night such as this could have conjured up a wicked potion of Louisiana lust, but Billy was asleep, sprawled at the front of the boat. Temple held a lantern over his head. The glow on his face, and the white shawl around his body made him look ghostly.

She had known Billy since they were kids. Billy the brat delighted in putting spiders and other insects in her sandwiches. In Junior High he once hid a baby alligator in her backpack. She hated him with a passion until High School when Temple fell in lust with Billy's thick, black hair, and the Elvis Presley curl of his upper lip.

Billy's folks were once poor potato farmers until oil gushed from their land. After that Billy was the catch of the county, and marrying him was a guarantee to the good life. But that was not enough to keep Temple home.

She did not need a crystal ball to foretell what a future with Billy would bring. He had never said or done anything that was not absolutely and totally predictable, if he had, there was an outside chance Temple would have given up her dream, fallen into his arms and stayed.

And there was no way Billy would go with her to New York City. For Billy to move out of Grand Chenier was unthinkable. The LaVoi family had lived in Louisiana before the Civil War, they were mangrove trees with branches that formed vines that grew and spread into the swamp water and formed deeper roots. But Temple was a river, running unchecked, full of capricious twists and turns leading to inlets of dark lagoons and secret hiding places.

Billy rubbed his eyes and looked at Temple. "Hey, Princess."

Temple unpinned her tiara. "Oh, this silly thing."

"It suits you. I've never seen you look so pretty."

"Thanks, but Cinderella has left the ball."

"I guess I really tied one on." Billy suddenly stood, causing the boat to wobble wildly. Billy lost his balance, and was about to tip over when Temple caught him.

"Billy, for God's sake, you'll capsize the boat."

Temple cupped her hand into the water and splashed Billy's face. The shock of cold water woke him. He stumbled to the bench beside Temple, reached into a pocket, and pulled out a small, black velvet box, and opened it. By the lantern light the diamond ring flickered like a swarm of fireflies.

Temple could hardly breath, "Billy, you know I can't."

"I know you're the only one for me. Come on, sugar, marry me."

"Billy, you will always be in my heart, always. But there is something I wanted all my life. Please try and understand." Billy put his head down. Temple brushed his hair. "If it doesn't work out...maybe I'll be back."

She knew that was a lie, a whopper. Temple had resolved never go back, no matter what, even if she had to sweep sidewalks. She wanted her life to be more than the weekly regimen of Grand Chenier: the

Friday night High School Football game, the Saturday night at the Grand Cinema, Sunday night at Prima's Pizza, Monday Night Football, Tuesday night TV, the Wednesday night clam bake, and the worst night of all, Thursday night dinner with the in-laws.

Temple returned the box. Billy pushed it back. "Come on, take it."

"No!" Temple forced the ring into his hand, and looked out into the darkness.

Billy snapped the box closed, and stood on the bench. "Hell! If you don't want it, then let the Bayou have it." Billy brought his arm back, and threw a fifty-yard pass into the swamp.

"Billy! No!" Temple jumped up to grab his arm, but too late, the box soared out of sight. Billy teetered on the boat. The boat lurched wildly. Billy fell forward and clutched at Temple, but the satin fabric of her dress slipped through his hands, and he splashed into the swamp.

"Billy, Billy!"

Billy's head bobbed to the surface, seaweed and vines entwined in his hair. Temple put her hands to her mouth, tried to stifle a smile, but could not, and laughed uncontrollably.

"What's so damn funny?"

"I never thought you would do something so crazy."

Another splash was heard in the water. Temple screamed, "Billy, get in. Hurry."

Billy heard the panic in her voice, and recognized the danger. He swam madly to the boat, grabbing its side, and putting one leg over the boat. Temple struggled to haul him inside, when she saw the gator head for Billy's dangling leg. She picked up an oar, and swung madly, hitting the creature on the snout. It stunned the alligator long enough for Billy to fling his whole body into the boat. Temple picked up the closest thing, her tiara, and threw it at the gator. It bounced off his head and into the water. The gator slinked away.

Temple and Billy collapsed on the floor of the boat, gasping for breath. For a long time, Temple held the oar, to stop her hands from shaking. When her pulse had stopped racing, she let go the oar, and released a soft, quiet cry. Billy crawled to her.

"Baby, it's all right." He took her in his arms. She snuggled her face in his neck. "It's all right."

"That was so reckless."

"Sorry."

"But so…romantic."

"Yeah, it was, wasn't it? So come on, marry me."

Temple smiled. "I can't now, there's no ring."

Billy reached into his pants, and pulled out the ring. "Presto!"

The smile left Temple's face. "You took out the ring and threw away the box."

"Well sure. You think I'm crazy?" Billy slid the ring on her finger.

Temple tried to slip the ring off, but Billy stopped her. "No, I can't. Take it back, please."

"I can't. I got it for you. I'm not going to put it on someone else and always be thinking of you. Besides you saved my life tonight. It's a token of my thanks. Maybe some day it might bring you good luck." Billy slid the ring on her finger.

Temple felt the strings tugging on her heart, the strings that could keep her from her dreams. She held back the tears and would not cry, she would not let the vines of the mangrove trees drag her into the black swamp of the Bayou.

The boat nudged at Temple's dock. Temple took off her high heels and climbed an old wooden ladder. On top of the dock she knelt down, kissed Billy on the mouth, a smoldering, 'you'll-never-forget-me-kiss.'

Billy cupped his hands around her waist. Temple felt a rush of arousal through her body. She gripped his hair and pushed his face to her neck. He kissed her softly then bit into her neck. She whimpered slightly then groaned as Billy pulled away enough fabric to expose her shoulder. His tongue, wet and warm, then encircled her neck. She jerked her head back. The sudden movement made the boat sway under Billy's feet. He grasped her tightly, and pulled her towards him.

"This is our last night, babe, let's make it unforgettable."

Temple placed her shoes on the dock, and climbed down the ladder. Temple entangled her arms firmly around the ladder. With one foot she pushed hard, the boat rocked wildly into the channel.

"Good night, Billy."

"Why'd you do that?"

"So that we'll have this passion whenever we think of each other."

"I don't get it."

"One day you will."

Billy knew the battle was lost, all that was left was the formality of surrender. "How 'bout I see you off tomorrow?"

"No, let this be our last memory."

"Damn!" Billy dipped his oars into the water, and called as he drifted away. "I'll always love you, Temple. And I hate you for it."

Temple stood on the dock, silhouetted by a large yellow moon, she blew a final kiss, and waved as Billy disappeared into a river of flickering golden moonbeams.

CHAPTER 2

Temple Drake stood at the front of the subway. Her hands tightly gripped two metal bars as the train snaked through the tunnel, screeching and careening back and forth on winding tracks. She watched the black tunnel illuminated for a few seconds from the white sparks of the train's steel wheels. Concrete pillars in the tunnel were rooted deep in murky brown water. It reminded her of the mangrove trees in the swamps and that make her think of Billy. She closed her eyes, and reproached herself not to look back.

A muffled voice from a loudspeaker shouted, "Spring Street. Let'em out, please." Temple slung her backpack over her shoulder. The doors opened and she was sucked out of the train by the crowd, whisked up a flight of stairs, and deposited on the sidewalks of New York City.

The sunlight was blinding. She shaded her eyes to read a map; but it seemed incomprehensible, little boxes with lots of squiggly colored lines running amuck. She was about to ask for directions, but she heard her Aunt's voice, "In New York they kidnap young girls, then sell them into Harems and they're never heard from again." Playing it safe, Temple walked straight ahead, if after five blocks Mercer Street did not intersect Spring Street she would then know she had to gone in the wrong direction.

Spring Street was a bazaar of sidewalk salesmen, vendors hawking Yankee baseball caps, walkmans, MP3's, sunglasses, toys, belts and plastic jewelry. Temple walked by the black, wrought iron doors of La Grille; the cafe doors were open and inside a young bartender in a crisp white shirt with red suspenders smiled at her. Temple smiled back, then quickly turned her head, thinking it not proper to flirt with the first good-looking man she saw in New York.

She peaked through the window of a Boutique where a gaggle of secretaries rifled through racks of leather skirts. The chattering secretaries hardly ruffled the trance of a salesgirl with orange hair and skin the color of tofu. The salesgirl leaned casually against the door and scanned Temple's outfit, a pale yellow, puckered cotton dress with a stiff white collar.

Temple looked at the salesgirl's flimsy long black dress with combat boots, then looked down at her white flats, realized she looked like a tourist, shrugged, and continued walking along the street passing more jewelry stands. She stopped to look at a pair of earrings. The vendor, a short, ruddy-faced man with a missing tooth turned to his friends, and spoke from the side of his mouth, "Real gold, little girl?"

There was a genuine insincerity in his voice, and Temple returned the earrings and resolved to have nothing more with street vendors, until she reached the corner. There in front of her was a wide brimmed straw hat with a brown band with white polka dots. The same hat Julia Roberts wore in 'Pretty Woman.'

She tried it on and looked at herself in a hand mirror. It made her look and feel sophisticated.

"How much?"

"Forty bucks."

She would negotiate the way she haggled at the fish market in Grand Chenier. "I only got twenty."

"Then you ain't got a hat, Miss."

She poured extra syrup on her Southern accent, "Surely, you could part with this hat for twenty dollars."

"Surely, you could be arrested if you don't put it back."

Temple admired herself from another angle then advanced to another tactic. "The sun is baking my brain. I could die on this street of heat exhaustion without a hat. Can't you find it in your heart to help a hot and hatless visitor to your fine city."

"Stop! Stop, all ready! What are you an actress?"

"Oh, no, a dancer."

"A dancer in New York City? What are the odds of finding a dancer in New York City?" The vendor laughed. "You're good, sweetheart. OK! Take the damn hat. Twenty bucks."

Temple gladly handed him the money. "You are so nice. When I become famous I'll write about you in my autobiography."

"Write what? About the poor schnook who went broke giving away hats. You keep me out of your book, or I'll sue you."

Temple laughed and started to walk away but stopped. She reached into her jeans, and pulled out another twenty-dollar bill. "Here."

"What's this?"

"What I did was shameless. Please take it."

The vendor shook his head. "Sorry kid, all sales are final."

"No really. Please."

The vendor pushed the money back. "When I was your age I was something of a piano player. Then I met a girl. Then came a little one, and then another one, and another one, and another one. Now I sell hats. You got a dream, right?" Temple nodded. "Then go for it! Now get out of here before I double the price."

Temple winked. "If only you were not a married man."

"Who said I was married?" Temple, caught by surprise, put her hand over her chest. "Hey, I'm joking."

"Oh, of course. Well, thanks."

"Forget it. It's my humble frame for a beautiful work of art."

The vendor watched Temple walk down the street, he let out a soft whistle, "I wish it wasn't joking."

Somehow Temple found Mercer Street. She turned right, and in the middle of the block stood St. Mary's Boarding House, a double-width brownstone with two crusty brown columns framing a flight of broken and cracked cement steps. Temple opened the stained glass door, and trotted carefully across the creaking oak floorboards, and put her backpack down at the receptionist desk.

She was eyed through the bifocals of Miss Libby Haig, a gray haired woman with a long face.

"May I help you, dear?"

"I'm Temple Drake."

"Oh, yes, the scholarship student. Welcome to St. Mary's."

In a single motion Miss Haig reached underneath the counter, grabbed a sheet of paper and slid it on the desk.

"These are the House Rules. Breakfast is Eight AM sharp. Dinner is six sharp. I hope you know the meaning of the word 'sharp' or you will be one hungry young lady. Curfew is midnight. No drugs, no alcohol, no boys allowed in the rooms. No loud music at any time. Any deviation will result in the loss of your scholarship. Any questions, Miss Drake?"

"Yes. Where is the room?"

Miss Haig slid a key along the counter. "Room Three Hundred and five. You can take the elevator over there."

Temple picked up her backpacks and heaved them onto her shoulders.

"By the way, Miss Drake."

"Yes."

"It's lovely to see young ladies wearing hats again."

CHAPTER 3

A taxi screeched to a stop in front of St. Mary's.

"For God sake, driver, you almost missed it."

"But I didn't miss it, lady." The driver looked through the mirror at Ruth Fain, a woman in her late forties, but trim with a chiseled face, a Roman nose and full lips, brown eyes, and dark brown hair cropped around the ears, she wore a tailored navy blue suit.

"That'll be forty-five bucks, lady."

Ruth Fain handed him the money. "You drive like a maniac."

The driver was not interested in what Ruth had to say; he fixed his eyes on the other passenger.

Alison Fain, Ruth's only daughter, had inherited her mother's strong features, but her eyes were blacker with flecks of green light in them, her white skin was a sharp contrast to her jet black hair which she wore loose, letting it fall over the collar of her blue jean denim jacket, underneath her coat was a black halter top displaying more than ample breasts. The ensemble was finished off with black stockings and black boots.

The driver smiled at Alison. "This is a place for dancers. You a dancer, Miss?"

Ruth Fain was delighted her daughter was recognized as a dancer. "Why yes, she is. Do you like the ballet?"

"Are you kidding? That faggy stuff! No friggin' way."

Ruth lost her smile. Alison hopped out of the cab; her mother followed. The driver began to pull bags out of the trunk.

"Mother, it's not necessary to come up."

"Nonsense, I don't mind."

"You have a train to catch?"

"So I'll catch a later train."

"Mother, this is not first day of kindergarten."

A black man on roller skates carrying a boombox, circled Alison, whistled at her slim, muscular body in a short, tight black dress and black combat boots.

"And it's not Disneyland either, baby."

"Mother, I'm eighteen years old, I can handle myself."

Ruth sighed, resigned, and embraced Alison. "I suppose you can. I'll call tonight to make sure you're all right." She kissed Alison on the cheek. "Your father and I are so proud of you."

"Don't be so proud. I haven't made it in the company, mother."

"Don't be silly. Of course you will." Ruth turned to find the driver holding two suitcases and leering at Alison. "You can leave the bags, driver."

"No trouble, I'll help the little girl with these."

"You heard her. She can take care of herself. And you can take me back to Penn Station."

Alison dropped her suitcases at the receptionist's desk with a thud.

"A reservation for Alison Fain."

Miss Haig looked at Allison's semi-gothic attire and her mouth puckered as if she had just sucked a lemon. She slapped a paper on the desk. "These are the House Rules. We expect you to conduct yourself like a lady."

"Right. Can I have my key?"

Miss Haig pushed the key to Allison. "Room 305. You're roommate arrived a few minutes ago."

"Roommate? Hold on. I didn't ask for a roommate."

"You may not have asked, Miss Fain, but all our girls have roommates. That is our policy."

"Is it. Well, I'll be damned."

"No profanity, please."

Allison picked up her suitcases, and started to the elevator.

"Miss Fain, are you forgetting something."

"What, to say 'may I?'"

"The house rules." Miss Haig held out the paper.

Allison holding on to her suitcase, took the paper, put it in her mouth and held it between her teeth.

Allison waited for the elevator. In the mirror above the elevator she could see Miss Haig turn her back. Allison took the sheet of rules crumpled the paper, tossed it into the trashcan, and stepped into the elevator.

Allison twisted and turned the key in the lock, but it was locked from within; she pounded on the door.

Temple, half undressed, covering herself with a towel, opened the door a crack. "Yes?"

"Room service."

"Oh, I didn't order anything."

Allison laughed. "You think this is the Plaza. I'm you're new roommate. Open up, for God's sake!"

"Oh, sorry. Please, let me help you with your bags."

Allison strode in the room. Temple extended her hand. "I'm Temple Drake, pleased to meet you."

"Allison Fain," Allison wheeled three hundred and sixty degrees to check the room.

It was a small square chamber decorated with wallpaper of tiny bouquets of red roses against a background of moss green. A mahogany chest, carved with initials of former residents, stood between two beds that were opposite a mushroom colored stuffed chair. "What a dump." Allison dropped her suitcases on the floor.

Allison looked out the window. "Well, lookee here. This dump does have one amenity."

"What's that?"

"The fire escape leads down to the backdoor of Howard Johnson's which happens to be open twenty-four hours a day."

"In case of fire?"

"In case of fire!" Allison laughed a laugh that came from the wind-pipe, but landed in the nose resulting in something between a snort and a sneeze. Allison laughed so hard she landed on the bed.

"No, you ninny. In case of…men!"

Temple sat across her on the other bed. "I see. Well, I'm not here to date."

"You don't have to date to get laid. You understand this is a boarding house not a convent. You don't take a vow of chastity."

"I'm not looking to get involved."

"You're gonna lock your legs in fifth position all summer…" Allison rolled on her back, and kicked open her legs, "when second position feels so good."

Temple inched backwards. "Are you some kind of pervert?"

"Why as a matter of fact, yes…I am." Alison flicked her tongue.

Temple turned quickly to continue unpacking her own suitcase.

"Hey, I'm just fooling." Allison picked up Temple's new hat from the bed. "Hey, we can play Frisbee with this hat."

"Please put that down."

"Nobody wears hats under the age of eighty."

Temple picked up the phone on the night table.

"Who are you calling, the hat police?"

"I'm calling to have my room changed."

"All right, all right. I'm putting down the hat." Temple hung up the phone. "Sorry, I didn't realize you have no sense of humor. Here, I'll help you unpack."

"No thanks."

"I'm not going to steal your panties."

Allison sat on the bed beside Temple. "Is that Scarlet O'Hara accent for real?"

"What accent?"

Allison stopped for a second, smiled, "You got me on that one."

"Is that a Brooklyn accent?" Temple retorted.

Alison stiffened. "No, it is not. My family moved out of Brooklyn when I was a kid. I took speech classes in high school. So I don't have any accent. OK?"

"OK, sure. Sorry."

"So where you taking class?"

"I'm on scholarship with the National."

"Oh, yeah, me too."

Temple, genuinely surprised, tried not to show it. "You're a dancer?"

"What'd you think, kid? This is a boarding house for bun heads." Allison noticed Temple hair was up in a bun. "Oh, no offense."

"You mean everybody in this place is a dancer?"

"Yeah, plus another three or four hundred girls going for openings in the company.

"God! So many?"

"Well, yeah. Did you think it was like getting a job at Macys? Do you have any idea what your odds are of getting in?"

"As good as anyone else, I guess." Temple shrugged. "But if I don't make it I'll try out for smaller companies, or I'll get an agent and try for soaps, or commercials, or I'll do extra work, anything, waitress work if I have to. Anything to stay in New York. What about you, what's your plan?"

"To get in the company, of course."

"So I'm a long shot, but you're getting in. You're pretty confident."

"Actually, I'm pretty great." Allison rolled on her back and kicked her long muscular legs in little *scissons*.

"Well, I'll have to watch for you in class."

"And I'll be looking at you, kid." Allison, her head upside down, made her hand into a pistol, fired a round at Temple, and blew the smoke from her fingertips.

CHAPTER 4

Dancers in the National Ballet's Studio warmed up for class by extending their muscles, curling their legs behind their heads, twisting and contorting their bodies on the floor like dying cockroaches. Temple walked to a rear corner of the studio and deposited her ballet bag. She lifted one ankle on the wooden barre, and stretched the muscles in her slender but powerful legs. Satisfied her muscles were limber, she concentrated on plies. She glanced, neither to the right or left, but focused her eyes on the body in the mirror, and watched her long legs come perfectly to an arch as legs began to bend and straighten in a series of perfect plies. Tiny beads of sweat glistened on her pale blue leotard. A few strands of fine gold hair came loose from a tight chignon and wisped lightly over her swan-like neck.

Temple felt other eyes watching her. Eyes that judged the line of her body, the curve of her instep, the arch of her foot, the delicacy of her hands, the flatness of her stomach, the slimness of her hips, the gracefulness of her arms. She knew she was getting high ratings, and the higher the rating the greater the threat. Every girl in the studio wanted the same thing. Temple did not look back at her jury, but snuck a glance at the clock. Five minutes before her first class in New York, the moment she had dreamed about since she was eight. She would have to be on. Nerves began to take over, her heart pounded in her chest like a jackhammer; her palms were dripping wet as she gripped the barre.

"Concentrate," she encouraged herself. "Think of what your body is doing. *Tendu.* Starting right, and one, and two and three and—"

She felt a slap on her bottom, and turned quickly to see Allison smiling.

"Keep your hips in, for Christ's sake."

Temple was as surprised by the slap as she was by looking at Allison. Could this be the same girl who yesterday looked like a Hell's Angel?

Allison had decorated her hair with tiny baby breath flowers encircling her lustrous, black hair. She wore a pink leotard and tights with a transparent, filmy pink shirt. Her make-up was impeccable, and enhanced with diamond stud earrings.

Penny Dennison, a former Principal of the National Ballet, clapped her hands. Dancers assembled in straight lines at the barre. Temple positioned herself at the front, but Alison found an extra inch at the barre to nudge herself in front of Temple.

To anyone walking in off the street, all the girls resembled each other, all slim and pretty with long necks. But Temple could easily see the differences between herself and Allison. Temple's muscles, although strong as steel, looked soft and fluent. She was a 'romantic' dancer, trained in traditional tutu ballets like *Les Sylphides* or *Spectre de la Rose*. Allison had tight, rippling muscles: a back chiseled in white alabaster, thighs sharply etched, arms assertive, and fingers long and thin like scissors. Years of training shaped her body to dance the sharp, angular, discordant ballets of Stravinsky and Balanchine.

After warm-up, the class moved to the center of the studio for the next test. Many girls looked like ballerinas at the barre, only to flutter like birds with broken wings in the center of the floor.

Miss Dennison introduced the first combination, a dizzying assortment of jumps and turns. Many girls could not execute the steps; some could not even follow the combination. Timidly, a few girls slipped to the back of the room, gathered their ballet bags, and sneaked out of the studio.

Allison had no trouble performing the combination, looking almost bored, as if flaunting her technique. Temple had difficulty with a pique turn; her foot slipped causing her to jiggle her body so as not to fall out. A slight mistake, but she was able to finish.

Allison was invited to the front of the class to demonstrate the next combination, a series of *glissades*, quick gliding steps, and *bourees*, and fast little steps with the feet close together like the stitches of a sewing machine. Miss Dennison instructed the pianist to play at triple speed. A tempo impossible for a few more girls who grabbed their ballet bags and headed for the nearest exit. Temple breathed easier, it was a combination similar to the first act of *Raymonda*, a piece she had danced in a recital.

Allison had difficulty with the fleet footed steps and lagged hopelessly behind the beat. Miss Dennison slapped her hands together. "Stop, stop." She peered through the lines of girls. "You!" Heads turned to the back of the room and focused on Temple. "The blue leotard. Yes, you, come here."

Temple inched her way to the front. Allison shuffled off to a side of the room.

"Show how it should be done." Miss Dennison nodded to the pianist. Temple performed the steps exquisitely.

Miss Dennison applauded. "See, girls, it's not just steps, this is dancing."

In the dressing room Allison began to untie the pink ribbons of her toe shoes. Behind her, two girls opened lockers and began shedding their leotards.

"What a bitch of a class."

"Yeah, I'm going to soak in a hot bath for two days."

"Are you coming back tomorrow?"

"Why bother, you saw the competition."

"Yeah, and how about the technique of that one girl."

"And her legs and feet. I could kill myself."

"Or her." Both girls laughed.

Allison pricked up her ears, smiled secretly, thinking they were talking about her.

"And so pretty."

"And blond, no less."

In one sharp movement, Allison ripped the ribbon from her shoe.

CHAPTER 5

In the next few weeks of summer the National Ballet slashed the candidates from three hundred to fifty. Temple and Allison lasted the early rounds of cuts, and despite the heat of competition they became friends. Although it was not spoken, both girls felt the head to head rivalry. But simple mathematics was hard to ignore. From the remaining fifty students the National, one of elite companies of the world, would select only two dancers for the corps de ballet.

Temple and Allison were rumored to be among the top five candidates. Their years of hard study were evident, although they were schooled in different styles; both were products of impeccable training.

Allison was trained at her mother's school, The Ruth Fain School of Dance and Tap. Ruth was a gifted teacher, and once a dancer with a promise of a professional career, until she met and married Dominic Fainucci, a name Ruth had shortened when Allison was born. Dominic was a dashing Italian when Ruth first met him, but as he grew older his face widened as round as a Bottici ball, and his belly inflated like a beach ball. He arrived in American when he was sixteen, by twenty he opened his first pizza shop, by thirty it grew to a chain of fifteen. With success came a move from a Brooklyn apartment to a mansion in Great Neck, Long Island, with a swimming pool, tennis court, a rose arbor, and two Mercedes.

He underwrote Ruth's ballet school, which he considered a nice hobby, as long as Ruth was home to cook pasta dinners. Dominic assumed Allison would dance for a time, but then marry and bring him grandchildren to play on the tennis court.

Ruth had other plans. She married on Domenic's condition that she give up dancing. She traded her career for security, she would be a good wife, mother and cook. At the time those were the choices in a world that offered few choices. But she knew there was more, and her Allison would have it. Allison would be a dancer who received applause, flowers strewn at her feet, who traveled, wore furs, and rode in limousines. Ruth fed Allison on those dreams, and Allison ate them up with her mother's peanut butter and jelly sandwiches.

Temple had a less direct path to the world of ballet. Her father, Matt, was a drummer in local New Orleans blues bands. He had long blond hair and sparkling green eyes, but his soul had a darker side, he was laughing one minute, cursing the next. He made extra money passing cocaine around the bands, but soon lost those profits in private poker games.

Temple's mother, fed up with life on the downside, packed out when Temple was five, after that there was a long progression of 'aunts.' Temple had learned sex from peeking through the keyhole. Her father caught her and wanted Temple out from underfoot. One of the aunts, 'Aunt' Catherine, took her to a ballet matinee. It was there Catherine suggested that Temple take ballet lessons.

From the first class Temple was captivated. She loved the patches of yellow light on the sanded oak floors, the musty smell of rosin, the comforting tinkling of the piano. The studio was a private world; a safe world rivaled only by Temple's love of her father.

Her first recital was at the Grand Chenier High School Auditorium. It was a concoction of ballet classics, *Swan Lake Pas de Deux, Sleeping Beauty Pas de Deux,* and so on. There were no males in the dance program so the girls had to be Prince Siegfried or Prince Florimund. Temple was given one of the leads and was sewn into a green body suit and green tulle skirt that made he look like a dancing umbrella. She was at the back of the stage with dozens of other girls, but even then she could feel the heated pulse of the audience, and it was electrifying. At that moment she knew this was her destiny.

Temple was only fourteen when her father died of an overdose of cocaine and heroin. They tried to keep the cause of death hidden from Temple. But Temple overheard the kids from school talking about how her father stole a kilo of coke from the mob, got caught and committed suicide before he was to be killed.

Dance was the only other thing in Temple's life that she loved. So she clung to dance desperately, afraid to let go and be left with nothing. At the age of fourteen her only one love was her only ambition—to be a dancer.

There was only one week left before the final auditions. The days of summer were a blurred memory. It was all work, five hours of classes plus an adagio-partner class. Each day was aches and pains, and Temple and Allison pushed their bodies harder and harder. If Temple learned a new step, Allison had it mastered by the end of the day. Neither girl wanted to lose an inch to the other.

They were together all day, and yet could not satisfy their appetite for dance, and spent every night in the theatre. They saw the American Ballet Theatre, the New York City Ballet, the Bolshoi, and the Royal Ballet of London, Paul Taylor, Martha Graham, Joffrey, the Dance Theatre of Harlem, Alvin Ailey, and all the companies and all the stars.

By the end of August Allison ran out of ticket money. Her father would send no more. So Allison expanded, in a more deliberate way, her plan to get to know somebody in every dance company. Men preferably. Free tickets and invitations to watch from backstage were part of the deal that often included midnight rambles down the fire escape.

Once in the room, the girls exchanged reports about a glance thrown them by one of the male stars, a Warren Ashley or a Christopher Beckett. They drooled over photographs in souvenir books like groupies over rock stars.

"Allison, I would give anything to dance on stage with Christopher Beckett."

"I'd rather be in bed with him."

"Is that all you think about? There's more to life than—"

"Save the sermon for Sundays, prune face, I got a date. Bye."

Allison carefully slipped out the window, trying not to tear her stocking on the rusty fire escape, and disappeared into the night.

The last days of August were sizzlers; temperatures soared to ninety-five degrees converting the studio into a sauna. From open windows came black fumes from buses and trucks, a large metal fan scarcely stirred a breeze to cool fifty sweating students.

Miss Dennison suddenly stopped class. "Girls, we have a special treat today, a guest teacher for center work."

Juri Agarte, short and dark with curly black hair, walked into the studio with his two Yorkshire terriers. Applause immediately encircled the room.

"Thank you, ladies. A pleasure to be here. Hopefully I will see some of you in my ballets one day. Shall we begin? On *pointe*, arms out, and *tendu* left, and…"

After class the students applauded, then rushed out of the doors to the corridors. Allison and Temple flopped on a bench. Temple took off her pointe shoes, and looked at her feet.

"Damn, they're bleeding."

"Here." Allison reached into her ballet bag for a wad of cotton. "Stuff this in the shank of your shoes. It dries the blood, and you're feet won't cut as bad."

Juri walked past the girls, petting his dogs and absorbed in an intense conversation with Miss Dennison.

Allison leaned over to Temple. "So who's the dog face?"

"Where have you been? He's the hottest choreographer in New York,"

"Choreographer? His combinations were crap."

"For your information that 'Dog face' is also on the audition panel."

"Really?"

"Oh, I meant to give you a little tip. When you're in port de bras hold your hands tighter, not flopping around like they do at Center Ballet."

"Yeah, thanks, I'll remember." Allison stood quickly. "Listen, I'm cutting Vulkova's adagio class."

"What? Nobody cuts her class."

"Do me a favor, tell her…it's that time of the month."

"Wednesday?"

Allison hurried down the corridor to the dressing room, flipped off her toe shoes, wrapped a skirt around her waist and hastened for the street.

She saw Juri waiting for his dogs to pee on the tire of a parked car. She walked to the end of the block, crossed the street and then walked back in the opposite direction. She stopped and bent down to pet the dogs.

"What adorable little doggies."

One of the Yorkies snapped at her finger; Allison withdrew it barely in time. "They must not like dancers."

"Are you a dancer?"

"I was in your class today."

"Sorry, there were so many girls. I am Juri Agarte."

Allison extended her hand. "Allison Fain."

"You live around here?"

"Down the street at St. Mary's."

"Maybe some day when I walking dogs, I'll stop in, and we'll have a drink."

"Oh, but they don't allow men."

"Well, that is too bad, isn't it. Nice to meet you, Miss Fain." He picked up his dogs. "Come on, boys." He started to walk away.

"But…there is…a fire escape."

"Excuse me?"

"A fire escape. It goes up as well as down."

Juri smiled.

Chapter 6

"You're sure you don't feel well enough." Temple had her hand on the doorknob.

"Temple, I'm sure. You go."

"But City Ballet is doing *Barocco*."

"Yeah, I know. I'd love to see it, but I'll listen to the music on my Walkman, and run the steps in my head."

"You sure you'll be all right?"

"I'm sure. I'm sure. Now go, or you'll be late."

"I'll tell you all about it when I get back."

"I can't wait. Go!"

Allison closed the door behind Temple. She rushed to the vanity table, and took out her makeup bag.

The door opened. Temple stuck her head in the room. "And thanks again for the ticket."

"My pleasure. Enjoy."

Temple saw the make-up kit scattered on the table. "What…what are you doing with your make-up kit."

"Oh, just sorting things for tomorrow."

"Worry about that tomorrow, and get to bed."

"I will. I will. Temple, go!"

"OK, Good night."

Temple closed the door, in a New York minute Allison slapped on a fast face. She was in the middle of brushing her hair when she heard the rattle of the fire escape. She quickly cursed, then dashed to the closet, and slipped on a slinky dress. She grabbed a new pair of high heels, and ran to the window in time to see Juri Agarte struggling through the window while holding two Yorkshire terriers.

"I feel like a burglar."

He put the dogs on the floor and took Allison in his arms. "And you look so delectable."

Scherzo, one of the dogs, growled at Allison.

Juri put his hand behind Allison's head, and brought her lips to his, and kissed her passionately.

Scherzo nipped Allison on her big toe. Allison screamed and fell back on the bed. Justin grabbed Scherzo.

"Scherzo, bad doggie. Don't be jealous." The other dog growled; Juri picked him up. "And I love you too, Scherharezade. Yes, I do. Oh, yes I do." Juri kissed Scherharezade on the mouth. He put the dogs on the floor, but they jumped on the bed, both barking at Allison. Allison jumped up. Juri put them back on the floor, and knelt on the bed, kissing Allison.

"Juri, you have to do something."

"They'll stop barking in a few minutes."

"In a few minutes I'll be thrown out of here."

Juri looked around the room, and saw a pair of toe shoes on Temple's bed. He ripped the ribbons from the shoes and tied pink ribbons around the dogs' snouts, and dropped them in the bathroom and closed the door.

"Sorry, darling, they're just not used to another woman."

"Another woman?"

"Victoria, you know…"

"Victoria?"

"Victoria Bennett, my wife."

"The Principle dancer of the National?"

"Yes. Everyone knows we're married."

"I didn't." Allison's first reaction was total incomprehension. She wanted to slap him, but instead found herself standing like a statute in the middle of the room "She doesn't use her married name?"

"No, she kept her stage name."

Juri looked at his watch. "Listen, Allison, I don't have much time."

"But, what if—"

Before she could finish he kissed her neck. His fingers unbuttoned her dress; it slipped off and dropped to the floor. Juri touched her breasts. He cocked his head to one side and smiled.

Allison pushed her hands against him, but Juri put his weight on top of her and they sank on the bed.

"Juri, what if your wife finds out?"

"Are you going to tell her?" Juri smiled.

"No, but word has a way of getting around."

"Only you, me and the dogs know. I can blindfold the dogs if you like."

"But Juri—"

"Don't worry. Everything will be all right."

Allison opened her mouth to speak, but Juri put his mouth on hers, smothering her with a kiss. It didn't take long. He pumped hard and fast; she scarcely had time to realize the sequence. He rose quickly with a raised, red flush on his white neck, and drew on his clothes. In a few minutes he had collected the Yorkies from the bathroom and was gone.

Allison lay naked on the bed, trying to grasp what had just happened. Did she love him? No! She hardly knew him. And he was a married. So, of course not. But he was on the audition committee, and a major choreographer. He could help her. Of course, it was necessary to be talented, hard working, and dedicated, but one must also be practical, if one had the opportunity to have an edge one would be foolish to turn it down. And except for the fact that she was sleeping with someone else's husband, what could be the harm? If a tree fell in the forest and no one was there to hear it does it make a sound? No! So where was the sin if nobody got hurt? Besides he was using her so why shouldn't she use him? Hell! Allison wrapped a sheet around herself. Anyway, she was not bound by some old-fashioned Victorian morality. She was a twenty-first century girl. And Juri was right. Unless the dogs talked, no one would ever find out.

CHAPTER 7

The National studio was a flurry of activity on the last day of auditions, hallways overflowed, and the ladies room was jammed with girls whose intestines gave way to nerves. The fifty finalists warmed up. All were good, and each had a specialty. Some were 'jumpers' who could spring across the floor in a single bound; others were 'turners' who could knock off five pirouettes in a blur; others were elegant 'adagio' dancers with rubber-band bodies that could straighten a leg and hold it perpendicular to their ear.

Temple pinned a sheet with a large number eight on Allison's back. "Temple, I'm going to puke, my stomach's like a volcano. I can't even feel my legs."

"Just relax. What's the worst can happen?"

"How about—not getting in the company."

"So? Your life goes on."

"What life?" Allison looked at Temple as if she escaped from a mental institution. Allison pinned the number seven on Temple's leotard; her fingers slipped and pushed the pin into Temple's back.

"Ouch."

"Sorry."

Temple took her hands. "You're hands are trembling."

"I can't go through with this. I can't."

"Allison, pull yourself together." Temple squeezed her hands tight. Allison looked Temple in the eyes and nodded.

Rebecca Borden, Founder and Artistic Director of the National Ballet, entered the studio, surrounded by a flotilla of clipboard assistants. The finalists lined up in neat rows. Miss Borden held a white poodle in her arm and eyed the dancers like Nero before feeding Christians to the lions. A few seconds later she was followed by Madame Vulkova, once one of the most fragile Giselles of the Kirov Ballet, but over the course of years her body ballooned, and she rolled in the studio like a Russian tank. Miss Dennison and Juri Agarte with his two Yorkies hurried in and took their places at the long table in front of the mirrors.

Vulkova conducted the audition class. It was one of the hardest classes that either Temple or Allison had ever taken. Temple whispered to Allison that she stole the steps from a handbook on Chinese torture. One more minute and Temple muscles would turn to Jell-O.

Miss Vulkova motioned to the pianist to stop. "Ladies, please step outside."

For the next hour Rebecca Borden, Madame Vulkova, Miss Dennison and Juri Agarte shuffled through audition forms. The names of ten semi-finalists were tacked to a wall in the corridor. Girls collected around the notice, most shuffled quietly away; only an occasional muffled moan broke the silence. Allison watched two girls from St. Mary's who had weeks ago confided to Allison that they would not join the company without each other. Allison watched them sling their ballet bags over their shoulders and leave; at least, Allison thought, now they didn't have to worry about being separated.

As the crowd thinned Allison stepped to the notice, and spotted Temple's name at the top of the list. Her heart stopped. Not for a second had she considered the possibility of Temple making it and not herself. If it happened she would not know how to hold her head up ever again. Allison ran her finger down the list. Thank God!

Her name was last on the list.

Allison found Temple sitting on a bench at the farthest end of the corridor. "You haven't looked yet?"

"Too afraid."

"What happened to the courage you had before class?"

"Gone. Well—?"

"I made it!"

Temple closed her eyes and leaned her head back against the wall, holding back the tears. "Well, at least, one of us made it. Allison, I'm so very happy for you." Temple hugged Allison.

"Be happy for yourself."

"What?"

"You made it too."

"I could kill you." Temple put her hands around Allison's throat, then laughed, then cried.

Allison held Temple's face in her hands. "Don't celebrate yet. There's eight more dancers we have to get passed."

The ten finalists were called back to the studio. Madame Vulkova, her chubby arms folded, stood at the front of the studio.

"Ladies, you have all proven you have technique. Now let's see who can dance."

The pianist played an elegant Chopin waltz as Madame Vulkova demonstrated the steps.

Temple was brought center to begin. She danced as graceful as the petals of a flower opening in spring. No one who followed, even Allison, could match Temple.

The final notes of the piano finished; the girls applauded, and retreated to the rear mirrors. A conference gathered around Rebecca Borden. "Well?"

Madame Vulkova was first to respond. "There is no question, Temple Drake has elegance of Kirov dancer."

"Which one is she?"

Vulkova whispered, nodding to the rear of the studio. "Number seven, the blond."

"Oh, yes, she's lovely. Who else?"

Juri was quick to speak. "The girl with the black hair. I believe she's number eight. What's her name?"

One of the clipboard assistants shuffled through papers. "Allison Fain."

"We haven't heard from you." Miss Borden turned her eye to Miss Dennison.

"They're both wonderful."

"Yes, they are, but we can only take one." Rebecca Borden whispered more softly. "Since we will take Julianna Duncan for one of openings."

Miss Dennison's face could not hide her shock. "But she's not anywhere as good as the other two."

"Her father contributed a quarter million dollars to the company last year. He's on the Board of Directors of four major corporations. Conservatively, I would estimate Mr. Duncan could bring ten million dollars to this company in the next five years." There was an immediate silence. "So we have one girl to select."

Miss Dennison spoke up quickly," Then I agree with Madame Vulkova. Temple Drake is the most elegant dancer."

"Yes, she is." Juri interjected, "But how many ballets could we put her in? As you know, we're increasing the number of contemporary ballets this season and decreasing the classical works."

"She can easily adapt to modern with some more training. After a few weeks she would—" Miss Dennison tried to finish.

"Maybe." Juri continued, "But I don't want to take that chance. For my part I could not use now her in any of my ballets. With the budget as tight as it is, I don't think we can afford to carry someone who will not be used in any of the new works."

Rebecca Borden understood budgets, and the need to keep her principal choreographer happy.

"Then it's settled." Rebecca Borden stood. "Ladies, come forward. I wish we could take you all, but we can't. The audition committee has selected the following two girls, Julianna Duncan and…Allison Fain."

Gasped were heard throughout the room. Temple thought she saw Juri lock eyes with Allison and smile.

Miss Borden petted her white poodle. "On behalf of the National Ballet, we thank you, and wish you the best in your future careers."

Temple rushed to hug Allison. Tears ran down Allison's cheeks. "I don't believe it. Oh, God, I made it." Allison took Temple's hand. "But what about you."

"I'm just happy for you, so happy for you."

"You should have made it too. That other girl isn't half as good as you."

"The committee didn't see it that way."

"Temple, what are you going to do now?"

"Somebody will want me." Temple tried to hold it back, but the tears came. Both girls hugged each other and cried, one from the sting of rejection, the other from guilt.

CHAPTER 8

Three weeks before Christmas, snowflakes whirled through Central Park. Icicles clung to the tree and the cornices of building lining Fifth Avenue. Traffic cops held scarves tight against bitter, sharp winds blowing in from the Hudson River. Doormen in circus band uniforms with noses as red as Bowery bums, blew whistles for taxis, then quickly stuck their hands back in pockets.

Even Fifth Avenue dogs—as well bundled as any dog on earth—trotted as fast as their legs could carry them to keep their paws off the frozen pavement. Carriage drivers and their horses waited outside the Plaza hotel; without clients willing to brave a trip through the park, they stood, as motionless as ice sculptures.

Hurried shoppers spun through the revolving brass door at F. O. A. Schwartz, one of New York's leading toy stores. Passerbys looked at its windows with life-sized gorillas, giraffes and jungle cats; miniature, antique doll houses; computer toys, and tiny, lead soldiers reenacting the Franco-Prussian war. While just down the street at Tiffany's, the ladies from Great Neck bought watches made by Rolex, Piaget or Patek Phillipe.

On the West Side, the restaurant and boutique windows blinked holiday decorations. At Lincoln Center longer lines than usual queued at the box office with customers eager for the best seats for the National Ballet's annual *Nutcracker*.

It was not much of a trick to spot a dancer on the street, even in winter wraps there was an elegant carriage of the upper torso and head, muscular calves, and, of course, the peculiar duck-waddle walk. Victoria

Bennett turned more than a few heads as she crossed Lincoln Center Plaza for Amy's Health Food restaurant, not her favorite, but close.

Hat and scarf on the seat beside her, collar open, she rubbed aching cold hands, then massaged her left calf, sore since a rehearsal of the day before. Hers was definitely a theatrical presence, a face haughty, expressive; the hands and arms quick, continually moving. Her long black hair had gray streaks that were no longer disguised. Her age was a secret guarded by the company, ignored by the press, and a matter of frequent speculation among her fellow dancers. But no one dared openly to compare the number of birthdays with her younger husband, Juri Agarte. Those who were kind put her in her late thirties; those who were unkind were unkind.

"Where is she?" A close look could catch the jaw setting into place like a trap door as she closed a sentence, but neither did that, nor the quick, hard frown detract from the startling beauty of her face with its Eskimo-wide cheekbones and luminous black eyes.

Victoria had once danced with the famed Ballet Russe de Monte Carlo; by her account she was thirteen at the time, and only fifteen when she joined the National Ballet. She harbored many memories from those days, often with a pang when things got tough in America. The hopes and dreams of her youth would then flood back to her on shimmering waves. She remembered exciting opening night performances in the Baroque theatres of Europe's great cities, the glamorous parties, girlish romances in languages she could not speak, the lovely, then unspoiled French Riviera, and the special magic of Monte Carlo, a gingerbread kingdom and play-world of the rich and titled. In those days Victoria had not learned the price of success, nor had she been required to pay for it.

The windows at Amy's were opaque with condensation and frost. Victoria wiped a hole on the window surface to see outside. She saw

Nanette Gorham tearing across the street. The waitress placed a sun-flower seed and wheat germ yogurt in front of Victoria.

Nanette slid into the seat opposite Victoria, out of breath from wind and hurry.

"Sorry I'm late." She flashed Victoria a quick, cursory look.

Nanette's skin was the color of watery milk stretched tightly over del-icate bones that looked as if they would snap and crunch if touched ever so lightly. But these delicate features of a woodland nymph disappeared immediately when she opened her mouth, and two protruding teeth turned an enchanting forest creature into a beaver.

Victoria spooned yogurt into her mouth. "Well?"

"Well, I'm not sure how to start."

After twenty years in ballet Victoria developed a radar system for impending danger. "Is it about Juri?"

"Yes." Nanette was genuinely surprised.

"Is he having an affair?"

"Yes."

"Let me see…who would it be…is it… Allison Fain?"

"How did you know?"

"Because he never looks at her."

Nanette squinted, confused. "But how does that—"

"When a man looks at a beautiful woman it's natural. When he does-n't, he's hiding something and he's guilty as sin."

"Victoria stared out the window at the faces, wools and furs going by in a blur, forcing out the next question, the one that could hurt. "Is it a fact or just a rumor?"

"Oh, no, not a rumor. I saw them."

Victoria was a pro, only her eyes showed the wince. She kept her hands clenched under the table to keep from strangling Nanette. "And just what did you see?"

"After a rehearsal, I went to the dressing room for a sweater. I saw Allison bent over a table, her tights down around her ankles. Juri saw me in the mirror. I ran out, but Juri chased me. He told me he would take me out of his ballets if I ever said anything. So, of course, I promised. It wasn't until I got home that I realized I wasn't in any of his ballets."

Nanette looked down at the table and added, "Then I thought about you...and how the company would laugh behind your back. So I had to tell you. Victoria, promise me one thing."

"What?"

"You won't tell Juri, I told you. I mean, there's always a chance I could get in one of his ballets."

"And maybe even take the role from Allison?"

"Oh, I hadn't thought of that."

"Of course not. Have you told anyone else?"

"No."

Victoria grabbed Nanette's hand and pinned it to the table.

"And you had better not."

Nanette bit her teeth on her lower lip. "What are you going to do?"

Victoria did not return an answer, but Victoria resolved herself to school Allison Fain in the consequences of a backstage romance.

CHAPTER 9

In her private dressing room at the Metropolitan Opera House, Victoria Bennett stretched and twisted a pair of new toe shoes to break their stiffness. The room, essentially a concrete cell, had a few touches of luxury—a stuffed lounge chair, a portable space heater, and silver framed photographs of Victoria and Juri in favorite roles.

Victoria visualized Allison's face on the wall as a loudspeaker squawked "Fifteen minutes to curtain." Anger and adrenaline mixed with blood. Whack! She pounded a shoe against a vision of Allison's face on the wall.

It was part of Victoria's routine to psych herself up for a performance by picking a fight. A wrinkle in a costume produced a tirade at the wardrobe mistress; or a misplaced prop provoked foul words for a stagehand. But tonight she needed no scapegoat.

Juri bounded into the dressing room. Victoria looked at him through the fluorescent halo of the mirror; his handsome face glowed.

Victoria surgically painted a thin, scarlet line around her mouth and dabbed some extra powder at the corners of her eyes to conceal tiny crow's feet.

"Thank God for make-up. With enough blush and a pink spotlight I'll be able to totter around stage until forty. Then I'm put out to pasture somewhere in New Jersey to teach little rich girls to dance like butterflies."

"Don't be ridiculous. You look as young as a teenager."

"Juri, do you ever think about being with a younger woman?"

For a moment Juri was caught by surprise. "Why would I think such a thing."

"Oh, no reason. But for being so sweet and so honest I am dedicating this performance to you."

"You are an angel." He kissed her lightly on her hair so not to ruin her makeup. He whispered '*merde*,' the dancers' good luck wish, then closed the door.

Victoria shut her eyes and breathed in the spirits of the dressing room. She believed dressing rooms retained the cosmic energy of its former legendary inhabitants, Bernstein, Pavarotti, Alonso, Markarova, Gregory and Fonteyn. Two weeks after the National Ballet's season another superstar would be sitting in her place. Victoria smiled, gazing in the mirror of the future. "Where will you be then, Miss Fain?" Victoria asked, but knew the answer.

Temple waited in a corridor by the chorus dressing room. She watched dancers race out of the room and fly down the aisle to prepare for the performance. Allison, in costume, dashed out of the room.

"Allison!

Allison turned and screamed. "Temple! My God, I didn't know you would be here."

"I wouldn't miss your first performance for anything in the world."

"But I'm just one of fifty dancers in the corps. You won't even be able to find me."

"I would find you even if I were sitting in the last row. Which, by the way, is where I'm sitting." Temple laughed.

"Why didn't you call me. I would have gotten you better seats."

"I did call."

"Oh, right, right. Listen, I'm sorry I haven't been in touch, but with all the new ballets, well, you understand, don't you?"

"Of course."

"Are you still at St. Mary's?"

"Yes."

"You poor thing. Have you found any work?"

"I'm a cocktail waitress part time."

"Oh, no. Well, just hang in there. You'll land a dance job one of these days."

The loudspeaker announced 'Places.' Allison kissed Temple on the cheek. "I gotta run. How about meeting later for a drink."

"Sure, that would be great!"

Temple waved as Allison ran to the stage. Temple felt a bump on her side, knocking her into the wall. She recovered to see she was pushed out of the way by Victoria Bennett who was rushing down the corridor.

Victoria entered the wings, the shadowy alcoves on the sides of the stage where dancers peeled off knitted leg warmers and awaited a cue that would catapult them into the blazing lights of the stage.

Allison was grinding the tips of her pointe shoes into rosin, the sticky yellow powder that gives shoes an extra bit of traction. Allison saw Victoria and stepped out of the box, a courtesy to a principal dancer. Victoria raided the rosin box so quickly that Allison stumbled, falling into another dancer.

The curtain rose, and shafts of steel blue light shot from towering booms on all sides of the wings and focused on exquisite, lithe dancers moving in perfect unison. The National Ballet trained dancers like Swiss watches, precisely tuned and built for a lifetime of wear. On cue, Victoria bolted like a meteor on stage, accepting thunderous applause, a reward for memories of past triumphs. She whirled through a series of furiously fast diagonal turns, finishing into the upstage wing where Allison stood waiting to go on.

As soon as Victoria was out of the audience's sight, she slapped Allison viciously across the face. Allison reeled backwards; not sure what happened. Allison picked herself up, and on cue followed the line of girls on stage, but her bright smile was dimmed, her eyes clouded. She only knew she had to finish. She struggled through the coda then ran back into the darkness of the wings. Victoria was waiting.

Victoria slapped Allison again, this time slicing stiletto-like nails across Allison's cheek. Allison screamed, crashing back against the black velour drapes. Horrified dancers looked at Allison sprawled on the floor, blood trickling down her neck.

Victoria leapt back to the stage, pulling off a set of pirouettes that seemed to send sparks from her shoes. Allison staggered, too stunned to cry, too frightened to think. Victoria returned to the wings. She grabbed Allison by the hair and flung her to the ground. Two stagehands wrestled them apart. Once separated, Victoria spit at Allison. One of the stagehands put a towel to Allison's face and helped her to a dressing room.

At curtain calls Victoria glittered like the gems in her tiara. Fans hurled roses at her feet. She bathed in their adulation with a modest smile, but there was a sparkle of victory in her eyes, a celebration of victory and revenge.

Chapter 10

The following morning a secretary called Allison to report to the office of the director of the National Ballet. "'Immediately,' Miss Fain, that was Miss Borden's very word." The voice was officially crisp.

"I can be there in an hour."

Even getting out of bed in the early morning Allison looked like an Italian goddess, long and straight black hair, black eyes, a thin elegant nose, and skin as white and pure as cream.

Allison scurried to the bathroom and assembled her makeup on the counter. One look in the mirror froze her. The scratches across her cheek swelled during the night to three long, red scabs. She covered her face with trembling hands, "Not so ugly, please God." Frantically she applied base to her cheeks, then powder, then rouge, but it made her look more hideous in a desperate attempt to hide the obvious marks. She gripped the edges of the sink; then slowly opened her eyes. "Why hide it? Let Miss Borden see what Victoria did."

Allison selected her most conservative day dress, a blue print with an antique lace collar; and a pair of matching high heels that hurt like hell, but she was acutely conscious Miss Borden preferred her dancers to look like ladies, not gypsies.

Allison announced herself to the receptionist who pointed Allison to a seat. It was Allison's first time inside the administration office, and she looked with awe at the walls covered with autographed photos of the legendary stars who had appeared with the National: Violette Verdy,

Melissa Hayden, Alicia Alonso, Rosella Hightower, Nora Kaye, Ivan Nagy, Fernando Bujones, Arthur Mitchell and Igor Yousevitch.

Allison tried not to think of the meeting she would have in a few minutes. She feared Miss Borden, as did everyone. Rebecca Borden held absolute power; and was aloof as one of her Persian cats, but with an unmistakable tinge of bitterness that some say was caused by failures she suffered as a young dancer.

"Miss Fain," it was the voice of the morning caller, "Miss Borden will see you."

Miss Borden did not rise from her Louis XIV chair. "Sit." Miss Borden's eyes remained lowered on some papers on her desk.

Allison sat in an upholstered leather chair, rested her elbows on the arms, but feeling it looked too casual, folded her hands on her lap. There were more photos on the walls, but more personal than in the receptionist's office: photos of Rebecca Borden with Stravinsky in rehearsal, Diaghilev with his arm draped her shoulder, a photo with Nijinsky on a beach, and photos of Miss Borden being kisses by Presidents, Kings and Prime Ministers. Near her desk on a marble pedestal was a bronzed toe shoe of Pavlova, and behind her desk a large oil painting in the sweeping style of Michelangelo. The painting depicted Miss Borden wrapped in swaddling white cloth and floating in a blue sky towards the heavens; a nude Adonis, flanked by a legion of cherub angels; Adonis had his arm outstretched, and was handing— Allison blinked, hardly believing! Adonis was offering Miss Borden a pair of pointe shoes, a divine commission to spread the sacred sacrament of dance.

Allison looked from the painting to the subject herself. Rebecca Borden was no more than five feet; and wore the trappings of old money: a dowdy oatmeal sweater, muted plaid skirt, and a pair of brown penny loafers. Her hair was a jumble of carrot-colored curls that made her look more like an elderly Little Orphan Annie than a cohort of Adonis.

"Are you aware of the scandal you caused?" The sudden outburst caught Allison by surprise. "Are you having an affair with Juri Agarte?"

Allison hesitated; not sure it was wise to admit.

Rebecca Borden picked up a letter opener from her desk. "Do you think I poured millions of dollars into this company so it could be a playground for whores." Her eyes pierced to the center of Allison's brain, Orphan Annie had become Tosca with a dagger. "I have seen to it that nothing will be printed, but I can not cut off the grapevine. The story of Victoria Bennett slapping a corps girl in retaliation for the seduction of her husband will be an episode of ballet gossip…although you will only be remembered anonymously as the 'corps girl.'"

"Miss Borden, I didn't seduce Juri, and I didn't do anything to Victoria Bennett. She attacked me." Allison tilted her face to show the scars, hoping for a crumb of sympathy.

"That's too bad. But you will not be permanently disfigured. Miss Fain, I am sorry, but you are dismissed from the company. And please do not ask for a letter of recommendation." She pressed the intercom, "Would you please show Miss Fain out."

Allison's head reeled, her lips trembled, but she fought back the tears, she would not show anyone her humiliation. Outside it was raining. She tried hailing a taxi, waving like a flag for fifteen minutes, but nothing was free. Accepting futility, she ran to a phone booth on the corner of 59th Street. She had to call Juri; he would intercede for her. No dial tone, she jiggled the coin release, her last coin was swallowed. Allison wanted to kick out the glass in the booth, but stopped, fearing she would break her toe. She ran to a luncheonette across the street, and asked the waitress at the counter for change.

"Sorry, Miss, you gotta buy something. That's our policy."

"OK, then give me a cup of coffee." It was not a bad idea, Allison was soaked and cold, the coffee would warm her and help get her wits together. "Where is your phone?"

"We just got this one." The waitress pointed to a phone on the side of the cash register.

"Could I use it?"

"This phone's for take-out orders; that's how we make a living around here."

Allison sipped the coffee. She could see from her reflection in the chrome refrigeration until that her eye makeup ran into black smudges, with her scars she looked like a vampiress.

"Do you have a bathroom?"

The waitress leaned on the counter. "Look, Miss, this is a luncheonette. If you want change, a phone and a restroom, go to a hotel."

"Could I have my change." Allison abruptly handed her a couple of dollars, took the change and started to leave.

"Hey," the waitress called, "Ain't you gonna leave a tip?"

"I came in for change if I leave a tip I won't have change for my phone call."

The waitress splashed Allison's cup into a tub of gray dishwater. "Damn deadbeats."

Allison found a working phone and dialed Juri. A woman answered. Allison did not breathe. Victoria slammed down the receiver as if she knew who it was.

Allison ran wildly through the street; she had to catch Juri before the start of company class. She entered the studio, and ran down the corridors, dancers stepped back as she approached. "Does everyone know," she asked herself, "or do I look like a madwoman." She saw Juri warming up in an empty studio.

"Juri."

Juri froze as if approached by a vampire, "Look at you. What happened?"

"I was fired."

"Fired?"

"Can you talk to Rebecca Borden?"

"About what?"

"Changing her mind."

"You want me to ask Rebecca Borden to change her mind? You can't be serious?"

"Then what am I going to do."

"There are other ballet companies."

"But what…what about us?"

"Us? Do you realize the situation you put me in with Victoria?"

"That *I* put you—"

"Victoria was quite unpleasant last night, I assure you."

"I'm sorry, but—"

"Darling, this is very difficult…if I had met you before Victoria, who knows…but you knew she was my wife."

"Yes, but—"

"And now she's asking for a divorce…but she'll calm down in a few days, she always does."

"This has happened before?"

Juri smiled. "Allison, don't be naïve. Listen, if there is anything else I can do for you, let me know." He looked at his watch. "But right now, I am very late for class." He put both his arms on Allison's shoulders. "Allison."

"Yes?"

"You understand? We have to be adult about this."

"Yes."

"OK then. Good luck, I mean that."

Juri pecked Allison on the cheek, picked up his ballet bag, and dashed for the door. Allison stood. Everything was spinning like some carousel ride that would not stop. She backed out into the hallway, she could feel the eyes of the dancers on her, but no one said a word. She looked at Nanette who lowered her eyes. Allison understood. She was an outcast, these dancers once friends would never talk to her again. She wrapped her coat around her body, pushed back her wet hair, summoned a scrap of dignity and walked out.

In her apartment Allison waited for the anger to explode, for the tears to gush, but everything was frozen inside her. She pulled a robe tighter around herself, and sank into a corner of the sofa. She poured a glass of champagne, a gift from her mother to celebrate her first performance. She wished she had something stronger, some drug to make her forget last night, to forget Rebecca Borden, Juri, Victoria, the whole rotten day, her whole rotten life. The phone rang. Allison let the answering machine take the message.

"Allison, Allison, are you there. This is Temple. I waited for you last night. What happened? Anyway, that's not important. You won't believe this. I was offered a contract with the National. Can you believe! There must have been an opening. I'm so excited. We'll be together again. Call me. Call me, the moment you get this message, we have to celebrate."

Allison threw a glass of champagne against the wall. It exploded; then so did her tears. Allison realized all she had worked for, all she had planned, was gone. Her career, her hopes and dreams now taken by, of all people, Temple Drake.

How could she have been such an idiot, falling for such a jerk? And a married jerk! And besides that a lousy lover. The only good thing about him was that he was fast, and out the door. Jerk!

But how the hell did Victoria find out? Somebody must have seen Juri going in St. Mary's. Oh no! Of course—that day in the dressing room…Nanette. Nanette, the little bitch!

Well, none of that was important now. What mattered now was what to do about the rest of her life. There was always suicide! She would swallow a bottle of pills. But all she had in the house was a bottle of multi-vitamins and a half bottle of aspirin. Maybe she could just throw herself out the window, but the way things were going she would screw that up too.

Maybe she would just run away to Europe. Disguise herself, get a new identity. Allison brushed away some tears. No, she would have to face her mother, after all she was almost twenty-one, she would handle this like an adult. She leaned back her head and lifted the bottle of champagne to her lips and poured it down her throat.

CHAPTER 11

It was the season when New Yorkers huddled around hissing radiators, or hustled rapidly to their favorite bars for extended periods, like bears in a cave. Scattered black leaves on white snow littered Central Park; the skies had turned dark gray, and the winds began to bite. In the middle of the park, in luxurious isolation was Tavern-on-the-Green, a shining circle of glass and steel, a restaurant whose sparkling crystal chandeliers, soft green carpets, and attentive waiters provided shelter for tired, hungry, and wealthy New Yorkers.

Ruth Fain ordered a salad and a salmon en croute for herself and a junior steak for Allison. Ruth drummed her fingers on the table.

"Why are you wearing sunglasses at table, Allison?"

Allison pulled down her glasses to reveal bloody red eyes.

"You've been crying."

"Yes."

"Are you sleeping?"

"No."

Ruth reached into her handbag; from a bottle she poured a tiny pile of pills into her hand. "Take these." Allison held out her hand. "They've helped get me through some rough times." Ruth's voice turned unusually brusque.

"Your father doesn't know what's happened. And I am going to try and keep this from him. You are his angel. This would kill him."

A young waitress, Fran, a pretty girl with a dancer's body, placed salads on the table. "Fresh pepper?"

"Yes." Ruth smiled.

Fran twisted the pepper grinder.

"What are your plans, Allison?"

"I don't have any plans. Maybe…I'll just quit dancing."

"Like hell you will." The words were lashed at Allison. The waitress stopped grinding. "I haven't devoted my life training you so you can quit. I quit my career for your father. That's enough quitting in this family!"

Allison had never heard such ferocity in her mother's voice. "Besides what else can you be…a waitress?"

Allison felt the embarrassment of the waitress standing over her. Allison wanted her to have a graceful escape. "A glass of wine, please?"

"What kind, Miss?"

"Any kind."

The waitress was equally relieved to have a reason to exit.

Ruth continued, "Well, what else can you be? You can't be a secretary. You don't know how to work a computer. You even failed typing. Remember when you quit dancing before, and we sent you to that private college? You failed every course, even with that teacher you were having an affair with."

"What are you talking about!"

"That cute drama professor!"

"I wasn't having an affair. We were just friendly."

"And you expect me to believe that?"

"All right, so maybe all I'm good for is to get married."

"And where is your Prince Charming?" Ruth looked around the room. "You see anyone interesting here? Or maybe your Prince is in the kitchen washing dishes. Why don't you go take a look?" Allison turned away. "No Princess, life isn't some ballet fairy tale. There are no Prince Charmings, only men. If you're lucky, you'll find a Santa Claus like I did. Someone who can afford a Lexus instead of a Chevy."

"God, mother, you can be so nasty."

Ruth reached across the table and clutched Allison's hand. "I'm not trying to bully you. I just want you to see things as they are. All you have is dance. You must make it…at any cost. If you don't, you will have nothing. Nothing!"

"But you don't understand, mother, no company will take me after this scandal."

"Maybe not in New York."

"Not in this universe."

"Not quite, I found you a position."

"You-? Where?"

"Atlantic City."

"There's no ballet company in Atlantic City."

"I didn't say 'ballet,' I said a 'position.' I spoke to Miguel Alamar. You remember he was one of my students years ago. He now choreographs shows at Bally's."

"A casino? Mother, you got me a job as a showgirl?"

"No, they have ballet sections in the shows."

"Are they naked?"

"No, the ballet dancers wear toe shoes. Seriously, Allison the ballet parts are…somewhat dignified. I told Miguel you would be there on Monday. While you are exiled to obscurity in Atlantic City you can, at least, work on your technique, and when this incident fades from memory, you'll be able to return to New York."

Allison looks at her mother, stunned. "Mother, I don't know—"

"I do." Ruth reached into her handbag. "Here's your bus ticket." Allison gaped at the ticket in her mother's hand.

"While your mouth is open, eat your steak, dear."

CHAPTER 12

Miguel Alamar met Allison at the bus station.

"Allison!" He embraced her enthusiastically. "Darling, it's so good to see you. How long as it been?"

"Five years."

"You were just a tadpole, and now you're a—"

"Big frog!"

"Not at all, you are beautiful. Come, my car's across the street."

Once in the car there was no stopping Miguel. "Chiquita, you are the answer to my prayers. I don't have one dancer on your level. They're all bloated jersey cows. And every day is a crisis. 'My boyfriend left me.' "I need an abortion.' 'I'm broke.' "My feet hurt.' Nothing but problems! On top of all that we have a new conductor. A total schmuck! No sense of tempo. My dancers are dying. He plays every piece of music like a funeral march. And we're stuck with this guy because he's Italian. I'd like to stick a gigantic cannelloni up his butt." He waved his arm wildly out the car as he drove through the city. "Oh, merde, I forgot you're Italian. I'm sorry. But you're not like them."

"It's OK, I—"

"Ever been to Atlantic City before?"

"No, I—"

"You'll hate it. Glitzy neon palaces surrounded by slums. There's nothing to do outside of the casinos. It rains all the time, except in summer, and summer is so crowded you can't squeeze your ass onto an inch of the beach." He ran his fingers through his tight curly black hair. "But enough of that for now. Here we are." Miguel stopped in front of a one-story building.

"I arranged for you to stay with one of our dancers, Giselle, a nice girl, not bright, but agreeable. You'll like her. Get some rest, I need you in rehearsal tomorrow."

"Welcome, Allison. I hope Miguel didn't talk your ear off." Giselle kissed Allison warmly on the cheeks. Miguel was right, Allison liked her immediately. Her short-cropped hair gave her an elfish look; her China blue eyes wide-set with a trusting expression. Allison thought she was a bit hefty for a dancer, but appreciated the ease with which she carried the luggage to her room. The room was even smaller than the one at St. Mary's. A slanting ceiling indicated the proximity of the roof. A tall armoire took up most of one wall, and in a corner was a tiny sink below a framed mirror. One straight chair and that was all.

Giselle fussed, straightening knick-knacks, pillows, and then put her hands on her hips, and smiled. "I bet you'd like a shower?"

"That would be the safest bet in Atlantic City."

In the weeks that followed, Giselle was a co-worker, friend, mother, and teacher of bus routes. She knew the stores that sold good dresses at good prices. "Avoid the shops at the Casinos," she warned. She took Allison into the poorer sections of the city where they could get inexpensive, quality leotards and tights at outlet prices. They spent evenings after the shows at the secret after-hours clubs where the bartenders and casino dealers went after work. Giselle also had a ready supply of drugs, mostly marijuana and occasionally cocaine. Allison resisted the first few times Giselle offered, but after her resistance broke down she found she liked marijuana, the way it altered her moods, the way it eased the pain of exile. With her mind opened to new music she was exposed to alternative rock and roll, blues and jazz, and she loved it. To her surprise, she even liked Atlantic City, there was a different energy than New York, but there was an urgency in getting about the daily business of the city—making money.

She also made an effort to get to know each showgirl and each member of the ballet troupe. They were different than the dancers at the National, accessible, down-to-earth, even lusty, and funny, nobody took too seriously what they were doing. There was not the life and death struggle of ballet competition. And the city provided Allison a respite, a shelter to heal her wounds, a time to think, to analyze her mistake, to plan a way back to New York, to work on herself, and if necessary, to recreate herself.

After the first two months in Atlantic City Allison began to take inventory, in the mirror at the studios, in the company of other dancers, in the small framed mirror above her sink at home, and in the make-up mirror in the dressing room. "Who am I? Who will I be? What is it I want? And how do I get it? She was certainly pretty, but was pretty enough?"

The magic scalpel of a certain plastic surgeon came up in many conversations among young dancers. He was credited with the touch that made many of the showgirls breathtaking beauties. An implant here, some silicon there, a nip, a tuck and a scrape could change one's future. Allison followed up the leads to the source and finally learned how to contact the doctor. Spectacular was what she needed to be, not just pretty! Pretty was definitely not enough to go back to New York and be the Prima Ballerina she had to be.

She would need money. Her father, Domenic, was reluctant at first when she called and asked for ten thousand dollars to furnish her bedroom and buy a second-hand car.

"Baby, Atlantic City is temporary, you'll be back soon."

"Daddy," she put on one of her best sobs, "you have no idea how barren my bedroom is, and how depressing it is to always have to bum a ride with Giselle."

He wired the money, and an extra thousand. Allison immediately called Dr. Parson's office, and made an appointment during her next free period.

On the train to New York she had second thoughts. How much pain would she have? Was she too young? Suppose the operation failed and she was left scarred and ugly?

"Hell! If I want to be a star, a big star, I have to do it."

Allison remembered the rumors that the legendary Prima Ballerina Margot Fonteyn had not been proud to tamper with nature, and she had her eyes slit at the corners to make them bigger. Fonteyn's big eyes were one of her greatest assets. Allison would never forget when she was a little girl watching Fonteyn and Nureyev in the video of *Romeo and Juliet*. Fonteyn's wide-eyed pleading for Romeo held an audience on the verge of tears. Allison wanted that ultimate power of making an audience weep.

Dr. Parson's office was a severe monochromatic gray broken only by a large violent abstract painting by Jackson Pollock. Dr. Parson's deep tan was set off dramatically by his crisp white frock. His close cropped silver gray hair blended perfectly with the gray walls and carpet. Allison wondered if the room was inspired by his hair. She imagined him sitting in a silver gray Mercedes in a silver gray garage.

"The operation you are requesting, Blepharoplasty," the voice was cool professionalism, "is generally performed on older woman who have developed fatty tissue around their eyes. We make the eyes larger, and consequently our clients younger and more attractive. But you are young and pretty. Why would you want this?"

"To help my appearance on stage."

"There are ways of applying make-up that give the illusion of bigger eyes."

"Yes, but I want…more."

"I cannot promise you the radical difference you might be picturing or hoping for."

"Will there be an improvement?"

"That is not the point. I can not recommend this."

"Doctor, will it make my eyes larger?"

"Well, yes, but—"

"Then let's do it."

Doctor Parson wrote in his silver gray appointment book. "Very well, and we'll fix that little bump on your nose."

"And I want a breast reduction."

"Miss Fain, any normal woman would be happy to—"

"I'm not normal. I'm a dancer. Choreographers who do 'leotard ballets' want the girls to look like the pencils."

"I see…and is that it?"

"No. My calves are too thin…I understand that silicone could enhance the curve."

"Miss Fain, I really think you should give more thought to what the consequences could be to—"

"I know what I'm doing, Doctor."

"I see," He jotted a final note in his book. "We're creating the Bride of Frankenstein…a beautiful one."

The surgery was not as painful as Allison feared; although she was given a sedative, she regained partial consciousness near the end of the operation; but still doped she hardly realized what was being done. After the operation she spent twenty-four hours with bandages wrapped around her head, each hour was an eternity. She was told not to laugh or cry since use of the facial muscles might be harmful to the healing process. She was permitted only liquid nourishment.

When the nurse snipped off the bandages, Allison was handed a mirror and warned the sight would not be pleasant. Allison gasped at the black and blue swellings that almost closed her eyes.

"It is temporary," the nurse consoled, "the swelling will go down tonight. After that you should be pleased."

For the rest of the night, between sipping soup and eating creamed spinach, there was nothing to do but wait. After a few days the swelling went down, the black and blue faded, the tiny scars vanished. There was an incredible difference! Her eyes were stunning! Mesmerizing! Allison looked at her image in the mirror, "The new Allison Fain."

Allison was so satisfied she decided to take a detailed inventory. Her legs were excellent, well-shaped from years of *relevees* and *tendus*, but the upper part of her calves had been a trifle thin, until the tiny injection of silicone make her legs absolutely perfect.

Her feet were slim and delicate, and the arch curved gracefully like the crescent of a moon; but she had to admit her arch was not nearly as good as the Russian dancers. The Russians and Europeans had an advantage. It was not uncommon that mothers of potential dancers broke their children's feet as the feet healed twice as strong and generally with a higher arch. Allison regretted her mother did not have the foresight to do the same.

Allison studied her mouth, it was lovely, wide and full with a touch of sensuality, and when she smiled she flashed the perfect straight teeth, the product of years of braces. Her nose was now perfect; strong and distinctive, and it would 'carry' well on stage. Allison remembered the famed ballerina Cynthia Wright had a nose job three years ago, and lost the strong, sharp profile on stage. Allison had not made that mistake.

She took off her top to study the last modification, her breast reduction. It was only a slight reduction, but it did improve the line of her body. She wanted to be 'pencil thin' to have the perfect body to wear white millskin unitards in ballets such as, *After Eden*. Dr. Parson told Allison that the breast operation would leave tiny, but permanent scars under each breast. It was irrelevant to Allison; an audience would never see the scars.

Allison felt sore at night, and had to sleep on her back, but Dr. Parson gave her some valium to get through the night.

In the morning she put on a white body leotard and stood in front of the mirror. She did not know how many hours had passed; she was in a dream, in love with the gorgeous new face and body in the mirror.

Dr. Parson's wished her farewell. "Send me reviews when you dance ballet again. I like to keep up on the success of my ballerinas."

"You've done others."

"Oh yes, many."

"Who?"

"I don't discuss my clients."

It crossed Allison's mind as she kissed Dr. Parson good-bye that she would give anything for an hour to look through his files.

Now to celebrate! She had money left over and a week to kill. She checked into the Plaza with a room overlooking Central Park. She felt delicious telling the desk clerk that she would be staying 'alone.'

For evening she selected a voile shirt of pale lavender with a low-cut top. Dinner in the Plaza's Edwardian room was superb: poached salmon with fresh fill sauce, tender white asparagus in a light butter sauce, a splendid vegetable salad and the best pastry she had ever eaten. Over cappuccino she stared at the other diners. There was a heavy, very dark Arab in a turban with three blond women who could have been Hollywood starlets. On the other side of the room there was a stocky, graying man with cauliflower ears, sun-seared skin and a black mustache in a navy blue blazer with gold braid on the sleeves, accompanied by a pigeon-breasted female with a hooked nose almost reaching her lower lip and tiny eyes like a ferret. Their daughter, about fifteen, seemed to have inherited the worst of each. "Even Dr. Parson couldn't help her!" Allison thought.

She walked along Broadway after dinner to Lincoln Center. She wore sunglasses when she purchased her ticket to see the National Ballet, although there was no reason to worry about being seen since she knew no one in the ticket line.

She did not take her seat, but choose instead to stand in the rear of the orchestra. She did not move a muscle during the first two ballets, pretty classic romantic ballets. It was during the last ballet that Allison had to grip the railing. It was Juri's ballet and Temple was dancing in the part created for Allison. Allison could not deny Temple's stage presence. Beyond technique, beyond the impact of her natural beauty complemented by her brilliant blue eyes and golden hair, she had the spark that animates all great performers. The ability to communicate and demand attention which springs from the innermost being of the great actor, the great dancer, which captivates, enthralls and enslaves an audience, demanding 'Bravos!' and spewing flowers across the footlights.

Temple Drake, late of Grand Chenier, Louisiana, so timid with men, so reserved in company, so modest, was fully assured and electrifying on stage. So much so that she moved with a hint of daring that transfixed an audience into approving, observant silence and then rapturous applause. Temple took her curtain call, a standing ovation; roses were tossed onto the stage. In the back of the audience, partially hidden behind a red velour drape, Allison stood. A tear could be seen falling from below her black sunglasses.

Allison returned to Atlantic City with a resolve that one day she would take her place in the spotlight, somehow, some way, and at whatever cost. She had re-made herself, sculptured herself with nips, cuts and injections into the image of the perfect ballerina. She vowed on her life that all her effort would not be in vain.

Meanwhile she would make her stay in Atlantic City as pleasant as possible, except for the impending visit of Temple during Easter vacation. She cringed at the thought of Temple seeing her in a Showgirl extravaganza.

Allison had pleaded with Temple not to come, but Temple would not be held off. It was just a few months ago that Temple had stood outside Allison's dressing room, and Allison had signed her program. Was

Temple laughing about that now, now that she was a rising star of the ballet world? Allison wondered, despite Temple's sweetness, if somewhere in the bottom of Temple's heart had she relished Allison's demotion. Was Temple coming to see her in Atlantic City to gloat and revel at her humiliation?

CHAPTER 13

After Temple signed her contract with the National Ballet she immediately leased an apartment at 70th Street and Broadway, a good location. The 104 bus stopped at the corner and in less than ten minutes took her to classes and rehearsals. The Broadway theatre district was just a few minutes away, and so were most of the midtown movie houses and restaurants.

Upper Broadway was an international marketplace with some of the best food New York had to offer: delicatessen specialties, health foods, German pastries, Italian pastas, French and Middle-Eastern breads, and all the ingredients for cooking Chinese, Japanese and Korean meals at home. If you were broke you could still afford the Chinese and Cuban restaurants, chow mein with fried plantains or black beans and rice on the side.

Temple's apartment was a floor-through in the middle of a Brownstone with three floors and an attic. It was owned by an actor who had bought it for a song, an actual song he did for a detergent commercial. He fixed up the apartment a little and left for Rome to live on the profits while he made Italian movies. But after a few years the spaghetti westerns lost interest in him. His face was bland, and as he grew bald he looked like an over-sized baby. He returned to New York, and spent most of his time practicing guitar, writing screenplays that nobody bought, and puttering in the garden behind the house.

"Temple, another glass of wine?"

"Sure." Temple propped her slender feet on a wicker stool next to a rose bush. "And tell me another story, Gerald."

He would tell her his war stories, how he was always on the verge of making it, and how he learned to survive without money. He taught Temple tricks a dancer could well use. How to scout the neighborhood for bargains in food, second-hand stores for good-label clothes, and the Salvation Army for furniture.

Gerald helped Temple decorate. Her living room was at the front of the house, with a ten-foot ceiling, parquet floors and tall windows whose shutters folded into frames, and a working fireplace. The kitchen was in the middle of everything. The bathroom had a claw foot tub and a stained glass window, probably real Victorian.

The living room was respected for its antiquity and painted white. The floors Gerald sanded, and gave them two coats of shellac. A closeout on wicker furniture at Pier One provided a couch and two chairs. Plants and ready-framed prints from a small gallery in Greenwich Village did the rest. It was sparse, no rugs or plush carpeting, but it was hers!

She decorated the bedroom in sand-colored paint everywhere except for the brick wall. On the walls she chose large black and white photographs of famous dancers from around the world. A bed, a white wicker table and chair, black pillows on a white bedspread, and the room was done. No lace, no organdy, no flounces. The bedroom with its shinny oak floor looked like a dance studio without mirrors or a practice barre.

She was happier than she had ever been; and she had everything she wanted—except a man. Now that she had a career, furnished her apartment, she was ready for romance, but where were the men? Her schedule of daily classes, rehearsals, and performances left no time for a social life. And the boys in the company with the exception of the two married men were all gay. Gerald, was the only heterosexual male friend she had, and although he was sweet, kind, funny and generous, he was thirty years too old. Gerald had once cautioned her about finding a man. "In New York, one-third of the men are gay, one-third are married, and the rest are running like hell."

Alone at night in her bed, she thought of Billy LaVoi, of his slender, muscular body over hers. She would look at his picture on the night table, and debated inviting him to New York for a weekend, her hand had reached for the phone so many times, but she always hesitated, concluding it was not worth re-igniting old fires.

Beside Billy's photo was a picture of Temple and Allison with their arms around each other, wearing funny baseball caps they had picked up on an evening's outing to Times Square. Temple felt sorry for Allison—and a bit guilty. Temple did not know it was Allison she was replacing until her first day at the National. Of course, it could have been any girl that was fired, but it wasn't—it was Allison. When Allison finally called back, two weeks after the firing, Allison assured her she was delighted, "Honest, Temple, if I could have picked anyone to take my place, I would have picked you."

That did not make Temple any more comfortable. Make no mistake, she was thrilled to have the job, but she was the second choice after Allison. The auditions were fair and impartial, and as Allison had mentioned on the phone, the affair with Juri was not until after Allison had joined the company. And it was Juri who seduced Allison. It should have been Juri that was fired!

Easter vacation break was only a few weeks away, and Temple would finally have free time to visit Allison in Atlantic City. After months in a dark theatre, she was ready to see and feel the warmth of the sun, and she longed to see her friend, her very best friend.

CHAPTER 14

Temple sat in the audience as the lights of Bally's auditorium went black, and the sparkling gold curtain opened to the courtyard of a sumptuous Egyptian palace, swaying with ferns and sprinkled with floor pillows draped with naked Nubian slave girls. Then a row of muscular black male dancers in gold G-strings, and twenty more chorus girls with ostrich feathers marched into the courtyard.

"Mating season at the ostrich farm," was Temple's professional opinion.

The ostriches wore black and white plumed headdresses about a yard tall. Sequins covered the narrow straps that ingeniously, somehow held the minute pieces of their costumes on their bodies. More dancers wiggled up like cobras out of baskets, arms straight up, boobies from side to side, wigs not moving over the heavily painted almond eyes. From the shoulders of each sprouted six falls constructed of bouncing wires with honeydew melon sized balls at intervals. With every movement the contraptions gyrated and jumped like serpents. The all-over effect was a barrage of beautiful flesh, over an expanse the size of a basketball court.

Temple had never seen such perfect bodies. The central dancer was a tall black girl with magnificent breasts almost exposed. The costumes were designed to support the lesser bosoms with wired cups, but the fuller and firmer ones were simply exposed between straps crossing the chest and torso. More dancers moved down silver-spangled stairways, slid under the legs of the male dancers, formed a variety of woven patterns and paraded along the lights at the edge of the stage. A predominant movement was simply the arms held straight out from the body, the torso swaying, the legs and breasts and headdresses showing to maximum advantage. The technique was interesting for Temple, but the performance lacked one thing crucial to ballet: a story line. Therefore it was gaudy and sensual, but not romantic.

A thunderous puff of lavender smoke produced the next act, a magician, who did the usual tricks adequately; and then attempted the lady-in-place-of-the-tiger trick, made famous by David Hemmings. He was flanked by six tall showgirls in even more elaborate costumes. Then came a Wayne Newton clone in a gold tunic who swayed at the microphone as he belted out "See the Pyramids Along the Nile," to six violins.

Several spots focused on the ceiling, and suddenly a litter descended with peacock feathers at the corners and a Cleopatra on a gold lounge. She was lightly draped with sheer, embroidered veils.

"Oh, my God, it's Allison," Temple gasped.

Allison as Cleopatra rose up and stood on the litter, she flew around the stage, veils blowing away from her body as pink, yellow and blue spots played over her. The royal litter descended to the stage where the slaves stripped the remaining veils from Cleopatra and she chased them back to their pillows with a long black bullwhip. At the left end of the stage entered a silver-haired man in a short pleated toga and wide arm and leg bracelets, tossing off his toga to show a dancer's buttocks encased in a G-string made of leaves. Anthony and Cleopatra swirled about in a passionate *Pas de Deux*. Even in this exploitative dance, it was obvious that Allison was well trained. The beautiful curve of her arms, the grace with which she moved them and the straight carriage of her back were unmistakable.

Anthony spurns Cleopatra's love, leaving her crawling on the floor, she opened a jeweled box, an asp rose, bit her neck, and Cleopatra died in her tomb.

The curtain closed, performers cleared the stage, and the stagehands rushed to move scenery in preparation for the next performance. Allison heard clapping; she turned to see Temple walking from the wings.

"*Bravisima!*"

"Temple! You're here."

Both girls rushed to hug each other.

"I'm so happy you came," Allison covered her face, "but I wish you hadn't seen this."

"I thought you would need a friend on opening night."

"I do, believe me. You are good. Come. Walk me to the dressing room so I can get out of this costume. I've got a special surprise for later, and then you can tell me everything that's happening in New York."

Allison and Temple walked through the enormous backstage areas, and passed the well-equipped wardrobe rooms. Ten women were sewing sequins and feathers, hooks and eyes and straps.

"Our costumes don't cover much, but we have lots of them." Allison grinned.

They walked down a corridor where dozens of cages held live animals. A tiger roared at Temple who jumped back in fright.

"Don't be afraid, Temple. She doesn't bite as bad as Rebecca Borden."

"You getting over it?"

"Sure." Allison shrugged. "Sure."

Outside of the dressing room Miguel stopped Allison, and planted a smoochy kiss on her forehead. "You were wonderful, darling, you have the spirit of Cleopatra. Although, I have one correction, you have to work on the whip...it has to crack when it hits the floor. Use your wrists, like this." Miguel demonstrated. "Like this...Whap! Whap! Whap! Got it?"

"Whap...whap."

"That's it. More whap."

"Got it. Miguel, I would like you to meet Temple Drake."

"Oh, my dear, I've heard so much about you."

"From Allison."

"No, no, Allison never mentions you. You're on the ballet grapevine, honey, the word is you are hot stuff, a future ballerina."

"I'm just in the corps." Temple modestly looked away.

Miguel turned to Allison, "What do you say, as soon as we get a break, we go to New York, and see this gorgeous creature on stage."

"That's a great idea, Miguel." Allison smiled widely.

"Good, well, I've got to run, kids, don't stay out too late. Remember we got a show tomorrow." Miguel smooched Allison on the cheek. "You were great tonight, Allison, you could dance here forever."

Miguel hurried off down the corridor. Allison and Temple looked at each other, and harmonized together, "Choreographers!"

They went into the spacious dressing rooms, much larger and nicer than the ones at Lincoln Center. Allison took off her gold snake tiara, and the black Cleopatra wig.

"Maybe I should dance here forever."

"Don't be ridiculous, Allison, you're too good for this. You'll be back in New York."

"Thanks, Temple. Sometimes I need to be reminded. Listen, what Miguel said about seeing you in New York, I'm not ready for that just yet. I hope you understand."

"Of course, I'd feel the same way if I were in your shoes."

"I mean, to face those dancers again, and Juri, and...see someone else in my role, I couldn't take it."

"I...I'm doing...your role now."

"Oh? Oh, well, then congratulations. If it had to be anyone I'm glad it's you." Allison wiped off the last traces of her stage makeup. "You and Juri...you're not..."

"No. No married men. That's a house rule."

"I should have lived in your house."

Allison led Temple through a labyrinth of corridors to a pair of huge rosewood doors. Allison lightly knocked on the door. Chichi, a short man with well-groomed blond hair, dressed in a white T-shirt and white pants, opened the door to the Hotel's multi-million dollar spa.

"Hey, girls.

"Hi, Chichi. This is Temple."

"Hi."

"Nice to meet you, Chichi."

"Well, Temple, take your clothes off, and we'll get started."

"What?" Temple looked at Allison in a panic.

"Chichi's gonna give us a massage."

"Oh, no, I'm OK, I don't really need one."

"Don't worry." Allison laughed.

"Listen, Temple," Chichi smiled, "You and I have a lot in common. We both like the same thing."

"What's that?"

"Men."

Temple listened to the sound of the ocean drifting through an open glass door as Chichi's fingers dug into her back. The tensions in her muscles washed away in waves of serene surrender.

"Temple."

"Hmmmmm."

"Promise me one thing."

"Whatever you want."

"You won't come back to see me in my next roles."

"What's that?"

"Scarlett O'Hara. I dance while Atlanta burn. After that we're doing a mermaid piece. I'm supposed to dance in this large fish tank."

"That I wouldn't miss for the world." Temple laughed.

Chichi slapped Temple on her naked bottom. "You're done, kid, and I'm out of here."

"Oh, let me get my handbag."

"It's taken care of. Goodnight, girls, and have fun." Chichi closed the door.

"Allison, you shouldn't have."

"I didn't. It was Chichi's pleasure."

"But he said he was gay."

"He said he liked men. But he likes girls too."

Instinctively Temple covered herself. "Oh, my God."

"Too late now to be modest." Allison laughed, and took out a bottle of white wine from the refrigerator. "Come on, Temple, it's Jacuzzi time."

Allison opened one of the glass panels, letting in the crisp cool wind. They jumped into the bubbling spa. Allison poured wine into Temple's glass.

"I'm turning into a noodle." Temple purred.

"Good, you need it after a season with the National Ballet."

"Maybe you're right. I need to be more relaxed."

"You're about to be more relaxed." Allison fished in her purse and took out a small orange plastic bottle with an unusual top. She turned it over, tapped it, and opened a flange. "Here."

"This isn't—?"

"Oh, yes, it is."

"Where did you get it?"

Allison smiled, "It's as common as sand around here. Go on. Don't worry, you're not going to die." Allison held the bottle to Temple's nose. "Just inhale."

Temple sniffed at the bottle.

"No, inhale hard."

"Wow, that goes right to my head."

"That's the idea. You feel very nice in a few seconds." Allison took a hit.

"All we need now is a couple guys."

"Screw men!"

Temple laughed, "Right, screw 'em."

"No, I mean 'screw 'em."

"Right."

"No, I don't mean 'screw 'em, I mean 'screw 'em. Do you know what I mean."

"Sure…what-the-hell do you mean."

"I mean..." Allison formed her arm into a scoop and showered Temple with water. "Screw 'em."

"And screw you." Temple retaliated by splashing Allison.

"And double screw you." Allison pushed Temple's head under water.

Temple reached up and grabbed Allison's hair, and dragged her down into the frothy water. The girls wrestled underwater, legs and arms emerged and disappeared from the boiling caldron. Running out of breath, both girls surfaced, gasping, laughing and holding each other. Temple let go of Allison's hair, but Allison ensnared her fingers in Temple's hair, and pulled her close.

"Allison, what are you—"

"Shut up."

Allison kissed Temple softly but firmly on the lips. Temple did not react or resist; her head began to spin, a cumulative effect of a massage, the Jacuzzi, wine, cocaine, and the hot, passionate, forbidden kiss. Allison kissed Temple on the neck and moved her hand down her body finding her breast and cupping it lightly.

"Allison, please, I..."

"Doesn't it feel nice?"

"Yes, but it's wrong."

"It's not wrong. It's beautiful. I'll do everything. Just let yourself go."

Temple's resistance, already weakened, gave way to Allison's touch. She felt Allison's tongue on her neck. She watched. Allison looked so pretty kissing her. And it felt so good. Allison moved Temple in front of one of the Jacuzzi jets and her hands slid down Temple's legs. Temple had never felt so warm, or felt such freedom or abandon. She had always wondered what it would be like, not just with any woman but with Allison. There were moments when they were putting on makeup in front of the bathroom mirror that Temple wanted to hug her and kiss her for being her friend. No, that was not quite true, that was just rationalization. There was more. Something she forced out of her mind. There was a secret attraction and an unspoken jealousy. Temple wanted to be as free, as outgoing, as bold, and as ruthless as Allison was. Temple swayed back and forth between fascination and resentment looking at Allison. But now her defenses were cracking. She gasped. No. It must stop! Temple flung Allison's hand away. Allison roughly reached for Temple's hand and twisted it behind her back, then grabbed a handful of Temple's hair and leaned her head back closing her mouth over Temple's lips. Allison had Temple trapped in tangled arms and legs. "No," Temple moaned, then closed her eyes, and let it happen.

Temple's eyes did not reopen until the crack of noon. She found herself in one of Bally's lavish suites. How had she got there? The last thing she remembered was…oh, God! Oh no! As hazy clouds cleared her brain, she felt an arm around her waist, a naked body lying close. It was not a dream! Memories of the night before became all too vivid. Temple was startled and afraid. She tried delicately to extricate herself from Allison's embrace without awakening her; but the movement aroused Allison.

"Where're you going?"

"Sorry, I tried not to wake you."

"Why are you sorry? I can't think of a nicer way to start a day."

Temple covered her face with one hand. "About last night…that must never happen again."

"You seemed to have enjoyed yourself."

"Allison, I am not a…lesbian."

"I'm not either, honey. One night with a woman doesn't make you a lesbian."

"How many nights does it take?"

Allison bolted up, and knelt on the bed. "Listen, Temple, it doesn't work that way. No woman could totally satisfy me. I want a man just like you. But where are they? I've given up stopped sitting on bar stools waiting for some faceless fantasy to pick me up so I can get laid."

"But this is no way to—"

"Hey, if we were a guy and a girl we'd be saying nothing happened last night."

"That's totally different."

"No, it's not. Nothing happened. You're not pregnant, are you?"

"For God's sake. Be serious."

"OK. Tell me you never fantasized what it would be like?"

Temple paused. "Alright, I have. But never, never did I think I would ever do it."

"Last night we gave each other pleasure, warmth and kindness, and I find nothing debasing or degrading about it."

"Allison, I'm scared how this changes our relationship."

"Temple, don't worry, I'm not going to ask you to marry me." Allison took Temple's hand. "Love will be there whenever you need it."

"No!" Temple pushed Allison's hand away, and jumped off the bed. "It must never happen again, never! It's perverted." Temple snatched her clothes from the floor, dashed into the bathroom and slammed the door.

Allison reached for a pillow, clutched it with her arms, then she suddenly stood on the bed and threw the pillow at the door. "God, what a prude you are." Her mouth then widened and she started to laugh.

CHAPTER 15

Giselle looked at Allison through the make-up table mirror. "You didn't make it home last night. You and Temple must have had a good time."

"Oh, yes." Allison carefully lined her eyes.

"Well, any luck picking up any guys?"

"No."

"No guys, and you had a good time?"

"It's possible."

"So what are you two doing tonight?"

"Oh, Temple had to go back to New York."

"I thought she was staying for a week."

"She was…but she was called back for an emergency rehearsal."

"That's too bad. Oh, listen, Center Ballet's in town. Kari Reed and Michael Windsor are dancing. How about we catch the matinee tomorrow?"

"I don't know if I could bear to watch."

"I know how you feel. Sometimes I daydream about being in a real ballet company. I even think about leaving my husband…but I never think about that at night."

"At least, you have someone." Allison threw her lipstick on the counter."

"For God's sake, Allison, you could have anyone you want. You're beautiful and talented."

"Really, then why isn't that enough?"

Giselle reached up, and took a red casino chip that was taped to the mirror.

"This is the first chip I won when I got here. I met my husband the same night." Giselle put the chip in Allison's hand. "Play it tonight after the show. Who knows, you might get lucky."

"No, I couldn't. It means too much to you."

"My family taught me a tradition. You pass good luck around. If you do it comes back to you. Go ahead, take it."

"You're sweet. You don't know how much I need a little kindness now, and a friend. Thanks, Giselle."

"Just make sure when you play that chip, my husband is not in the casino."

Both girls laughed, Allison leaned over and kissed Giselle on the cheek.

After the evening's performance Allison strode through the casino, her ballet bag slung over her shoulder. She walked to the center of the casino to one of the green felt blackjack tables. With a shrug she placed Giselle's chip on the table. She is dealt two nines. The dealer shows a four. She stays. The dealer draws to nineteen. Allison loses.

"So much for Giselle's lucky chip." Allison thought.

"You could have split." A sonorous, voice behind her came form a thick, raven black-haired man about thirty. His strong nose, narrow nostrils, steady gray eyes and full mouth combined into a classic European face. Allison caught the expensive tailor-made suit, and the butter-soft leather shoes, and knew he was rich.

"I don't know how to split."

"May I show you?"

"OK."

He took the seat next to her and placed a stack of chips in front of her.

"Oh, thank you, but I couldn't."

"Deal her in, please."

The woman dealer, a redhead with glossy red lipstick, maintained a cool exterior; nevertheless there was a hint of jealousy as she flipped over Allison's cards. "Blackjack for the lady."

Allison asked to be paid with Giselle's chip and she put it safely in her purse.

An hour later Allison was ahead five hundred dollars and decided to call it quits. The stranger's sonorous whispers, the beguiling aroma of his cologne, his clothes gently brushing against her bare arm had begun to mesmerize her, like a drug.

"You brought me luck. May I buy you a drink."

The gentleman looked shocked. "No. But I would be honored if you would have a drink with me. I know a quiet place with an excellent view of the harbor." The mysterious stranger took Allison's hand; she could say or do nothing but follow.

They walked along the marina where trim white yachts bobbed gently in the harbor. Allison was falling in a trance, fascinated with the way he gestured and clasped things, the way he opened his lighter, or lit a cigarette with squarish, slim-fingered manicured hands.

"I saw you dance on stage tonight, you're very good, Miss...?"

"Allison Fain."

"Have you ever thought about dancing in New York for a real ballet company."

"Oh, it crossed my mind once or twice. And are you going to tell me your name, or is it a mystery."

"Which do you prefer?"

"I'm a sucker for a good mystery. As long as there's a happy ending."

"And an interesting plot."

"Yes, that makes it even better. So where is this place?"

"I had this in mind." He pointed to the largest ship in the harbor.

"Yours?"

"No, a friend's."

"It's beautiful, gorgeous."

He took her hand, and helped her on board. "Welcome aboard, sailor."

In the ornately carved oak living room the stranger filled Allison's crystal fluted glass with champagne. Allison did not need any more wine, she was already intoxicated. A Chopin *ballade* played softly in the background, and a warm fire crackled in the green marble fireplace.

"I know you are professional, but would you condescend to a dance?" He slightly bowed from the waist.

"I would be delighted."

They waltzed around the room. Allison floated as in a dream, for the first time in her life she knew what it was like to be swept off her feet. "You dance divinely." Allison purred.

"You inspire me." He stopped dancing, and brought her close, he held her so tight she could scarcely breath. His lips close to her. Allison pulled back, paused, she wanted to be kissed more than anytime in her life, she wanted to be taken, ravaged, but first she had to ask the question. "You're not married, are you?"

"You want to throw in your hand now?"

Allison shrugged, "I just want to know."

He smiled, "I'm very single."

"Then keep dealing."

Before she closed her eyes to await his kiss, she glimpsed through the porthole the other yachts bobbing on the water, their lights glimmered in her pupils. All she knew was there were stars all around her, in her feet, her knees, her head, and her eyes. And then lightening struck. His kiss was like no other she had ever experienced. He clasped her more tightly and the pressure of his lips pushed her mouth open. Tongue on tongue, thigh to thigh, the sound of cords slapping against a hundred masts, a fireplace, champagne, Chopin, the classic handsome stranger, and Allison was completely out of control for the first time in her life.

"Darling," he whispered, and caressed the back of her thigh. He pulled her dress down over her shoulders and cupped her breasts in each hand. Allison let out a small scream—she had forgotten the surgery.

He put his mouth against her neck below her ear, as one hand pulled off her dress. She forgot the soreness of her breasts, her name, where she was. Her body between navel and knees broke into waves of lust and motion. She heaved, melted, ached as he pulled her down.

"Please, please."

He drew back, watching the lovely, writing body begging before him. In a moment he was pushing, pushing like a bull. Allison had never experienced anything like this before—the full strength of a man fully overcome by the lust that had no name, no identity, no thought, no past or future. Allison rocked against the sofa with a terrible force, lost in the waves of the harbor, the sea, the dark and starry night. The meteor of her first orgasm flashed through her in temporary brilliance. The stranger looked at her wet face, and laughed. Allison felt like a wild animal possessed her, she began to cry.

The next morning Allison awoke in an empty bed. She opened her mouth to call out for him, but realized she did not know his name. Where were her clothes? Oh, yes, scattered all over the ship. She wrapped a sheet around herself, and went topside.

The handsome stranger was on deck, wearing a black and white striped boat shirt and tights. To Allison's amazement he was stretching, holding the railing and using it as a barre.

"Good morning. Did you sleep well?

"On fluffy pink clouds." Allison answered with a dreamy smile.

"Good! There's coffee and orange juice on the table."

Allison took a sip of coffee. "You're a dancer!"

"I'm guesting with the Center Ballet."

Allison almost spilled her coffee. "Oh my God, Oh, my god, I didn't recognize you, you're Michael Windsor!"

"The mystery is solved."

"I'm so embarrassed." Allison started laughing hysterically.

"What's so funny?"

"A friend told me that I would have luck in the casino last night, and I didn't believe her. Well, it only goes to show—"

The sound of approaching footsteps startled them. "Ahoy!" A voice came from the below. Allison turned to see a tall, handsome blond bound up a ladder. "Michael, I missed you terribly. " His smile twisted to anger as he saw Allison from the corner of his eye. "So!"

"Keith." Michael smiled. "I want you to meet Allison. Allison, Keith. This is his yacht."

"It's very beautiful." Allison wrapped the sheet tighter around herself.

Keith dropped some packages on the table, sneered at Allison. "I see you enjoyed yourself on it."

Michael laughed, "'Variety.' Isn't that the word you used last night when you went off with the little college boy."

"You bastard." Keith kicked over the table; the coffee urn, cups and plates went crashing on the deck.

Allison jumped, barely getting out of the way of the steaming coffee. She looked at Michael and understood immediately that she had been used as a pawn, "You bastard!" Allison ran to the living room, gathering up her clothes and hurriedly dressing. Michael followed her.

"Allison, wait…I'm sorry."

"Right."

"I didn't mean to hurt you."

"No, I just played a little role in your game of revenge."

Michael grabbed her shoulders, "No. I had a lovely night with you."

"I'm glad." Allison's hand shook uncontrollably, she began to cry.

"Hey, come on, stop crying, please, let me make it up to you."

"You don't have to make up anything for me."

"But I want to." Michael sat her down. "Listen. Come to the matinee today. I will talk to Gregorov, and arrange a private audition."

"Gregorov!"

"Yes, God himself. I can't make any promises, of course, but there is an opening. How about it?"

"You mean it."

"You know Sleeping Beauty Pas de Deux?"

"Yes."

"I'll dance it with you. Believe me, I'm a very good partner."

"I already know that."

Michael kisses her on the forehead. "I have to go. Be backstage after the performance."

Michael ran off. Allison picked up her purse from the floor, opened it, and took out Giselle's lucky chip. She flipped it in the air, caught it, brought it to her mouth, and kissed it.

CHAPTER 16

Sitting on the edge of her bed at home in Great Neck, New York Allison stared out the window at the barren trees and mounds of mud awaiting the first whisper of spring. It was hard to believe she was back in her old room. A room that had been meticulously designed by Allison's mother, and intended to be an incubator for a creature that would grow to be part-Sleeping beauty, part-Swan, part-Juliet. Lilac walls, organdy curtains, with pale pink window shades, and a white lace vanity table were a color scheme inspired by a Degas painting 'Ballet Dancers at the Opera House,' a print of which hung opposite the bed. It amused Allison to recall how Degas was fond of calling ballet dancers 'the little rats.' Allison herself, when she was a teenager became ensnared in the ballet web, and hung photographs and posters on the remaining walls, Baryishnikov, Nureyev, Susan Jaffe, Alessandra Ferri, and, of course, the gorgeous Christopher Beckett.

The room seemed now a juvenile jest, "Little girl's dreams!" Allison wanted to throw a bomb into the room, but instead rubbed moisturizing cream on her face.

"I brought you some green tea, dear." her mother walked into the room.

"Mother, I asked for coffee."

"Green tea is better for you. It has antioxidants." Ruth placed the cup on the vanity table, and looked intently at Allison. "The surgeon did a very good job. Your eyes will look good on stage."

"So you noticed?"

"I'm your mother! Did you think you could keep anything from me? Did you think I didn't suspect where all that money was going?"

"I was going to tell you."

"Of course you were." Ruth sat beside Allison on the bed. "I don't know why you had a breast reduction, in my day breasts were considered an asset." Allison started to explain. "It's all right. Anyway, there is something else I wanted to talk to you about."

"Yes, mother."

"You remember our lunch at Tavern on the Green before you left for Atlantic City."

"Oh yes, I certainly haven't forgotten that."

"Since then I've often wondered if you thought that I...forced you into dance."

"You've forced me all my life, mother. I never chose dance. You chose it for me."

Ruth summoned up her courage to ask the question that gnawed at her insides. "Do you hate me for it?"

"Do I hate you?" Allison heaved a long sigh. "If you only knew how many times I wanted to drive a knife into your heart. I danced to make you love me, and I hated you for it."

"But why? All I wanted for you was—"

"Because one day I woke up and realized you were training me to be you."

Ruth nodded, "And you still hate me?"

"No, mother, I could have quit, many times. But I didn't. And you know why?" Ruth shook her head. "It wasn't for you, and it wasn't for art, or music, or the beauty of the dance. It was because dance made me special. Maybe that's not very lofty, but that's the truth. And you had nothing to do with that. It's something that was always inside of me."

Allison stood and walked to the window. "No, I don't hate you mother. If there's anyone I hate it's me. I don't even try to hide the vanity inside me. I'm vain and conceited and I know it. When I was kicked out of the National I wanted to die...not because I would miss the bleeding toes, the daily grind and sweat of the studio, but because without it I was just ordinary."

Ruth went to her daughter, "Nonsense, Allison, you're too hard on yourself. I should have shown you other careers that could have offered you the—"

"No, mother. Not like dance. Can you picture me as a Madeline Albright or a Janet Reno or…Hillary Clinton?" Mother and daughter laughed.

"Mother, you are absolved. I love you for your support without limit. But now it's all me."

Ruth kissed Allison on the cheek, "Good, then I have some news for you. You father and I leased an apartment for you."

"What? Where?

"Across from Lincoln Center."

The air was taken out of Allison's lungs, "That must have cost a fortune. Mother, you really didn't have to, I would be happy renting a little place."

"It's a reward for getting into the Center Ballet. And by the way, the location will be perfect to entertain: ballet masters, critics, writers, and choreographers—single choreographers!"

"I don't know what to say."

"The decorating is almost finished."

"Mother, I would have liked to decorate it myself."

"Don't worry, it won't look like this room. It will be very sophisticated. Besides I didn't want the decorating distracting from your career."

Ruth opened her arms. "Come." Allison moved closer to her mother, and was engulfed by Ruth's embrace. "When you were fired, I thought my life was over. All my dreams destroyed. Allison, I want you to know there was nothing I would not have done for you, no sacrifice too great. You were raised to be a ballerina. Never let anything or anyone take that away from you."

Allison nestled her face on her mother's shoulder. "No, mother, I won't. You can count on that."

CHAPTER 17

Allison packed her new French leotard, cut high at the hips and low in the back to show off her body. Slinging her new Gucci bag over her shoulder, she darted for her first class with the Center Ballet. On Broadway she stopped at Elaine's Flower Shop and bought tiny "Babies Breath" flowers to decorate her classic, pulled-back chignon hairstyle. Waiting for her change, she surveyed walls adorned with autographed photos of New York dancers. She had given Elaine a photo of herself a year ago. It was gone. She should have expected it. One of the penalties for leaving New York is to be instantly forgotten.

The journey along Broadway was both familiar and new. Stores and restaurants like Amy's or Fiorello (where she used to share ice cream crepes with Temple), among new apartment buildings, new restaurants such as Gigots with waiters on roller stakes; and new boutiques such as Valeska, where Allison promised herself she would return to browse.

Entering the spacious studios of the Center Ballet was like being transported to the Parthenon. The two-story lobby was supported by four classic, white Grecian columns, which set off a white marble stairway that led to the studios, a gigantic painting of the virgin goddess Minerva was set behind a black marble reception desk. Mothers sat on black slate stone benches at the edges of the lobby waiting for their daughters, and doing the three things that all ballet mothers do—gossip, gossip, gossip.

Treading on soundless indigo carpet, she stood at reception desk, where a cherubic young man with an acne-scarred face and protruding eyeballs peered through round, rimless glasses at Allison.

"Yes, here is the form to enroll in Adult Exercise Classes." He handed her a paper.

That riled Allison. Surely she did not look like one of the cows that took Adult Exercise Class? "I'm here for Company Class," she replied indignantly.

"Company Class is for Company members," was the quick retort.

"I am a Company Member."

The young man looked startled. "You? Who are you?"

"Allison Fain."

"Oh, the showgirl." He extended the tips of his fingers. "I am Charles Sittler, the Company Manager."

"Nice to meet you." Allison politely shook his fingers while her face flushed red.

"I hope you'll be happier here. The dressing rooms and studios are up the stairs on the right."

Allison graciously thanked him, although she didn't like him she knew it was bad policy for a newcomer to be on anybody's bad side.

Allison entered the studio and winced as she noticed half the girls had flowers in their hair, instantly regretting she had stopped by Elaine's. She wanted to look, at least, a little different.

As 10:30 approached the constellation of stars streamed in the studio, and the air bristled with the electricity of the ballet world's most celebrated dancers, Regina Christian, Carlotta Gray, Georginna Haviland, and Valeries Vestoff.

Company class was not merely an exercise for beautiful athletes, it was deadly competition. Not just with each other, but with themselves. Super-egos scanned banks of mirrors that told no lies, that showed every flaw, each dancer faced a show down with their own reflection. Hands gripped wooden barres. Everyone concentrated. In class there were no excuses, no partner to blame for falling off pointe, no conductor to scold if a pirouette was too slow.

Precisely at 10:30, Vaslov Alexi Gregorov entered, as he had for twenty years. He nodded to the assemblage of the world's greatest dancers. The studio was hushed in reverence.

Dancers chanted in unison, "Good morning, Mr. Gregorov."

"Good morning, my children."

Feet automatically fell in place for first position. A sense of contentment relaxed the dancers; the familiar routine warmed and protected them, for the moment, from harsher realities.

Gregorov was dressed in casual western wear, a blue jeans shirt with sleeves rolled to the elbows, pleated gray slacks, and butter-soft leather shoes made of the finest leather and hand-crafted in Italy. An extravagance on a corporate executive's salary, but Gregorov did not take salary. Instead the company reimbursed all his expenses. He merely had to point to what he wanted, whether an apartment, a car, jewelry, or a painting. Gregorov was, after all, more than a cultural institution, he was a demi-god; and it was certainly not befitting a god to carry loose change.

Vaslov Gregorov had once danced in his native Russia with the Kirov Ballet, but there had been nothing outstanding in his early performance, nothing suggesting he would later revolutionize ballet history. He arrived in America without the fanfare that greets the Russian defectors of this generation. Unable to find work in any classical ballet company, he survived by choreographing Broadway and Las Vegas shows. His fortune changed when he met the affluent businessman Oscar Lipstein at a museum exhibition. Lipstein listened intently to the Russian's description of a new kind of dance, a neo-classical dance of the Twentieth Century. Lipstein agreed to meet Gregorov for lunch the next day, and by the time coffee was served from the sterling silver urn of the Russian Tea Room, a new company was in the making.

Gregorov was impressed by the financial manipulations that Lipstein undertook to insure the economic success of the venture. Unlike the Russian public, Americans regarded ballet as a haven for homosexuals; a mood of hostility that made it difficult to find supporters. But

Lipstein raised one million dollars in two months, and the New York Center Ballet was created. Gregorov then concentrated on building the company into a "living jewel." He carefully recruited the best available dancers from all over America. He turned his back on the popular syrupy-sweet classical ballets, and instead chose the music of contemporary composers such as Igor Stravinsky. The New York cognoscenti flocked to Gregorov's new ballet, and thrilled to his daring innovations—although the mass audiences balked at such unfamiliar work. But Lipstein never lost faith, and helped Gregorov for the next twenty years build one of the two greatest companies in the world.

Gregorov, a slender 5'6", was far from an imposing physical presence, but he vibrated like the puppet, Petrouska, with passion and activity. At sixty-five years of age he still appeared on-stage as the Rat King in Nutcracker. And his virility was legend; as well as his rumored fondness for young dancers. A preference evidenced by the fact that he advanced Georginna Haviland and Regina Christian to Principal roles when they were both only seventeen.

At the center of his class stood his rumored mistress, Regina Christian, Gregorov's favorite dancer. Her physical presence embodied the archetypal look of the Center Ballet: slinky long limbs, a delicate face, arrogant eyes, and a small head perched on a long, graceful neck; but which her many detractors characterized as "the head of a hamster on the body of a weasel."

Allison studied Regina. What was it she had? What special qualities did Gregorov see? Allison could not deny she possessed a disconcerting combination of sophisticated sensuality and childlike innocence. The corps girls of the Center Ballet copied Regina carefully. They imitated her in every detail, hoping it would turn Gregorov's attention to them. If Regina wrapped a flowery print scarf around her hair, the next day the entire corps appeared with flowery scarves. When Regina affected a Continental look of French espadrilles and long peasant dresses, the look became the "Center Ballet Look." Allison thought it foolish. The obeisance of the corps to the star doomed them to remain in the corps, and in her shadow. It was surely Regina's uniqueness that attracted Gregorov.

Gregorov surveyed dancers with intense black eyes. His fingers snapped, "And one, and two;" the ritual of class began. Occasionally, he would stop a dancer and correct a placement in the legs or hips. His insights were uncanny, the result of years of experience and the distillation of the secrets of ballet history. It was said that one correction from Gregorov could change a dancer's career.

From the rear of the studio Allison saw a dancer rush into class and assume a place at the front. Allison expected Gregorov to reprimand her, but instead, he merely shook his head and smiled. Through the rows of dancers Allison could make out the back of her head. Strands of blond hair falling out of her chignon, she looked a lot like—no! It couldn't be! Allison almost fell off the barre. "It was her! What was she doing here? Only members of the Center Ballet were permitted to take company class. No guest was ever allowed. And what was she doing in the front? Positions at the front were only reserved for Principals and Soloists."

Class finished with a burst of applause for the Ballet Master. Allison joined the applause, but felt a tightening in the pit of her stomach. Gregorov had not even looked her way for the entire hour and a half.

Allison maneuvered through the dancers. "Temple?"

Temple turned. "Allison!" She unloosed a scream so loud that every dancer looked in her direction. Temple recovered from shock to ask, "What are you doing here?

"I'm in the Company! What are you doing here?"

"I'm in the company too."

"How?"

"That's a long story."

"I want to hear it. How about we get together at my new apartment."

"Listen, Allison, I'm sorry for not getting back to you after all your calls and letters. But I...well."

"It's OK, I understand. So how's tomorrow night?"

"Well…I."

"Temple, I'm not going to rape you. Tomorrow at eight at my place?"

"OK, eight o'clock."

CHAPTER 18

Opening the door to her apartment Allison greeted Temple with a sweep of her floor length antique black kimono. She escorted Temple into the living room, shuffling a bit in floppy black ballet slippers. "This is it," Allison cooed, "How do you like it?"

Temple could not speak. The room loomed before her, a gigantic space. The front was nearly all windows. An ornate fireplace dominated one side end of the room. The furnishings were simple, but in faultless taste. Two large creamy velvet sofas, a polished African burl wood cocktail table and an intricately patterned antique Oriental rug created a "living area" in the middle of the vast space. To one side another marvelous rug, this one dark blue with red swirls and white and mauve flower patterns led the way into the bedroom. Temple opened a door to reveal a kitchen, another large room, red tiled with a formidable island of solid ash wood in the center, and gleaming stainless steel appliances handing from the ceiling.

"Allison, it's wonderful!" Temple turned toward her old friend, "especially compared to my kitchen, which is two feet wide. I could live in this room.

Allison sighed. "All I can do is boil water for coffee, or open a can of tuna fish."

"No!" Temple protested.

"Mother wouldn't let me learn any homemaker skills."

Temple had Allison in tow and showed the bedroom, a room done in Chinese oxblood and black pillows, the windows were covered by lighted Japanese sliding panels. "Gorgeous," Temple admired.

"What would you like to drink?" Allison offered sweetly.

"Wine would be fine, thank you."

Allison in her silk kimono swished into the kitchen. Temple thought how Allison looked so sophisticated in the setting of her prestigious apartment. Temple, in ripped jeans and white woolen sweater, felt like a poor school girl—all she needed to complete the image was a spiral notebook and a ruler.

Temple promised herself that tomorrow she would visit some boutiques to outfit herself in more chic New York wardrobe.

Temple heard the soft hiss of silk entering the room.

"Here, darling," Allison poured wine into two crystal Baccarat goblets. "A toast to new times."

"To new times." They raised glasses to each other and sipped. "Mmmm, great wine, Allison." Temple receded into the softness of he velvet sofa and stared at the fireplace. "I love that fireplace and those beautiful carvings."

"It will be my favorite luxury, to sit in front of it for hours recovering from rehearsals like today. So tell me, I can't wait a second longer. How did you get in the Center? All I kept hearing was how well you were doing at the National."

Temple took another sip of wine. "Yes, I was happy there. I loved the repertoire, to be honest, a lot more than the rep at the Center. Well, I was getting more and more lead roles, and getting very good reviews. When the new contracts were handed out for next season I was offered a corps contract. Meanwhile Nanette Gorham, you remember her?

"The girl who looks like Bucky Beaver."

Temple laughed, "The same. She gets a Soloist contract, and she had no lead roles, in fact, that girl can hardly dance. When I spoke to Rebecca Borden about it, all she could say was 'You're day will come, sweetie.' Well, at a party I met a boy, Roberto, from the Center and talked to him about it. He spoke to Gregorov, and Gregorov had seen me dance, and he offered me a soloist contract."

"So you outrank me."

"And I expect a salute whenever I pass."

"Yes, sir." Allison performed a mock salute.

"So what's your story? How did you get in?"

"No story, really. They had open auditions in Atlantic City, and…I made it in."

"That's it? I expected something more dramatic from you."

"Sorry, that's the whole story. I live a dull life lately."

Temple looked around the apartment, "So I see."

"Temple," Allison turned to her friend with an air of conspiracy. "Tell me everything about everybody in the Center!"

Temple raised an eyebrow, as if to say, I shouldn't say anything; but Temple knew if there was one thing Allison loved as much as sex, it was gossip.

"How did Regina Christian get back into the company after Gregorov fired her two years ago?" Allison asked.

Temple smiled. "Gregorov was madly in love with her when she was a seventeen year old student. He put her in the company and created three ballets for her. Then Peter Spenser joined the company. It was top secret that she was seeing Peter. For a year they sneaked dinner in Regina's apartment because they feared running into Gregorov at a restaurant. Finally, they eloped, and when Gregorov found out he fired them. They tried guesting as a Pas de Deux team, but it didn't work. She's so tall and he's so short they looked like a dancing Mutt and Jeff. Peter stopped dancing, and tried to choreograph; but everything he did looked like a bad imitation of Gregorov. So Regina asked Gregorov to take her back. Gregorov agreed, with the stipulation that Peter stay out of his sight; stay away from the studio, the theatre, and away from tour."

"What does Peter do?"

"Live off her paychecks, shop for her wine, walk her dogs, and treat her like a princess. I'm waiting for the day when Gregorov asks all of us to bow when she enters the studio."

"How about Mark Gerston and Galina?"

"Broke-up after eleven years of marriage. Mark didn't get it from Galina, except an occasional hand-job."

Temple continued. "Mark was guesting with Baltimore Ballet and partnering Ginny Evans; you remember her from our student days?"

"Yes."

"They're getting married!"

"My God, no! Ginny's a hot number."

Temple edged along the sofa closer to Allison. "We had a season at Jacob's Pillow. There were five male dancers, of course, all gay. So they put us in little wooden cabins behind the theatre. Five boys, Ginny and me."

Temple paused for a sip of wine. "Every night Ginny complained how horny she was, running around the cabin with her robe open. After three days all the boys moved out, and went to another cabin. So, I was left alone with her. One night I hear moaning. I look over. There she was naked, rolling around playing with herself."

"So? I'm sure you've done it once or twice."

"Yeah, but not with a Pointe shoe."

Both girls held hands over their mouths, like cheerleaders hearing a rumor at the junior prom.

"Then there's a girl in the company, Delphine La Fleur, who carries a suitcase full of vibrators. Nobody gets a hotel room next to her on tour because the room buzzes all night."

Temple stopped laughing "God, maybe I should try it," Temple pondered.

"Still no love life."

"I can't even meet a straight guy."

"Occupational hazard, girl."

"Listen, Allison, about that night."

"Yes, I tried calling you because I wanted to apologize.

"No, I'm the one who should apologize. You see I had those...types of fantasies before...and when the fantasy became real... it frightened me. I was scared and ashamed…I treated you very badly…as if you were a criminal, or a pervert. And all you were offering was love."

Allison took Temple's hand. "It's all right. It's forgotten. Allison chided. "We're friends again, that's the only thing that's important."

"Thanks."

"And it taught me a lesson. I'm going to become more like you, Miss Chastity Belt." She yawned like a lioness and looked at her watch. "But it's almost midnight. I'd love to talk all night, but we have to be on tippy-toes for early class tomorrow."

Temple rose, "Let's do it again soon." They kissed and hugged good-bye.

Allison put on a sweater over her kimono and walked out to her balcony. She wrapped the sweater tight around her against the chilling winds blowing off the Hudson River. She looked at Broadway below. She saw Temple walking out of the building. She did not notice buildings or people passing by, she was so busy fighting an attack of primal jealousy. Allison watched as Temple stopped briefly at the plaza of Lincoln Center, the soft spray of the Plaza fountain misted lightly on Temple's face. A fan ran to her, producing a book and asking Temple for an autograph.

In a few weeks there would be the first long tour of the season for the Center Ballet, after that the company would return to play the Opera House. The tour would be enough time for Allison to prove herself, enough time to return to the Opera House as a Soloist. While Temple was a soloist she could not endure playing corps girl. Rather she would prefer to be found floating face down in the Plaza fountain!

CHAPTER 19

The next few weeks preparing for the tour were anything but happy. Gregorov's rehearsals were as cheerful as a detention camp. As he grew older, the harsh discipline of Russian ballet and Russian life consumed his immigrant spirit, and he clung to this part of his youthful memory as though to life itself.

In the shrine of the studio, decorum was demanded above all. If one dancer hugged another, he frowned. A simple kiss made him glare in annoyance. The only place the girls were safe from the Stalinesque atmosphere was in the bathroom. There the unsteady young women gave way to tears and tantrums and expressions of joy and support from one another. More often, they held it all in until they were at home thus preventing letting it out when they least wanted to.

Allison was having a light supper one night with Temple at Fiorello's, across from Lincoln Center, when she first saw a young dancer become hysterical and uncontrollable in public. The girl was not someone they knew, but she could have easily been. As lovely and fragile as a hummingbird with honey blond hair in the classic chignon and a black lamb's fur jacket over her jeans, she was sitting alone at a corner table. Suddenly her shrieks echoed around the room, and she beat her head with her hands as though a subway train had been routed inside it and she would catch it or squeeze her forehead cone-shaped in the effort. The cafe's owner and a waiter took her gently by the elbows and hurried her out. It was not the first time they had saved such a scene.

Allison's comment was cynical. "That will make an opening for some hopeful young dancer some place tomorrow, 'cuz that one ain't gonna dance no mo."

Temple could not answer. The terror was too close. Temple took a quick swallow of wine.

Allison went on, "The girl I replaced, Karina Kaye, drowned in her parents' swimming pool a week after the management fired her. Karina was a high school swimming star before she became a professional dancer. But we were told not to mention the word 'suicide' to anyone."

"Why," Temple questioned as she swallowed more wine.

"It might leak to the press. Bad public relations hurts fund raising."

"OK, enough, let's not talk about suicides anymore."

"Temple, you're a big girl, you have to know about these things."

"I do know about these things…my father committed suicide."

Allison's mouth opened, "Oh, I am so sorry. I didn't know."

"Now you do." Temple stood, walked out of the restaurant and disappeared into a crowd.

Rehearsals fell behind schedule necessitating the company to work six days a week. There was no break. Rehearsals were all day, and at night it was wash tights and leotards, sew toe shoes, sleep, wake and repeat the day, again and again. There was no luxury of time that normal people take for granted, shopping, reading a novel, lunch with friends, or just sitting on a park bench.

No one in the company dared express their feelings about Gregorov's tyranny over their lives. Actually the dancers revered the old man as much as they feared him. So Temple and Allison would have to bear it and kept working. Both knew there would be no going back to the National as long as Rebecca Borden was alive.

"Hey, girls!" A pair of hands pinched Temple and Allison's rears.

"Roberto!" Temple screamed. "This is the guy I was telling you about, Allison."

"Oh, I've heard so much about you."

"I'm not as bad as people say…actually I'm worse, honey." Roberto, the company's sole Puerto Rican, spoke with a slow Salsa accent; he often caricatured himself for the style it gave him. Roberto with his triangular, skinny face, his twitchy eyeballs and frizzed hair, was all style. "*Que passon*, sweet things?"

"What else, steps." Allison complained.

"The coda in the Mozart piece." Temple added.

"*No problema*." He grabbed her hand, "Lez' go. We work it out over lunch."

"Where to?" Temple asked.

"Annie's of course. Where else can you get papaya yogurt?"

Passersby, if they cared to watch, could see an entire Mozart ballet staged only with hands by three young dancers who sat in the window of Annie's restaurant on Broadway. One finger twirled in the air was a *pirouette*; hands scissored together were a *scisson*, and two fingers tapping on the table meant *bourees*. Customers and staff hardly glanced at the couple with hands whirling off and on the table. Roberto, dressed in an olive-drab parachute jumpsuit and a rhinestone New York Yankees baseball cap, raised not an eyebrow in this little pocket of the dance world.

"Hey, girls," Roberto said with cavalier concern, "You been going out?"

Allison shrugged. "I can barely get my bones into bed at night. A hot bath is pretty exciting to me these day."

"Do you masturbate in the tub?" he asked with a wicked smile. Allison laughed out of embarrassment; but it was Roberto's style, he needed to know every detail of an affair, and was keen at ferreting the truth about performances in the sack. "I do not," Allison defended.

"Then where?"

"Roberto!" Her cheeks flushed.

Temple came to her rescue. "Enough, Roberto."

"Darlings, you got to go out and meet some men. Mira, there's a party at Stockton Cambell's. Don't say no. I made up my mind you will both be my date."

It hit Allison that Roberto wanted attractive girls on his arm, to make him more desirable to the men he wished to attract. She assumed he was after straight men, as they were tougher prey. Nonetheless Allison was delighted at the prospect of meeting some new people.

"Girls, someone's got to look out for you. You'll never make it through the Company alone." Roberto urged.

Bull's eye! He wanted a 'fag hag' to hang out with the other gays in the Company, and be privy to the latest gossip. The girls, if they considered Roberto's proposal would gain instant acceptance into a group of dancers, powerful allies whose lovers sat on the Board of Directors of Center Ballet. And gays were loyal unto the death to their 'fag hags.'

"OK, we'll go." Allison agreed.

"No, not me," Temple protested, "I have nothing to wear except a dress I wore to my Senior Prom."

"A prom dress would not exactly work at a Stockard Cambell party, but I'll take care of that." He attached a cigarette to his ivory holder. "Let's go shopping just to make sure you have the proper attire." He grinned broadly, tipped his Rhinestone Yankee hat; and they were gone.

Roberto seemed to know all the women's boutiques on Columbus Avenue. He greeted the salesgirls by name and selected the dresses for the girls to try on, with appropriate, hilarious commentary. Temple decided on a white satin dress cut "to the ass" in back and far enough "to let 'em know you've got boobies" in front. They then crossed over to Fifth Avenue and Fifty-seventh street to La Valse Shoes and picked out a pair of very high heels with narrow straps criss-crossing at the ankles. Roberto insisted on paying for the shoes. "I love the criss-crossing it would be wonderful for cross-dressing. You don't mind I borrow them sometime, do you, honey."

When he picked Temple up later, he clicked his tongue with approval as he viewed the total outfit. Temple paused to look in the mirror of the lobby and decided she looked like a high-class, East Side hooker. Had Roberto planned it deliberately, to tease and tantalize the other men? Was she a trophy or a worm on a fishhook? Whatever, it didn't matter. She felt adult for the first time since she moved up from Louisiana, she was becoming more sophisticated, maybe a little wicked, maybe even a little like Allison.

Stockard Cambell's place was a penthouse at the ritzy UN Plaza. The party was in full swing when Roberto, Temple and Allison arrived; the immense living room was full of smoke and chatter. A butler indicated the way to a black leather bar. Behind it opened a spectacular view of the East River with the lights of the bridges strung out like glittering necklaces, and beyond that was the distant shoreline of Brooklyn and Queens. Once they had drinks in hand, Roberto took Allison on a tour. The most surprising room in the house was a Japanese tearoom with imported mats and tables from Kyoto, where Stockard had taken lessons and later decided he couldn't do without a daily tea ceremony at home.

"He meditates, too," confided Roberto. "He's very spiritual. He spends hours every day just sitting on a pillow."

"What else does he do?" Temple asked.

"Makes money, lots of it, and he sits on several arts boards like any good culture vulture, and, of course, he chases boys."

Back in the main room with the two glass walls, Temple stepped gingerly over a girl stretched out on the thick white carpet flipping popcorn into her mouth while watching an old-fashioned porn film on TV.

Despite her new, sexy clothes Temple felt out of place among the high chic of the East Side's 'In Crowd.' The dimly lit room and the relentless pounding of the disco music, several decibels above tolerance, made a dull throbbing pain start at the back of Temple's head. She needed another drink, so she could relax and process the scene. This was her first real New York party, but she expected nothing like this. The casual but devastating snobbery was irritating to a simple, Southern girl. The only thing that tempered it was the utter relaxation of some people on couches who were snorting cocaine. She found herself in the middle of the room, feeling alone, she looked around for Allison, a friendly hand to quiet her nervousness.

Allison had headed straight for that cluster of elegantly dressed couples perched on a camel colored suede sofa. A woman in green spandex pants and a transparent black camisole handed her a joint as she sat down. Allison passed it on. Another joint followed, almost immediately. A slim, fashionably dressed man on her right turned a captivating smile on her. "Fresh today from Bloomie's men's room."

How could Allison refuse this charming gray-haired stranger? She puffed.

"I'm Stockard Cambell."

"I'm Allison Fain."

"I know."

Allison was surprised. "How did…?"

"Roberto," he interrupted, as he passed the joint back to her, "told me all about you." He slid his hand over her thigh.

The grass was stronger than Allison had ever had before; her head started to spin. She wondered if she looked as green as the spandex slacks that were now rubbing against her leg. Just what had Roberto told him? Of course, the story of her affair with Juri. The thought crossed Allison mind that maybe it would be easier if she just wore a scarlet 'A.'

Alison stammered, "I…I don't think I need anymore."

"Oh, don't be a silly puss. Have another drag. Here, let me help you with this roach clip."

He pulled a tiny gold scissors out of his breast pocket and clipped it on the joint. The eye of the scissors sparkling blue, Allison wondered if it were real sapphire. Inhaling, her lungs felt lined with gravel, her throat like a sandpit. As she tried to speak smoke spilled out of her lips with a torrent of coughing. But within seconds she began relaxed; strangely, the music became tolerable, although it didn't stop her eyes from oozing like a watering can."

Roberto plopped beside her. "So what do you think of Georginna Haviland?"

"She here?"

"Over there on the floor." Roberto pointed to the girl in faded jeans, still tossing popcorn into her mouth. "The ballet world's next Prima Ballerina."

"I didn't recognize her. She looks fourteen."

"She is fourteen. That's how Gregorov likes them. Right out of Junior High. Did you know she had silicone shot in her upper lip because her thick bottom lip made her look like she was always pouting? Weird, don't you think?"

A solitary popcorn plunked on Georginna's nose and landed on her flat chest. Allison thought about her own cosmetic modifications, and felt there was nothing weird at all.

"So what do you think of Stockard?" Roberto quizzed.

"He's nice."

"Nice he's not. But he donates a hundred grand to the company every year; this year he put up all the money for Christopher Beckett's new ballet."

"So isn't that nice?"

Roberto flashed a sarcastic grin. "Nice? He thinks it's a way to get into Beckett's pants."

"God, that's a pity." Allison was genuinely disappointed.

"Have another drink. It's time for me to cruise the party."

Allison went for another to wash down the gravel in her throat. "And why not?" she told herself. "After three weeks in the convent I deserve to let loose."

The party was getting amusing to Allison as more and more men in chic costumes began to walk in the door. Two frail blond boys packed into the party, twins or dressed up to look like twins. It was hard to tell since the party was thick with smoke. When her eyeballs cleared, she found herself looking at shadowy figures in black leather slouched in the hallways. Stockard ushered Allison and these men into his bedroom. The odor of sweat and the unmistakable scent of marijuana and amyl nitrate hit Allison. Men danced around the bed or lounged along the bar in the bedroom, some in jeans, others in full leather outfits, a couple in cowboy costumes. Two men in black leather jockstraps, boots and nothing else danced with Allison. Allison let loose, slithering from one man to the next, teasing, taunting. This is fun, Allison thought, and since they're all gay there was no worry that anything could happen.

Temple could not find Allison so she had thrown down a few drinks for courage, but she was clear-headed enough to notice that most of the women in the room had filtered out the doors, and now the party was now almost all men.

"Roberto," Temple tugged him away from a group of college age boys, "Where's Allison?"

"Having fun, I hope."

"It's time to go."

"Chiquita, the real fun hasn't even begun."

"That's why we're leaving."

"Baby doll, don't be a—"

"Now! Move it."

Roberto guided her through the throng, but Temple collided with a bald-headed man. Temple excused herself, then noticed his small leather vest partially concealed nipples pierced with silver rings.

Temple whispered frantically into Roberto's ear. "What the hell's going on here?"

"Why are you so upset, chicquita, you think the world is all pink tutus?"

Temple walked into Stockard's bedroom as the two cowboys were tying rope around Allison's wrists to the pillars behind Stockard's bed. For a moment Temple was frozen in the doorway. "That's enough."

Temple shouted. She quickly moved to the bed, and began to untie Allison's wrists.

"Hold on, girl," one of the cowboys smiled, "we could use another cowgirl." He pushed Temple down on top of Allison.

In one move Temple flipped her body over on the bed and swung her leg around, landing her foot dead center on the cowboy's head. He landed against the black leather headboard, his nose bleeding. Temple pulled the drunken Allison from the bed, and dragged her from the bedroom and through the party into the hallway.

Temple propped Allison up against an elevator wall.

"What are you doing?" Allison protested.

"Saving your drunken ass."

"Who asked you?"

Temple was astounded, "Allison, this is not our type of party."

"It's not your type of party, you country bumkin."

Temple instantly felt the sting of the slur; she stiffened her jaw to stifle her anger. "Do you have any idea what was going to happen to you with all those men."

"Why? Were you jealous?"

In a flash Temple's hand flashed across Allison's face. She paused for a moment, not believing what she had just done, and then ran from the elevator and out into the street where she hailed a taxi.

Allison stumbled out of the elevator on wobbly high heels. A skinny, Puerto Rican doorman, assuming she was just another drunk coming from a party, rushed to help her sit on a bench in the lobby.

"You OK, lady?"

"Sure." she assured him.

The slap helped clear some of the spider webs in her brain. Just what the hell was she doing upstairs at that party? Did she really need to add to her reputation? And why the hell had she said that to Temple? Who was the one who was really jealous? Why? Why? What was driving her?

What in God's good name was wrong with her? Allison started to cry, a little at first, but when the gates opened she began to bawl.

The doorman, somewhat sympathetic, somewhat embarrassed, but also desiring to maintain the dignity of his lobby approached her. "Can I call you a taxi, Miss."

"Call me a psychiatrist."

Chapter 20

The last few weeks of rehearsal whirled by like a triple pirouette, with costume fittings, publicity interviews, photo sessions for the souvenir book, and rehearsals. It helped take Allison's mind off the fact that Temple had not said one word to her since the party. Allison's only friend in the company was Roberto, but she limited their social contact to lunches and an occasional dinner. Most time went for steps.

Allison learned choreography for six ballets and understudied three others. Her brains were ready to explode with endless combinations of *batteries, entrechats,* and *fouettes.* A high school drama coach once told her that nineteenth century actors had to learn entire Shakespearean plays by heart; she was accomplishing a feat probably as difficult; if not more crucial. If an actor blows a line he can be cued back; but a missed count in a dance or a wrong step could send an entire row of corps girls collapsing like the row of dominoes! The tension between the former friends as they passed in a corridor, or changed in the dressing room added to the stress.

Allison knew Gregorov was watching her, although in three weeks he had not given her a single correction. The old fox could scan fifty dancers and point out mistakes, sometimes suggesting changes so subtle many teachers would have let them slip by. Like other masters trained in the old Russian schools, he had photographic eyes. After seeing a full-length ballet even once, he could re-set every step for every dancer the next day, although the number of steps and combinations totaled in the millions. Steps were Gregorov's language, the sacred vernacular of the religion of dance.

The studios of the Center Ballet had much of the aura of a church. Allison sometimes barely resisted the temptation to genuflect at the receptionist's desk manned by Madame Dudorska. The old dame had escaped Russia with Gregorov and dignified the entrance to his sanctuary with the face of a wrinkled icon, a perfect coiffure, manicured hands, and always wearing a designer suit and a stern expression. Once inside, corps girls assumed an unspoken vow of celibacy, as in a nunnery. The contrast couldn't have been greater with Gregorov's personal life, replete with three former wives and a trail of younger mistresses. Nevertheless he disapproved of romances within the company as though the identity of an heir were at stake. The last time a couple transgressed he banished them to an Australian ballet company, and they considered themselves well off, as he had been known to do worse. The First Commandment at the Center Ballet was that there were no idols before Gregorov.

Finally the New York Center Ballet was going on tour, an American tour, to cities such as Chicago, Detroit, Minneapolis, Kansas City, San Francisco, San Diego, Dallas, Memphis, Atlanta, Richmond, and Washington, D.C., plus a host of smaller places in between. A few days before leaving, Allison and Roberto sat swinging their legs over the edge of the fountain in Lincoln Center Plaza.

"I'm excited, I don't mind telling you. Aren't you?"

"Chiquita, it's my fourth season. The first couple of times it's okay, then it gets to be a drag. What crap parties they have in the provinces! Full of fat old widows who want to pat a ballet star on the ass."

Allison leaned back and turned her face into the sun working its way down between the tall buildings. The skyscrapers flashed like bronze mirrors. "I don't know if I can handle this tour, I already feel I'm ready to crash and burn."

"Allison, you have to learn how to shut down when you leave the studio. I was raised a Catholic, I know how to slam the confessional door when I finish with the priest. You're going to go crazy if you don't learn, like…"

"Like Karina?"

"Yeah, Karina, the girl you replaced. Nice chick, and they wrecked her. I told her to go back to swimming a hundred times, but she liked the lights. The magic of being on stage gets to you, you know? And the music. That's what got me, the music. It saved my life."

"Saved your life?"

"Yeah, I'd probably be hustling cheap tricks or selling dope. I was born on the street and would have died there if it wasn't for dance."

"But I never saw anyone who loves being out on the street more than you."

"Yeah, the street is in my soul. Where I lived in the South Bronx everything took place on the street. People spent eighty percent of their lives there—only came in out of the rain and in winter. They even screw on the street.

"So how did you get out?"

"You know how kids see a great dancer or a dance company and get struck by lightning? Well, with me it wasn't even a dance company. I'd never seen anything before I was thirteen up there in the Bronx, except cockfights and human fights. One day they set up a ratty old stage on my street. It was the Puerto Rican Traveling Theatre. That day I saw some goofy thing about a pirate named Cossi, from Puerto Rico. The guy had a black and gold cape, must have been made out of a curtain, and a wooden sword. But he looked terrific, that guy! I was really taken with the way he ran around the stage, waving that sword in the air. Right after that I begged Mama to let me become an actor. They didn't have any acting classes in the neighborhood, but she found a place where they gave free dance lessons to slum kids. That's how I got started. You think that's ridiculous, don't you?"

"No."

"Temple is sort of like me, the way she started. That's why I admire her so much."

"So you would admire me if I grew out of the slum."

"Easy, *mija*. I'm not making a comparison. But since you mention it, you had all the advantages."

"And you think that makes it easier."

"I'm sorry, Allison, but the way I grew up—the way Temple grew up—dancing was all we had. We only live when we're dancing. You aren't like that—until something happens."

"Until what happens?"

"Oh, I don't know. It can be lots of things…come on, Baby, it's almost six. I gotta see my Mama before I leave town. And you were to get your crap together. Go on, now, you got to buy stuff for the tour, Macy's is open until nine. Remember buy miniature stuff, miniature toothbrush, miniature toothpaste, etc. so you don't have to lug heavy suitcases."

Even following Roberto's advice, packing was agony. Allison managed to squeeze her clothes and gadgets into a lightweight suitcase, but the black fiber theatre case was more difficult. It had "New York Center Ballet Company" stenciled in white on the top, and her number,'32' Decals covered the sides: 'I Love New York,' and Snoopy doing a flat-footed pirouette. The case had previously belonged to Karina Kaye, and using it gave Allison the willies.

She rolled everything up into balls where possible, and pushed and shoved until it all fit: ribbons, toe shoes, leotards, tights, a travel iron, and a radio to take the dullness out of the dressing room.

The last thing to pack was the Gucci ballet bag. In went aspirin, street make-up, a sweater, and a copy of Vogue, Chapstick, packs of gum, sunglasses and an extra pair of tights and leotards.

They were leaving early in the morning; she laid out her traveling outfit. "Not glamorous," she thought, looking down at the jeans, plaid flannel cowboy shirt and mid-calf boots, well broken in. The only jewelry she would take was the diamond stud earrings her father gave her on her twentieth birthday.

"Allison, are you packed?" Her mother's voice was ecstatic over the phone.

"Yes, I'm all set, Mom. I wish you could come with me."

"I am with you, honey. I'm always with you."

"Thanks. So what's new, Mom?"

"Oh, my enrollment doubled this year. You made us famous! I lost Margaret, my best teacher, and I'm so busy I don't think I can leave to see you dance, except maybe in Chicago since it isn't that far. But I can't promise. Allison, I'm proud of you."

"I'm proud of you too."

"Take care, and stay out of trouble. And especially stay away from—"

"Don't worry about that, Mom."

She crawled into the sack, watched the eleven o'clock news, pushing the tour out of her mind so she could go to sleep.

"Why is it the news always makes me sleepy? I guess I'm getting like Roberto…only ballet is real."

Allison woke to the hissing of tires skimming along the streets of Broadway. She knelt on the bed and peeked out the blinds. Rain splashed against her window like Niagara Falls. Allison set her teeth in determination, she knew she had to move quickly to give herself extra time to get a taxi. She whipped up an egg and milk; splattered on basic make-up and, with the help of the doorman, managed to be on the street by 8:30. From out of the minor monsoon came a checkered cab screeching across three lanes of traffic, and halting in front of her. The doorman threw in the luggage, and Allison threw herself in the back.

"Kennedy or La Guardia?" The cabby barked, licking his lips over a fat fare.

"The back of the New York State Theatre, please."

The cabby jerked open the protective Plexiglas panel, "Are you crazy, lady; it's only five blocks to Lincoln Center."

"But I have all these suitcases, and it's pouring."

"Jesus, lady!"

"I'll give you a big tip."

"Jesus!" With a disgruntled snort he wheeled the cab
in the direction of Lincoln Center.

"So you a dancer?" he assumed a pose of resignation.

"Yes."

"What's the deal with all those fruitcakes?" he interrupted.

"What?"

"Those guys who run around in tights with their rear ends bouncing
around—silly twits."

"There are straight men in ballet, as well." She couldn't believe she
was defending the heterosexuality of dancers at eight-thirty in the
morning, but New York cabbies knew how to lure passengers into inane
conversations.

"It's tradition." Allison replied. Now she was defending her art. It
wasn't silly, how could she have devoted her whole life to something
that was merely 'silly'? She cringed; thinking that in some ways he had a
point; the plots of some ballets were plain ridiculous, but she would
never admit that to an outsider.

"Why don't those guys wear pants like the regular guys?" the cabby's
question roused her from her thoughts.

"Tights give freedom to the body and show off line." She stopped
from explaining what 'line' meant.

"Well, lot's of luck, little girl, wherever you're heading." Cabbies have
refined the art of appeasement as well as abuse. He was actually pleasant
as they neared the destination; and after all the abuse, Allison put the
extra tip in his palm.

She raced to a waiting circle of dancers holding umbrellas.

"The goddamn bus ain't here," Roberto wailed. "It's eight-thirty five
and the bus was supposed to be here at eight-thirty. The friggin' bus is

late, and it's friggin' pouring. My new clothes are soaked. A friggin' tour this is."

"Roberto, tour hasn't started, and it's only five minutes late."

"A bad omen, believe me."

A bus turned a corner and pulled up in front of the theatre.

"See Roberto, there was nothing to worry about. Nothing bad is going to happen on tour. It's going to be great. Great!"

CHAPTER 21

A company on tour is like a roving band of gypsies; everybody together all the time: breakfast at the hotel; class at the studio; rehearsal at the theatre; dinner at the hotel, performance at the theatre, and drinks afterwards at the hotel bar. Only after midnight does the group divide and shift into pairings and permutations that will last until the morning. Boarding the plane Allison looked at scattered couples holding hands and wondered how many would return holding the same hand.

She sat with Roberto, but he was flouncing up and down the aisle socializing more than he was in his seat much to the annoyance of the stewardesses who were trying to serve breakfast. For the trip Roberto was wearing light purple cotton billowing trousers that were tied at the ankle over a pair of fancy red cowboy boots; for a top he chose a simple black T-shirt with an iridescent print of a pair of roller skates. A three-headed creature from Mars would get scant attention from unflappable New Yorkers, but Roberto managed to get even New Yorkers to gawk.

When Roberto did finally sit, he complained about airline food for the entire trip. Allison was delighted when the plane finally landed at the first tour stop in Richmond, Virginia. They were booked into the Virginia Museum Theatre, an elegant but tiny theatre, seating five hundred people. It had been selected to work the kinks out of the production before encountering the harsher critics of the larger cities.

Housed inside the museum, the theatre was part of an elaborate security system installed to protect a collection of masterwork paintings and sculptures. Entrances to backstage areas and dressing rooms led to a Byzantine maze of corridors with bulletproof guarded glass check-booths.

Each dancer was assigned coded security badges that had to be pinned to costumes. Roberto pinned his on his rear cheek, and laughed as one of the security guards reddened as he sashayed past.

Gregorov called the company together even before they unpacked with news of the first disaster of the tour. "Children, I have bad news, but nothing we cannot combat. The van with our sets has broken down outside of Washington, and we have to dance tonight without them. What is worse, we will not be able to put down our linoleum dance floor. You will have to do your best, your very best, on these horrid freshly waxed floors they have prepared for us. Of course, the surface is dangerous, and your union would be against you dancing on it. But as always, we will have a company vote. What will it be? Do we dance, or not?"

No one voted to perform. One slip could mean an injury that would end a career. Gregorov looked at them dejectedly, his white wisps of hair falling around his ears.

"My little ones, in Russia we danced on ice if the Czar asked us to! But in Russia, we danced for love of dance. We were artists!"

The vote was re-taken. All the dancers without exception voted to perform.

During rehearsal Allison had trouble balancing on the slippery floor, she fell on almost every turn. Temple, watching from the wings, could not take it anymore. She pulled Allison off to the side of the stage.

"Allison, here's a trick." She produced a thin two-inch square of soft rubber. "Sew this on the tips of your pointe shoes. It will give you traction."

It worked, and Allison finished rehearsal without slipping again. A few girls did fall, and a chorus of curses resounded through the corridors and in the wings. The loudest shriek was Regina Christian's as she landed on her *derriere* during a treacherous step in Gregorov's ballet, *La Chanson Innocent*. She begged him to change the step to make it safer. Gregorov acquiesced, but no other dancer was permitted such an option.

After the rehearsal Allison sat next to Temple in the dressing room. "You saved my ass."

"It's OK," Temple said, occupied with untying her toe shoes.

"Listen, Temple," Allison took a deep breath, "the last time I tried apologizing to you. You turned it around and apologized to me. This time it's definitely my turn. I was jealous. I saw you getting all the soloists roles while I was dancing in the back row. It's something I have to get over. But maybe this has made me grow up a little bit. I wouldn't blame you if you never talked to me again. But if I promised not to be such an asshole in the future, I hope you'll let me be your friend once more. I've missed you, Temple. I missed you a lot."

Temple heard a genuine hurt in Allison's voice, and her heart melted. "I missed you too. And I can't handle the silent treatment anymore, it's too exhausting."

Allison extended her hand. "Amiga?"

"Si, amiga." Temple laughed, and warmly embraced Allison.

Allison's heart sang; she had fallen from grace, and she was redeemed. "Nothing will ever come between us again. I promise."

The opening night of the tour was to a full house, granted not a great feat with only five hundred seats to sell. A large percentage of it was elderly aunts and dance mothers and the like, the pampered rich of Richmond who had the taste and the time for the good things in life.

The company danced as if tiptoeing on eggshells, but no one fell until the final coda. Allison did a *grand jete*, and her front foot skidded across the polished floor. Her other leg was stretched out behind her for the jump, and she splayed across the stage with a thud. The audience gasped. She quickly sprang up, re-aligning herself into the choreographic patterns, not hurt but embarrassed.

After the performance, to a decent quota of applause, Gregorov opened the door of the dressing room. "Miss Fain."

The room of cackling girls suddenly went as silent as a glacier in the Alps. The old man had rarely been in the corps dressing room; Marina Thomas was so startled she didn't think to cover herself, her bodice hanging down below her waist, her breasts exposed and so remaining. Allison waddled to the door, still in her toe shoes, and held up the top of her tutu, which was unhooked and open in back. "Yes, Mr. Gregorov."

"Miss Fain, for the rest of the tour try and stay on your feet." He briskly turned away.

The girls remained hushed. Not wanting to face the others, Allison stared at the closed door as long as she could. When she turned, the girls averted their eyes. For weeks she had tried to get Gregorov to look at her, and now her hopes were shattered by one crushing sentence! She wished she could, like the heroine of Shakespeare, call for the sting of death, if not an asp then a quick cyanide capsule.

The opening night party was in the ballroom of the Howard Johnson's where the company was staying. Allison couldn't face anyone—cast, crew or public—and crumpled into a crying fit in her room.

"Allison, let me in." It was Temple. Allison opened the door.

Temple sat on the edge of the bed. "The girls are laying ten to one you won't make it through the tour." She knew Allison, and the mettle she was made of under her tutu.

Allison stopped crying at once. "Damn them! By the end of the tour I'll be a soloist!"

"That's the spirit!" She took Allison's hand and looked into her eyes. "You're all right now." Temple smoothed Allison's hair, and squeezed her hand. "Remember tomorrow is another day."

Temple closed the door, and Allison mimicked her voice, "'Tomorrow is another day.' God, she can be such a Pollyanna." To get through the night Allison needed something more than good advice.

Temple pawed through her bag and produced a joint that Roberto had given her.

"I shouldn't be doing this," she chided herself, "but it beats staying away all night."

She put it between her lips, took one puff, and another. After two more hits she lay back on the bed, relaxed and calm. Allison waved good-bye to the light in the ceiling. Her arms flopped down beside her, and she was out.

The next week went more smoothly, but the company lacked fire. Nothing soared, even the best *jetes*. The audience response was lukewarm. Gregorov called the dancers on stage after curtain calls.

They toweled off sweat and pulled up their leg warmers, tense with the knowledge that a lecture was coming. The stagehands quietly slipped out of the theatre and headed for a local bar, a good place to be when Gregorov was on the rampage.

He walked to center stage like a General at West Point suspecting mutiny during parade. In front of a work light, he was silhouetted in supernatural radiance with his white hair like a halo. Some of the dancers unconsciously edged behind others, afraid they would be singled out for an offense.

Gregorov's voice was almost inaudible as he addressed them. "Tonight's performance was 'nice', but nice is not enough. There must be more, much more. You belong to an elite circle. And you pay the price for it. When you began in dance you knew you would never be wealthy. You leave your families, and give up loved ones. You tour six to eight months a year. In New York we have class, then rehearse six hours and perform at night. You have no personal lives; you are slave to the dance! But for a reason! A dancer has the opportunity of reaching a unique pinnacle in the quest for ultimate perfection, a place where ordinary people can never go."

He gestured with his right arm, shaking his open hand at them like a prosecutor challenging a jury. "This is why you chose to dance, yes? On stage you are above the world, absolute, supreme—more than human!"

A company of tired figures, glitter stripped off, looked like raggedy urchins in towels, bathrobes and tights, was silent. Each dancer knew individually, they all knew as a company, Gregorov was right. All were addicts, hooked on those fleeting moments when they were "more than human." The hooks had been inserted when they were children. They were suspended from the hooks high above ordinary streets and places, dangling like puppets—to be let down on the bright stage when it was time to dance. The gloominess and unforgiving discipline, the loneliness and poverty outside the stage drove the hook deeper every year. Yes, they had chosen. Dancing was life; the rest was a walk through shadows.

Gregorov pushed their consciences to the limit. "We need more rehearsals, my children. But we are strapped to a budget with no overtime. I cannot ask this of you because of the union contracts, but you may **want** extra rehearsals. Talk among yourselves, and let me know if you are willing to volunteer a little extra effort to create masterworks. Good night."

"Good night, Mr. Gregorov," they whispered in unison.

With some grumbling, they voted. As Gregorov knew it would be, the result was in the affirmative for more rehearsal time. For no extra pay, the day increased to a workload of a Russian peasant before the Revolution. It began at seven with quick coffee and a bagel. At eight they boarded the bus for a six-hour trip to the next town. They were allowed a fifteen-minute rest stop every four hours and one-hour for lunch, usually at a Howard Johnson's. The bus went directly to the theatre, where the dancers dressed to be on stage for a spacing rehearsal, then warm-up, class and back to the dressing rooms for make-up. Dinner was a vending machine sandwich. After the performance, it was hamburgers or pizza and beer at a local bar, if there was a bar still open.

Allison endured the tour of ten southern hamlets with the only sentiment permitted: patience. But she was getting as horny as the last hen in the hen house while keeping up the appearance of the Iron Maiden. Male dancers in the corps scratched at her armor, but she fended them off fearing somebody would run a scandal back to Gregorov. At night she fantasized about making love in hotel rooms, in the Greyhound bus, in dressing rooms, or on stage in view of the audience. Typical fantasies of a corps dancer, they all took place in her narrow world. Most of the other girls had the same unfulfilled needs and dreams, part of the shadowy, off-stage dancer's life. So on they worked beautiful birds in brilliant plumage soaring among the music and the lights for a few hours, but afterwards only gray sparrows in metal cages.

During a lunch break Temple and Allison sat in a corner booth of a Howard Johnson's.

"Aren't you horny, Temple?"

"No?"

"No," Allison was dumbfounded, "when's the last time you had any action? A year?"

"Oh, about two weeks ago."

"What?" Allison almost fell over. "A boy in the company?"

"Good God, no."

"Then who? Who?"

"Nobody you would know."

Allison pulled on Temple's arm. "OK, tell me, tell me."

"There's not much to tell."

"If you don't tell me everything, I going to drop this pizza on your head. Come on, tell me who, where, when!"

Temple recovered some aplomb after a few sips of coffee. "OK, it was before we left for tour…when we were not talking. I needed to clear my head after a day of Gregorov rehearsals. I had a million steps jumping in my brain."

"I know." Allison sympathized.

"So I took one of the cruises around New York Harbor."

"What? You did it on a boat?" Allison waited a moment for a denial from Temple, but none was forthcoming. "Oh, my God. I hope nobody saw you!"

"I was sitting in the back of the boat…nobody else was there, except this guy…he was just sitting real quiet…feeding his dog potato chips. I thought I recognized him, a boy I used to sing with in my high school choir."

"So was it?"

"Yes."

"So what did he say, '"How are things in church, let's screw."

"He didn't say anything."

"And what did you say to this mute, sex-maniac?"

"I said 'hi.'"

"Did he recognize you?"

"I could tell from his smile that he did."

"Then what happened?" Allison put her hand to her mouth, "Oh, my God, he raped you?"

"No.!"

"You raped him?" Allison asked, confused.

"No! We sort of raped each other."

"So where did you go?"

"Nowhere."

"Nowhere? But there's no room on the boat. The seats are so narrow you can hardly sit much less—"

"Who has to sit?"

"What? You did it standing?" Allison was stunned.

" Allison, it's just a different angle. What's wrong with that?"

"Oh, nothing. For a year you're the Virgin Mary, now you're talking angles like an engineer."

"I thought you would be happy for me. It's something you would do."

"Yeah, but I thought you would hold out for something a little more romantic."

"In a way it was. There was a boat, a breeze, moonlight, and he was cute."

"So are you seeing him again?"

Temple shook her head, "No, he's just a boy."

"What's his name?"

"I don't know." Temple shrugged.

"So if there's a kid what are you going to call it—'Circle Line?'

"There's not going to by a kid."

"Temple, you've gone loopy. I should have you committed."

"I already am." Temple looked at the last slice of pizza on the silver tray. "Are you going to eat that pepperoni?"

"No."

Temple reached across the table and swept up the slice of pizza.

CHAPTER 22

One small town remained on the tour before the company traveled on to the major cities. And it was a homecoming of sorts for Temple. Lake Charles, Louisiana was about fifty miles from her home. She had agonized but in the end had decided not to call anyone. It was only a one-night engagement and since she had no family except for some distant cousins and she had not kept in touch with her few friends from Grand Chenier High School she thought it best to not let anyone know she was passing through. Actually she was hoping to sneak out of town without anyone noticing—especially Billy LaVoi. She had an apparition of him showing up at the stage door with a bouquet of flowers in his hand and a grin on his face. "I'd knew you be back, sugar. So let's get married and have us some kids." The thought made her skin crawl. She remembered what Johnny, Billy's linesman, said the night she left Louisiana. "Don't forget where you came from." But that was exactly what she wanted—to forget. She knew the other girls in the company giggled at her Southern Belle accent and smirked when she wore the wrong shoes with the wrong dress. She was resolutely working to gain the big city sophistication that came so easily and naturally to Allison and the other girls. She would not slip back. She was a New Yorker now and would not be sucked back down into the swamps of the Bayou.

Stepping down from the bus in front of their hotel, Temple and the Center Ballet was greeted by the Lake Charles Ladies Guild for the Performing Arts. The ladies, most of them as hefty as truck drivers and with the self-important countenances of Louisiana's Daughters of the

American Revolution, announced that a parade had been arranged through town. No choice was involved; the dancers were obliged to hike through the business district in the shimmering mid-day heat, between the brick hardware stores and frilled white wooden porches. In an attempt to hide Temple wore a hat, a scarf and sunglasses. Roberto marched beside Temple and loudly proclaimed to the rest of the troupe. "Everybody here sounds just like Temple."

The extravaganza included three high school marching bands, a float left over from a New Orleans Mardi Gras, and the Ladies Guild committee waving handkerchiefs and fanning themselves under broad-brimmed hats. "It's all to drum up business!" said Mrs. Alvira Peterson, extremely proud of her P.T. Barnum savvy. She wore a badge with 'President, Ladies Guild for the Arts' among the pearls and sand dune sized mounds of her bosom. She crinkled her eyes and Sunday school smile at Roberto. "Wasn't it a brilliant idea, the parade? Aren't you having a wonderful time?"

Roberto's smile out-shone hers as he told her in Spanish that she looked like an elephant in a one-ring circus and told her where she could shove the marching band.

The cavernous barn of the Veteran's Memorial Theatre was packed to its three thousand-seat capacity for the special Guild's Matinee performance. Dancers scurrying for places in the wings accompanied by the cacophony of the orchestra's tuning. A baton raised, signaling the prologue to *Nightfall*, a quivering flute played a lugubrious, portentous melody.

On stage a young couple joyously dancing amidst a lush verdant pastoral setting. Unconscious of time, their daylight turned to darkness. Frantically, they searched for a way out of the woods, but were impossibly lost. Then suddenly they were attacked by a pair of criminals; the boy tried to protect the girl, but the criminals strangled the boy, then brutally raped the girl, leaving her unconscious nude body atop her murdered lover.

Georginna Haviland, as the girl, gave a deeply touching performance. She expected enthusiastic ovation, but was greeted with only mild applause. Disappointed, she shuffled towards her dressing room, but was ambushed by a regimen of mothers trailed by small children. They encircled Georginna like an Indian raiding party. Georginna stood before them in a white terry cloth robe, a slight figure in comparison to the scowling harpies confronting her.

Mrs. Peterson spoke. "The Lake Charles Ladies sponsored this performance to benefit under-privileged children. We brought three hundred children to be exposed to culture, and what they see is filth!" Georginna retreated a step. "Where is ballet? Where are the tutus?"

"We did a modern ballet." Georginna pointed to her turned-out feet, "I'm wearing pointe shoes, it's still ballet."

"Can you justify the obscene display of your naked body as anything but pornography?"

"I'm wearing a leotard." Georginna opened her robe to exhibit a flesh colored leotard.

"Good God, woman, stop flaunting yourself?" She huddled her own two daughters under her flabby arms. "I can see your bosoms through your costume." The children strained their eyes to see what terrible bosoms she was talking about. The other ladies grunted approving like a family of grizzlies.

Georginna repeated, in disbelief, "My bosoms?" Mrs. Peterson, I'm as flat as a ten-year-old boy."

"Holy Mary, watch your mouth, can't you see children here?"

Temple and Allison witnessed the commotion and snatched Georginna by the arms and led her down the corridor to a dressing room. They closed the door, but not fast enough to miss one of the ladies sling the word "whore."

Inside the dressing room Temple looked at Georginna with her fawn-like eyes; and her heart went out to her. A major star at the age of eighteen and yet so petite, fragile and alone. Temple held her hand, and Allison put her arm around her, Georginna was trembling; she clung to Allison and burst into tears.

Mrs. Peterson spotted Gregorov walking down the corridor. "How can you display pornography in front of under-privileged children?"

Gregorov looked at the two girls. "Are these your children?"

"Yes."

"Then they are the most under-privileged." Gregorov fixed a smile. "If you do not like the performance, you have the option of leaving."

"So we shall!" she shouted to her compatriots. "Come ladies! And Mr. Gregorov…" Gregorov turned as he reached Georginna's dressing room, "The Ladies Guild shall never invite your company back to Lake Charles again."

"Thank you for your kindness." Gregorov's face was a mask of glacial indifference.

Gregorov found Georginna crying in the dressing room, she pleaded, "Mr. Gregorov, I can't go on for the evening performance. I can't!"

"Babushka, you are only one who can do *Symphony Variations*."

"Regina knows it."

"Regina is off tonight…"

"You have to find her. Please, I beg you."

"You must go on, that's all there is to it." Gregorov marched off towards the stage.

Temple turned to Allison, "Listen, Allison, I've got to get ready for the first ballet, could you stay with her?"

"Sure. I'm not on until the last piece."

"Everything will be all right, Georginna." Temple patted Georginna's hand and rushed off down the corridor.

Georginna's hands were shaking uncontrollably. Allison stroked her hair, "I have something to relax you." She reached into her ballet bag and found a bottle of valium. "This will take the edge off." She filled a glass with water. Georginna swallowed the pill.

"Thanks, Allison, you're an angel."

During the evening performance Allison was amazed that Georginna could finish the performance, seemingly so calm and relaxed as if the incident had never happened.

On the plane to Denver the next day Roberto told Temple and Allison that Christopher Beckett would join the company at the next stop.

"Christopher Beckett!" Allison grabbed Temple's hand. "Remember how we used to collect his photos, and tape them on the walls at St. Mary's."

"He's even more gorgeous in the flesh. But be warned, no woman can resist falling in love with him." Robert waved a warning finger at Allison, "And his wife, Zhandra Amaya, would cut out the heart of any girl who gets near him."

"I'm just talking, Roberto. If there's one thing I've learned, it's to stay away from married men."

"He's choreographing a new ballet," Roberto added. "A small cast, maybe five or six dancers."

Allison sighed. "To be on stage with him just once would make my life complete."

That night, the opening night in Denver, Allison was in the corps for the opening of the white classical ballet, *La Bayadere*, at the Music Hall, one of two dozen girls dancing in unison. Suddenly she felt a cramp in her stomach. Her menstruation started, and she had forgotten to protect herself. She hoped that the stage would open up and swallow her, but no miracle. Hours seemed to pass before she could get to her dressing room. The stage manager called through the door.

"Gregorov wants to see you in his hotel room.

"Jesus!" Allison cringed.

At the hotel, Allison timidly knocked on the door of Room 414, the bridal suite.

"Come in, Miss Fain." Gregorov was wearing an elegant, long black Chinese robe.

"Will you take a glass of wine?"

"The last meal," she thought. "Then the firing squad." She took the wine, hoping it might calm her nerves. She looked around the room like a prisoner fascinated by the torture-chamber. Four icons perched on a table, flanked by photographs of Gregorov and his parents, himself as a student at the Kirov Ballet, and as a dancer in his first roles. No picture showed him past the age of thirty. On a bureau was a vase of white roses.

She had not eaten since breakfast, and the wine shot through her head. Gregorov sat on the edge of the bed near her chair. Allison thought of the time she sat in Miss Borden's office. Gregorov was more civilized; the glass of wine was the blindfold.

"A disgrace, child."

"Mr. Gregorov, I'm sorry, I wish I were dead." The tears poured out. Gregorov reached over and rubbed her back.

"Don't cry, my dear. It is over. An accident, part of a woman's nature."

"I'm so embarrassed!"

"Little one, nothing more can be done." He sat her beside him on the bed, and continued to stroke her, sliding his hand underneath the back of her blouse. "Pretty shoulders!" Allison froze as she realized his touch was more than fatherly concern.

"Beautiful, firm breasts. May I?" He undid the top buttons of her white nylon blouse, and dropped the blouse off the left shoulder, then off the right. The clinging nylon shifted slightly to reveal her small breasts. Allison could not move, shocked that the venerable genius was really the man he was rumored to be, and fearful that if she did not let him have his way she would be on the first plane back to New York, her career over.

Gregorov massaged her softly. "Very pretty." His hands went to the midsection of her body, over her smooth flat stomach. He opened all the buttons of her blouse and let it slide down.

"Stand, please." His tone was no less casual than the voice in the studio giving correction. His hands reached behind her and unzipped her skirt. It fell to the floor in a quiet hiss. "You don't mind?"

Allison wasn't sure she had the power to move. Sensing this, Gregorov gently lowered her to her knees. Strangely, Allison was relieved as it took away a feeling of paralysis. He loosened the belt of his robe, "I am not young anymore, but still I have desires. You understand?" The touch of humility surprised Allison. "It wasn't necessary. Couldn't he have whatever he wanted?"

She thought of Roberto's tale about Sir Lawrence Anthony, the prestigious choreographer of the National Ballet of America. He had been gay for all the seventy years of his life, as far as anyone knew. After ogling young boys at health clubs, he would call male dancers in the company to his apartment. Once he called Roberto. Now she understood his motive in going to Sir Anthony; it was survival.

Sure, she could file a sex discrimination suit, but that would mean never dancing at the Center Ballet, probably never dancing anywhere again. Besides her reputation gained as the seductress, the home wrecker of the National Ballet preceded her. What court would believe her?

One mistake in her life, a stupid affair, and she was branded for life as a company whore. The innocent pink tutu dreams of her childhood faded fast into dark, bitter, sharp realities of life in the professional dance world.

Finally Gregorov was satisfied. He slipped on his robe, and Allison dressed herself. He held her at arms length, to examine her body again.

"Such a beautiful girl. You looked lovely on stage tonight, but you must keep your foot pointed in *effece*."

"So," Allison thought, "we're back to business." Gregorov selected a white rose from the vase and presented it to Allison.

"Thank you." Allison's words were automatic as she backed towards the door.

"Class tomorrow at 9:30. Then auditions for Beckett's new ballet at 11:00."

"Yes, Mr. Gregorov."

Outside in the corridor she saw Regina Christian walking her way. Regina lifted an eyebrow. "A pretty rose!"

Allison watched Regina's departing figure. Was it her imagination, or did Regina know the meaning of the rose?

At class the next day, no one failed to notice Gregorov's attentions to Allison. At each correction Allison felt like a specimen on glass under a microscope especially from Regina. Gregorov slapped his hands together signaling the end of class. Allison bolted. There was only a half-hour before Beckett's audition, so she did not bother to change tights. Still wet with sweat; she wrapped a practice skirt around her and grabbed Roberto. "I have to talk to you.

"What about, baby?"

"First, promise not to breathe a word." Roberto raised two fingers in a girl scout's oath. "Last night, Gregorov called me to his room. I thought he was going to fire me—but he didn't. He—"

"Had his way?"

"How did you know?"

"Honey, that ain't no new thing. Don't you know what's goin' on? How you think Regina got where she is? She doesn't have half the technique of any girl in the corps. And Temple…"

"Temple?"

"Sure, honey. Rumor has it she paid her dues to get a soloist contract."

"No. Not Temple." Allison paused. "But then again, she recently told me a story that I thought…well, she is full of little secrets. What kind of business are we in, Roberto?"

"Just like any other business, sweetheart. We just create a better illusion. People think when you girls are on stage you're so pure you never even go to the bathroom. But we know what goes on backstage."

"Why does it have to be this way?"

"Come on, you think ballet is some Disney movie? When are you going to grow up! You think Regina's husband, Peter, doesn't knows that Gregorov is poking Regina? Of course he does! But Peter likes her paycheck. Did it ever occur to you why the Center is the largest school in America, filled with hundreds of eighteen years old girls? All for Gregorov's picking. Well, anyway, you must have been real good. You got second lead in the Debussy piece."

"What?"

"It was on the Call Board this morning."

"Roberto!" Allison hugged him. "I can't believe it." In an instant the humiliation of the night before was forgotten.

"So you've made your decision."

"What decision?"

"Morality or roles." Roberto trotted off, swinging his behind.

Within the hour Roberto broke his sworn promise and told Temple of Allison's night with Gregorov. In Allison's ballet bag, Temple had slipped a note on crisp white stationary:

> "Though we travel
> the world over
> to find the beautiful
> we must carry it inside us
> or we find it not."
>
> Emerson

Allison,

May you also see the beauty that radiates from you. I have seen your beauty and sensitivity. I have faith and trust in you as a friend. What you are now going through is a taste of ballet hell. I understand. Have faith for in the end, what is meant to be, will be.

Courage my love,

Temple

So was it true? Is that's how she got in the Center Ballet as a soloist? Allison never felt more stupid. The little bitch, always playing so damn innocent! Well, Allison could play that game, and she could play it better!

CHAPTER 23

Dancers applauded as Christopher Beckett entered the studio and waved a salute. The light from the studio windows lit his wavy blond hair, fine as a child's, turning it into threads of gold.

Allison edged to the front of the studio. His eyes were a cool blue, like a lake in the middle of a summer afternoon. He was over six feet; a body not painfully slender like so many male dancers, but solid with muscle as a Renaissance sculpture. His face was more long than broad with a strong jaw and a long, deep line in the flesh running down from below each cheekbone to its outer edge. This feature made Beckett seem older than he was, but the originality of his mature face made him the most mesmerizing male star since Nureyev.

The workings of his face and the movements of his body bewitched Allison on the instant. Knees weakened, hands shaking, she fixed her gaze rigidly upon him. She saw, she admired, she felt a deep, heated tingling, her brain spun in a vortex. She was in love. This was the man she must have, at any cost.

The audition was exacting, complicated combinations and fast steps. Allison gave a good accounting, nonetheless she didn't expect to be cast. She registered her depression to Roberto and Temple as they walked back to the hotel.

"Stop worrying. You were fine." Roberto encouraged. "So what did you think of Beckett?"

"I've never seen such a gorgeous man before."

"Even more beautiful than his posters." Temple added.

"I wish I had a bucket of ice water to dump on you two." Roberto chided, "He loves his wife. Don't get any fantasies, girls."

"For God's sake! Just because I think he's handsome doesn't mean I'm in love." Allison protested.

But it was a lie, caution was falling from Allison's brain like water over a dam, she was giving no thought to the consequences. Christopher Beckett was indeed a good-looking specimen, in spite of his thrusting jaw. His European apprenticeship had been in Paris and with the Stuttgart Ballet, at the time one of the best on the Continent— outside of Russia, at least—and some of the macho-cockiness of a European male had rubbed off on him. It went no deeper than his wide, ingratiating smile and the dramatic shifts in his voice. Something about him reminded her of Juri, but she pushed the thought out of her mind.

If there was anything in Christopher Beckett's head beside choreography, public adulation and the same hard work they all experienced, her brief contact with him did not show it. She always took note of where he was on stage and in the studio, but she never had the nerve to go near him. The opportunity simply wasn't there without her stepping, literally, out of place. She wished she believed in *santeros*, like Roberto, and could hire one to work up a spell. If not to make Beckett fall for her, at least to make him cross her path. In the rosin box? At the door to the studio, he imposing and gargantuan in his winter fur, she fragile and oh, so female with a long scarf around her magnificent head and neck like Isadora used to wear? How would it happen, or would it ever?

At the other end of the scale from her dreams of becoming close to Beckett was her dread of another session with Gregorov. He hadn't called for her since the night she earned her white rose, but the possibility kept her tense. His was a double threat, a Victorian ogre watching over the morality of his dancers—in case Beckett ever did pay some attention to her—and the feudal lord with powers to summon her to his bed chamber when he wished. Watching him out of the corner of her eye, Allison hoped that avoiding him would keep her out of his mind. Perhaps he was bedding Regina regularly, and that's why he hadn't called her…if he did, she would have to go to him…if she wanted to keep dancing.

Her attempts to avoid him went so far as dashing out of the studio after class if he was in the vicinity of the dressing room, hiding in the wings during rehearsals and leaving the theatre immediately after performances. What else could she do? "If he calls me, I'll go. I have to…it's that simple. If Temple can do it, and the others, what am I killing myself over this for? It's business that's all. Her father used to tell her that over and over when he had a bad day. It's just business."

But the repulsive fear sickened her and gave her nightmares. She actually woke up with a scream on her lips. She turned on the light and forced herself to order from room service in the middle of the night to bring herself back to reality. But as she munched away, trying to concentrate on a magazine, the realization hit her that her danger would come when Regina left for a month of guest appearances.

Allison threw the magazine on the floor, shoved a valium down her throat and climbed back into bed, putting the pillow over her head.

The nightmare was becoming real and closing in! During a performance Regina pulled Allison into the wings. "I leave for Europe tomorrow. I told Gregorov when I return I want to find everything the way it is now."

"What do you mean?"

"I am Prima Ballerina—you are corps de ballet. You make sure we keep it that way."

On cue for her entrance, Regina swept past Allison glowing on stage during her short variation. Regina returned, panting but managed her words, "I have friends…who will tell me if anything goes on while I'm away. You stay away from him, do you understand, little slut?"

Alison waited for a slap; her fists were clenched, prepared to fight back, but no slap came, only another invective.

"Stick to your gay boy friends, you company whore."

It was Allison's cue to go on stage, but her mind was whirling from the words whipped at her by Regina. What had she done to deserve that? Allison was just a soldier following orders. She had done nothing more than Regina, servicing Field Marshall Gregorov. Allison's body performed, but her head began sifting the new development, suddenly she realized Regina had granted the favor of excusing her from the battle. If need be, she would tell Gregorov that Regina had threatened her. It would frighten him too. She was saved! She was saved from Gregorov. A smile was forbidden in *La Bayadere*, but she smiled.

CHAPTER 24

Friday morning, with the weekend of performances to go in Denver, Temple and Roberto were finishing a rehearsal. Roberto had been pairing Temple in *Handel Variations,* and Gregorov was not satisfied with the final steps. The criticism and the extra rehearsals made Roberto grouchy. His grouchiness was reaching iceberg proportions as the tour progressed, Roberto's usual reaction as they went farther and longer away from New York. He was still a street kid, and on tour he had no connection to the streets. So he acted like a yokel off the farm in other big cities, and not knowing or not wanting to state the reason, complained about everything.

"The Denver stage is crap. Three-quarters in the round with no way to spot. How the hell can I keep from getting dizzy if I can't find a place to focus my eyes? One turn and I'll spin off the stage into the pit."

"Pick out some cute boy in the audience, and spot on him!" Temple retorted, annoyed with his constant gripes.

"Hell, you know I can't see anybody in the audience any better than you can! I got a mind to give my notice, I'm tellin' you."

She brushed him off like a pesky fly. "So why don't you?"

At such times Roberto never gave his real reasons for doing anything. He acted as though his need to dance, his fear of not being in a company did not exist.

"I need the money. I got lovers back in New York to support."

Temple ignored him. Roberto's bitchy chatter was annoying, but she had to dance with him and couldn't afford any bitchiness from him on stage.

"Temple" a shriek was heard from across the stage. "We're cast in Beckett's ballet!" Allison ran to Temple.

"My God!" Temple hung on to the curtain to keep from collapsing in shock.

They hugged each other, squealing like ballet students back at St. Mary's. Roberto was not smiling.

"He picked the only straight boy, Rich Paulson."

"Rick's a great dancer." Temple countered.

"Sure, but he wouldn't get picked if he were gay! When I get back to New York, I'm gonna complain to the union. I tell you." He slung his ballet bag over his shoulder and headed out. "This company is for crap. Everything is for crap."

"Temple, does this mean Zhandra wasn't cast?"

"No, he's double casting. Delphine's also in."

"Then we're not first cast!" Allison was quickly deflated. "It means not getting reviewed on opening nights."

"So, we get reviewed another time. Hey, we'll get our chance! We're not understudies, we're second cast."

"You're right. I should be happy. When's rehearsal?"

"Three o'clock."

"God, Temple, we made it."

By three o' clock, Allison's thighs were as tight as steel springs. Temple, Rick Paulson and Delphine LaFleur wore leg warmers, trying to save muscles ravaged by a long day of rehearsal. Everyone was searching for a new reserve of energy to be 'on' to impress the choreographer.

Beckett entered the studio wearing light gray practice tights that subtlety flattered his long, elegant legs, muscles rippling as he walked.

He was followed by his wife, Prima Ballerina, Zhandra Amaya, a dazzling Latin beauty with long, blue-black hair, large dark eyes, sensuous dark lips, and pale ivory skin. The room held a collection of stunning people, young, tight-wound with energy like bright plumed cockatoos ready for the ring, they were all colors, all magnificent. Zhandra and Allison, both dark beauties, wore lavender and red, respectively. Temple was in blue, which deepened her huge blue eyes. Delphine, also blond, had a pursed, Marilyn Monroe mouth and dreamy eyes, the just rolled-out-of-bed look. Her yellow practice clothes made her as bright and cheery as a buttercup.

The men were their equals, Rick with his chiseled features and dark skin making Allison think of Valentino. Not that he could compare to Beckett—who could!

Beckett stood in the center of the studio. "I want to check pairings." Temple stood next to Zhandra and Rick, and Allison next to Delphine, and so on for several permutations. Allison resigned herself to a second cast, but thought it sporting of Beckett to pretend she had a chance against Zhandra or Delphine. Temple had a good chance since she was a soloist, but Allison in the corps, accepted the pecking order.

Beckett called attention. "First cast is Zhandra, Allison and myself; second cast is Delphine, Temple and Rick."

Allison was not sure her ears were working.

"Let's begin. Zhandra and Allison in front; Delphine and Temple stand behind and learn."

Allison turned to look at the second cast. Delphine was transparently disappointed; Temple did not look at Allison, as if to cover her envy.

Allison finished rehearsal in a daze, muscles ached, and sweat saturated her leotard and tights. "I thought I'd never get through the rehearsal." Allison admitted to Temple in the dressing room, "Tonight I'm taking a long hot bath."

"Allison, congratulations!"

"Yeah, thanks, but I'm sorry you're not with me in the first cast."

"It's OK. I'll get my reviews later. How do you feel?"

"Dazed…I hope tomorrow I can remember one step."

Both girls laughed, knowing years of training would not forsake them. When the music played the body would follow.

Allison dumped a packet of Vitabath in the tub and submerged herself. It stung for a moment, but then the muscles loosened. The pain eased. Allison was used to the pain. She had come to expect it, even need it. It would not seem right if, after a day like today, that every inch of her did not hurt.

While the bath soothed, visions of opening night elated her. And she had done it on her own. No sex! She endured exile to Atlantic City, and the humility of the corps de ballet. And now finally the spoils—on stage with Christopher Beckett. Allison smiled. It was true. There was a Guardian Angel for dancers. Tonight the angel's wand touched Allison on top of the head. All was right with the world. There was only one thing more...one more assignment for her guardian angel...her body settled into the warm sudsy water...her fingers slid down her stomach...there was Christopher Beckett!

"Angel, do your stuff."

CHAPTER 25

The Company arrived in Atlanta, always a favorite stop on a tour. The weather was cool, crisp and clear, so the dancers could walk about the city on the two afternoons they had free. Regina was in Europe, but Gregorov left Allison alone. Much of his time was taken by rehearsals, as usual, but after performances Gregorov had social invitations and other business to attend. He was an old colleague of the director of the largest ballet school in Atlanta, as well as having numerous other admirers. Everything was going smoothly, no mishaps. Roberto was finally happy, he didn't spin into the orchestra pit, and on the first night he had an affair with a cabaret singer.

Rehearsals for Beckett's new ballet had gone well. He was ecstatic with the choice of dancers and the way they enhanced his work. To Allison he was polite, helpful and encouraging, but he evidenced only professional interest. She hoped he would warm to her in Atlanta.

Preludes, Beckett's piece, was excellent. Set in the sixteenth century to the music of a Schubert Quintet, it was about a young aristocrat with an appetite for love. He wooed a young virgin and professed his undying love, but when she was about to yield, another girl appeared. The boy fluttered to the new flower, extricating himself from the first entanglement to seduce the second. He maintained a double life despite some close calls until both maidens discovered the ruse. Enraged, they attacked each other while the young man referred. The girls demanded he chose between them, but he declined. Angered by his weakness, they turned their fists upon him and beat him to the ground. Then they joined hands and departed, leaving the boy alone.

Christopher explained *Preludes* was an exploration of the sequences that entice lovers. "The boy views love as a game. But one player cannot win, since there is no one to win against. He can only lose."

The work combined a delicate humor with intriguing steps and elegant music. It was assumed the ballet would receive good reviews, particularly since critics usually have only good things to say about choreography done by a star performer. Allison would have preferred a more bravura piece to show her off, but for that she would have to wait and hope. There was still the New York opening, several months away.

On stage of the legendary Fox Theatre in Atlanta, Allison studied the massive old structure, made famous by the first showing of *Gone with The Wind*. She marveled at one of the last standing movie palaces in America, with its wonderful ceiling displaying a constellation of moving stars.

There was no portable barre on the stage, so she used a stagehand's ladder to warm-up. She was absorbed in concentration on her muscles when a voice surprised her. "Mind if I join you?"

Allison covered her emotions at seeing Beckett with the sweetness of a Southern accent she had learned from Temple. "Why sure, honey, just help yourself to a hunk of this here ol' rickety ladder."

Christopher tried to ape the accent. "Thank ye, Ma'am, much obliged."

"That's a Texas accent."

"Gosh-darn, I jest come in har from Texas."

"In the south, they say…'an honor!'" Allison curtsied.

Christopher bowed. "An honor, if I might share this pillar of Magnolia with you."

"I'd be delighted, but as you can see," she waved her hand to the theatre, "we are unchaperoned. My honor would be reproached."

"A pity for us both." They laughed. Allison dropped the drawl. "How do we do this so we don't knock the ladder over? How about when I *tendu* front, you *tendu* back; that way, we balance the ladder."

"Let's try it, preparation, *Tendu*, and one, and two…"

The ladder croaked, but they finished a warm-up, with a few laughs for their efforts. Beckett straddled his arms around the ladder. "Do you have any plans after performance?"

"No."

"How about dinner?"

"OK, sure. I'd love to."

"Great. Stop by my room, Suite 1404."

For the rest of the day Allison floated like a swatch of chiffon on a summer breeze. After last rehearsal she swooped into the boutique in the hotel, and selected a dress of pink lisle with a camisole top that tied at the shoulders. Shuddering at the price, she told herself it was worth it, as it would be appropriate for one of Atlanta's gourmet restaurants. And it might impress Beckett! He saw her everyday in leotards, but a pretty dress could be just the stimulant to stir his mind to things other than choreography.

She told Roberto and Temple the news. They were curiously mute. She dismissed their lack of response as jealousy, although she was disappointed as she expected more from her best friends.

After the performance she showered and dressed. She put up her hair, twirled the strands over her ears around her fingers and blew them dry until the hair fell in long spiral curls to her shoulders. Where it was caught up, she sprinkled tiny pink flowers. With the camisole dress, she looked like Scarlet O'Hara on a good day before the War, which was exactly what she intended.

Beckett opened the door of his hotel suite dripping wet with a towel around his loins.

"Allison, you look stunning!"

"Thank you." Allison wondered "Is Zhandra undressed…is that why she didn't answer the door

He took her hand and led her in. "Excuse me while I finish drying my hair. I ordered room service—hope you don't mind."

"No, of course not." Alison lied and thought to herself, "Room Service! After I spent all this money for a night out."

The doorbell rang.

"Sign my name and leave a good tip, would you, love?"

"Love!" she was shaking like a leaf under her camisole.

"Three chairs, please," she said to the waiter as he set the table. "Christopher, there's only two place settings."

"I'm sorry, I thought you knew. Zhandra is in San Diego doing a guest appearance. I was supposed to go, but canceled. I needed more time for my new piece."

Suddenly Allison found room service absolutely wonderful. She lifted the dish covers and admired the food.

"And there's strawberry shortcake for dessert, Allison."

"My hips won't take that, I'm afraid."

"Your hips are lovely"'

He emerged from the bathroom in slacks and a loose knit shirt. "Champagne?"

"Thank you, I'd love some."

He worked on the cork. "Allison, you seem nervous. Sit down, and relax."

She sat on the edge of a chair, taking the glass and raising it to his. She was as nervous as if it was auditioning for her first ballet.

"To *Preludes*," Beckett lifted his glass. "To rave reviews in Los Angeles!" He laughed, very pleased. "And to ballerina Allison Fain, as well!"

The glasses clinked.

"How were you able to break the contract for San Diego?" her curiosity overcame the boldness of her question.

"I have an illness clause in my contract. If I say I am sick, what can anybody do about it?"

Allison liked his answer. It confirmed her impression of Beckett as shrewd and tough, the way she liked a man. Most dancers were too timid when it came to contract negotiations, and were easily taken advantage of.

He continued. "San Diego is lucky to have Zhandra; we both could have canceled."

"I would have felt so guilty!"

"The advantage of being a star is artistic exemption. It puts you above law, religion, and government, even Rebecca Borden. Although sometimes I'm not so sure about Rebecca." He laughed.

So he also knew about her firing at the hands of Rebecca Borden. Allison wondered how distorted the story must have grown. Allison watched him lolling against the back of his chair, legs outstretched, a perfect young god. Her stomach was fluttering like leaves on an ash tree before a storm.

"I'm not sure I understand what you mean."

"You will. When you're a principal you become arrogant, and the arrogance makes you more talented and mysterious…and therefore powerful. But, enough business, let's enjoy the moment."

"How can I endure this," she thought. "How can I eat pasta?" A wave of heat passed through her body like a rush of hot mercury. His lips were full, like her own. His deep black eyes had long, almost feminine lashes. She watched the thrust of his handsome jaw as he talked, and basked in his self-assurance, the freedom and power that oozed out of his pores, spinning her into his glittering web, making her feel like a star with him.

They ate in silence except for a few comments about the food. In reality they were both famished, and really good food was as much of a treat to Beckett as it was to Allison, for star dancers usually eat on the run and as badly as corps members.

After dessert he served coffee and brandy and placed a single white candle on the table, they sat in silence.

Beckett rose and turned off the room lights. "More romantic this way, don't you think?"

"Yes, more romantic!" she thought, her heart beating wildly, sending thumps through her bloodstream all the way to her toenails.

He stood up and came to her, enclosing her head and torso in his strong arms, pressing her face into his groin. She trembled as she rested her head on his thighs. He stepped back, took hold of her hands and riveted his eyes onto hers.

"Do you want me, Allison?"

His humility, however false, echoed Gregorov. But Allison could not think clearly about anything at that moment. She groped at the fastening of his slacks. Beckett helped her. He then stepped back, teasing. She looked up at him towering over her, and fell to her knees. He reached out and stroked her head, the tiny flowers over her ears, the curls, as a minister of the gospel might stroke a young convert, gently and in the manner of brotherly love…how Beckett loved these shy, frightened young dancers! Their reverence amused him so, after a daily diet of Zhandra's possessiveness. Always the first night—before the tears and demands began and he became bored and annoyed by them—was a taste of Heaven even being on stage couldn't give him.

"My angel."

Allison shook as though coursed by bolts of lightning in a summer storm, quick flashes driving away her fright and moving her to action. She kissed him with greed; her fantasies come real at last! This, she knew, was the man she had dreamed about all her life. When he finished, she didn't want to stop. He pulled away, laughing. "What a wild little one you are, Allison! And I thought you were a proper little girl."

Allison laughed. She loved him calling her wild. They walked to the bedroom. Her clothes were gone before she got there. Waking up hours later, she could not remember where she had lost them. It had really happened…he was asleep beside her. She closed her eyes and saw them dancing together center stage, the applause engulfing them, pounding like surf on an island beach. He awoke and looked at the clock.

"Allison, you have to go. The company has a thousand eyes. We don't want a scandal."

She dressed and left him in bed, quietly closing the door as she emerged into the hall outside the suite. Back in her room she went into the bathroom. Her stomach protruded like a third-world urchin's, stuffed with pasta and shortcake. She knelt over the toilet bowl, stuck two fingers deep down her throat, gagged and vomited. She rose and showered, her body felt so bloated, she hoped she could dance. But it was worth it. Now she was where she wanted to be! Except for one obstacle—his wife!

CHAPTER 26

Allison's one night with Christopher Beckett had been as sweet as honeysuckle, as tender as magnolia blossoms swaying in an afternoon breeze, and yet as passionate as stallions running wild in an open field. But when Zhandra returned it felt as though General Sherman's horse soldiers marched over Allison on its way to the sea. She had never noticed just how much attention Zhandra lavished on her handsome stud husband. It seemed that at every stage exit and entrance she pecked him on the cheek or blew him a kiss from afar. Beckett returned them, and instigated some of his own when he went on and off. They held hands like teen-agers leaving class and were constantly together after performances. If she was dancing well or badly, it was in the back of Allison's mind. She received her share of applause; just being on stage with Beckett inspired her performances, and she imagined he was watching her. Gregorov certainly was, and that was enough to keep every dancer in the company working at peak.

But it was with relief that Allison packed her things to leave Atlanta, the city that would always be one night of fulfilled dreams, the rest a blur. If the night were never to be repeated, perhaps another city would make her forget.

Allison's reflection in the airplane's glass window was sprinkled with quick flashes of light, like stars. Below was Los Angeles, the City of Angels; it twinkled like a field of diamonds spread out on black velvet. She hoped it was prophetic.

On the ground it was smog, noise, short tempers, and luggage-mix-ups, as usual. Allison put the inconveniences out of her mind, like the rather modest accommodations at a downtown hotel but close to the Music Center, and concentrated on what was to be her debut. It would be the first time the critics would have a go at her and Los Angeles critics were without question the roughest in the business.

On the opening night of Beckett's *Preludes*, Allison's dressing table was decorated with *merde* presents. Temple gave her a book with nudes in dance positions. Beckett sent two dozen deep red roses, and Roberto wrapped a vibrator in imitation tiger skin paper. Roberto had spent the entire afternoon in West Hollywood looking for it, cruising the porn shops in a 1950's pink Buick convertible he rented from Rent-a-Wreck, a favorite source of transportation for visiting writers and actors.

She flicked a stray grain of mascara off her right cheek and looked critically into the mirror. In spite of the flurry of dancers behind her at that moment she felt alone, as she would be on stage for the first time. There was something in her eyes that had never been there before, and she choked as she saw it—fear! The night before she had only been able to sleep for three hours, in spite of the pills. It was not her ability that she doubted, for she had danced the final rehearsal to high praise from Beckett, Temple, and even Gregorov.

She dreamed the dancer's nagging nightmare of a small mishap: tripping over a foot, being dropped by her partner or spinning off the stage into the orchestra pit. Would she blank out, forget steps or rip her costume? She remembered Jennifer Scanlon's horrifying crash on center stage at the opening night of a Jose Limon season, and her screams from the pain as her ruined leg crumbled under her, the audience too paralyzed to react.

But *Preludes* was a simple piece, and little could go wrong. The steps were stylized, not bravura. Still she couldn't shake the sound of Jennifer's screams out of her ears—for she had been in the audience that night—or the hundreds of things that could booby-trap her.

"Get a grip, Allison, you are a fine dancer, a great dancer," she lectured herself. "It's just nerves."

She took a pill from the small case broke it into a quarter piece with her thumbnail. Quickly she downed it with water, straightened up and smoothed her hair.

The dressing room door banged open. Girls rushed to change for the last ballet. Allison pulled on leg warmers and wrapped a robe around her body. Several dancers wished her *merde,* and she accepted their good wishes graciously.

"This is what dance should be about," she thought. "A garden to nurture artistic growth, not a damned Olympics competition!"

Behind the grand curtain she practiced last steps. The crowd beyond the curtain murmured, anticipating the world premiere by one of their favorite ballet heroes. A galaxy of film and music stars was reportedly in the audience: Warren Beatty, the Paul Newmans, Billy Crystal and God-knows-who else, Gregory Peck and Veronica, Jerry Seinfeld, Rob Lowe, Mira Sorvino, Britney Spears, Elizabeth Shue, Barbara Streisand, Tom Cruise without Nicole Kidman, Christian Slater, Marisa Tomei, Holly Hunter, Debbi Allen, Goldie Hawn and Julia Roberts. The Center Ballet always lured the stars, and many were among the most constant financial supporters of the company's West Coast season.

Allison ducked into the wings as the curtain rose on Christopher and Zhandra. The ovation was warm and enthusiastic for the handsome and popular couple, Beckett tall, light, blond and cool in manner, Zhandra petite, dark, mysterious, and fiery. Allison entered on cue. No applause; she was an unknown and hadn't expected any. But she would show them—stars, patrons, critics and the other dancers—they would notice Allison Fain!

With the speed of a dream the ballet was over. Christopher stood between Allison and Zhandra for the curtain call, leading both girls downstage to the edge of the apron and stepping back to let them bathe in the warm reception of the audience. The crowd loved *Preludes!* And they loved Allison! Roses flung from beyond the lights hit the stage with calls of "*bravo!*" The clapping and shouts resounded through the hall like a cannonade; it was the most wonderful music that Allison had ever heard.

She curtsied and looked into the audience, eyes glistening with happiness. It was her dream come true: success on stage, flowers and "bravos," with the man she loved! Except that he loved someone else. She looked at Zhandra's lovely small form bowing as gracefully as a Siamese, sleek and feline. She looked at Beckett, and he smiled. Taking a rose from a bouquet, she kissed it and handed it to him. Beckett held it to his heart. Zhandra plucked a rose from her bouquet, kissed it and handed it to Beckett in the same fashion. A swell of cheers rose from the audience. They were a hit! The curtain was rung down.

Christopher embraced Zhandra and called to Allison, "Allison, you were beautiful."

"Thank you, Christopher." She started for the wings. "Allison!" A scream turned her around. Temple and Roberto grabbed her. "You were absolutely sensational! We watched out front. The audience loved you."

Allison demurred, "Oh, I don't know, my pique turns were off."

"Nonsense!" Temple chided.

Roberto agreed. "And your scissons were perfect."

"Really?"

"Really!" Roberto assured her. "Now change into your most ravishing dress; you've got to look like a star for the party. We'll meet you at the stage door. Hurry!" Roberto shoved her off.

Allison wiped off her make-up while the music of *Etudes*, the last ballet, piped through her dressing room. She knew every step, and visualized the company's guest stars, Vladimir Nabolev and Carlotta Gray, performing the dazzling variations. She recalled the coda, the slap from Victoria Bennett. Allison wished Victoria was in the audience so she could watch Allison's ascendance into ballet prominence; but Victoria would hear soon enough, and that was almost as good.

The rear of the theatre was lined by balletomanes, the 'groupies' of the business. More intense in their devotion, more constant than rock groupies or stage door Johnny's, they followed dance companies from city to city, country to country. They lived for chosen dancers and wore life-long allegiance to certain companies. After every performance they were there, then disappearing like a cloud of smoke until the next performance.

The night of the first showing of *Preludes,* many of New York's most well known dance fanatics flew into Los Angeles. Propped against a wall nearest to the stage entrance was the Fat Lady, a three hundred pounder with the same nickname as Louise Nevelson's elephant sized sculptures in the New York State Theatre lobby. Obsessed with autographs, the Fat Lady had hundreds, but dancers never refused her. She valued the signatures from the corps as much as one from a star. Standing next to her were 'the Cuban Doctors,' a trio of middle-aged gays who shared a plush triplex apartment on the East Side and whose lucrative practice paid for lavish parties for certain dancers. When possible they flew to other cities for special performances. A tall, gaunt man in canvas sneakers stood next to one of the Cubans. Known as 'The Library,' he hoarded souvenir books, ticket stubs and reviews clipped from magazines and the newspapers.

Beside him stood Lucille, a black Puerto Rican who knitted leg warmers for her super-star idols. Her unusually beautiful and useful hand-made tights earned her the friendship of many performers, who shared intimate details of their lives with her. Lucille was the best source of gossip outside the company itself. Often she predicted correctly the assignment of a choice role or a dismissal. Many dancers even consulted her as they would a fortuneteller, trying to figure out the politics of the dance world and their place in it.

The balletomanes hung outside the stage door, waiting for their princes and sylphs to emerge. Sometimes one would be invited to a party, and the dancer who ushered his admirer could be rewarded with life-long fealty. Roberto, Allison and Temple stepped into the crowd.

"It's Allison Fain!" went up a shout. The crowd surged upon her thrusting pens and programs. She hesitated just a moment but then began signing the programs as if she had done it all her life.

"The first night of many," Allison thought, wondering if Roberto and Temple were very jealous, or just a little. A cavalcade of minibuses and limousines filed through the parking lot. Limos arrived for the stars, Nabolev, Carlotta Gray, Zhandra Amaya and Christopher Beckett. The corps de ballet was herded into minibuses for the wagon train to the Beverly Wilshire Hotel.

Nabolev saw Allison signing autographs, and hooked her arm, "Come, you ride with Carlotta and me." The handsome Russian escorted Allison to his limo, leaving Roberto and Temple behind. Allison waved. She felt a bit selfish, but how often does one get a ride with Nabolev and Carlotta Gray in a limo?

Hollywood is usually a quiet town at night, boutiques and salons close discretely at seven; and restaurants burn golden lamps, lighting the way to their legendary entries. But that night the fans came even from Beach Towns, from the Valley, from the hills of Ojai, to see the ballet and Hollywood stars enter the party.

Allison, Nabolev and Carlotta Gray climbed out of the limo. The crowds descended like seagulls over minnows in a tide pool. The paparazzi took aim, and hundreds of flashes burst in white explosions. Chauffeurs and policemen locked arms to encircle the stars and conveyed them through the throbbing, screaming crowds.

Inside the champagne flowed, and in honor of Nabolev, caviar had been imported from the Black Sea, and the appetizer was served Russian-style with chopped egg, radishes and onions, with a sliver of lemon, the glistening fish eggs on thin slices of dark bread.

The party was dotted with celebrities. Movie idol Ward Beaton was past fifty but still handsome, the better part of his days spent in the Hollywood gym and playing tennis. Like many of his colleagues, he had to choose between complete debauchery and Alcoholics Anonymous in his fifth decade and had made the sensible decision. Physical fitness was a cult that filled his non-working days, weeks and years. He cruised the crowd and settled on Delphine LaFleur. She recognized him and allowed him to edge her into a dark corner. Understanding the ego and longings of an older man, she hastened to flatter him. "I loved your film *Moment of Doubt!*"

"Yes, a good role," he began modestly.

"Was that made in the or forties or fifties?"

Beaton glowered. "In the late 1970's, my dear, and I was a teenager at the time." He let go of her elbow and quickly moved off.

A small group of locals carried on their usual talk of options, castings, budgets and re-writes. In Hollywood it was so much talent that mattered, or timing, or luck as much as 'the Deal.' The night of her first triumph the dealmakers were all around her, but she could care less, she only had eyes for Beckett.

When he arrived, he was immediately engulfed by fans who raved about *Preludes.* He received their enthusiasm calmly, well aware that the Los Angeles critics might demolish it in the morning papers. He had expressed his opinion of the critics to Gregorov backstage a few days before. "Only a few critics really understand ballet, and which of these is capable of evaluating *Preludes* in the historical context its choreography? I'll bet not one will catch the allusions to the classics."

Gregorov agreed. "Don't worry, dance for those who understand. The rest be damned!"

Zhandra glowed like an emerald in a slim green satin dress with a peacock train. She pulled Beckett down beside her on a marble fountain splashed with floodlights.

"I love you," she whispered, "and your ballet is magnificent!"

He embraced her, letting one hand slide down her back to settle on the comfortable roundness of her backside.

Allison, her eyes drawn to the figure of Beckett—the magnet that never let go—but she turned away and mixed into Nabolev's coterie of young men. They were the most easily spotted groupies of the evening. Dressed in 1930's suits from retro clothing stores at fancy Beverly Hills addresses, they had smug, private expressions under greased, slick hair. Nabolev had groups of them in every city; their function was not knitting leg warmers.

An elderly lady in black lace with high-buttoned, matching gloves, a hostess from the Los Angeles Friends of the New York Center Ballet, approached the wild Russian, smiling quaintly at the young men around him.

"Mr. Nabolev, we are honored to have such a great artist at our party."

Nabolev stopped chattering to his audience to look at her, the mischievous gleam in his eye that had earned him the nickname of 'Rasputin.' He cocked his Tartar head to one side, the beautiful long nose and slanted eyes worthy of Noguchi.

"Have you tried the tuna fish canapés," the lady inquired, holding out a silver tray dotted with hors d'oeuvres on Ritz crackers.

"Madame," he replied, his lip curling in disdain, "you give Nabolev tuna fish tonight, you get tuna fish performance tomorrow!"

His boys snickered, hands in their wide pockets. The hostess retreated, mumbling in confusion. A second hostess approached.

"Mr. Nabolev, you danced brilliantly tonight."

"No, I only dance so-so."

"Oh, no, you were wonderful!"

"I said, I was so-so, and so-so I was."

Flustered, the poor woman kept on, but no match for his determined rudeness. "Perhaps the orchestra was too fast."

"No, orchestra too slow!"

She took a step backward and closed with, "Well, I am pleased to inform you that Monsieur Chabier, formerly of the Tour d'Argent in Paris, has prepared a sumptuous buffet." She handed Nabolev a large white plate and a napkin wrapped around silverware. "We would be honored if you would be the first to open the buffet table." She gestured towards the long table. "Please serve yourself."

Nabolev took the plate. He had been in a foul temper ever since Beckett's arrival usurped the attention of the party. Now he could recapture his stature in the center of the party. Nabolev crashed the plate to the floor. The party stopped; abruptly enveloped in silence.

"Nabolev does not serve himself. Nabolev sits, and is served!" He flung the napkin at the woman.

"Come," he motioned to his cortege. "We go to restaurant where Nabolev is treated as he deserve."

Nabolev knew the LA gossip columnists would consume every word. The scandal would be wired to New York, and the morning columns would feature the event. The straight media would discreetly omit the group trailing Nabolev, but later in the week, the New York and Los Angeles gay papers would produce a more factual account.

Moments after the grand exit the party hummed with Nabolev stories: recalling the time he danced *Giselle* at La Scala with Alicia Marina, the Italian ballerina, and slapped her on stage for stepping on his foot. And of his performance in Cuba with Prima Ballerina Marta Alba, whom he dropped to the floor yelling she "weighed like a sack of potatoes." The Cubans went crazy; young men raced to the stage, whirling machetes and crying for Nabolev's blood. The Cuban police rescued him but threatened jail if he was not on the next plane. There was also the story of his appearance with the Robin Mailer Dance Company, where he left every dancer with a case of VD. Nabolev stories were eventually exhausted; and friends and fans forgave him with a resigned, "That's Nabolev!"

Allison's vision of Beckett and Zhandra cooled her excitement over her performance and the party. When Temple sat down beside her and asked why she was so glum on her night of triumph, she almost blurted out what had happened with Beckett and her love for him. But she could not bring herself to do it, it was so humiliating. Instead she stuffed her mouth from her salad plate.

"I got an idea. Let's celebrate by going to the beach tomorrow."

"I have *Sonatine* rehearsal." Temple protested.

"Call in sick. You can miss one day."

"And I could use a rest. OK, let's do it."

Allison hoped the beach might help her forget, and avoid the sight of Zhandra and Beckett for a day. He held Zhandra's hand the entire party. Allison had not even reached mistress status, just a half-night stand. She had little chance against Zhandra unless there was some way that she could break Zhandra's hold on Beckett?

The next morning Allison sneaked out the back door of the hotel as Temple honked from a rented car. They roared out of the parking lot under a bright blue cloudless California sky. Temple tossed Allison the morning paper.

Allison read, "'Allison Fain, a newcomer to the Center Ballet has a promising future.' Well, that's hardly a rave!"

"For LA it is. Last year the Times critic called Nabolev a 'side of beef.'"

Allison skimmed the rest of the review: "*Preludes* is an impressive beginning for Christopher Beckett, but he has more to learn before he can mount a masterpiece on the level of *Concerto Barocco, Jardin aux Lilacs* or *Symphonic Variations.*" She tossed the paper in the back seat. Like most dancers, that was the only part of the paper she would read.

They parked, crossed a stretch of swamp grass beyond the playgrounds and a scattering of nude bathers on the soft sand of a remote section north of Point Dume and put their towels down on the packed sand where the tide had slid out an hour before.

"How did you know about this place?" Temple asked.

"Roberto. Who else?"

Allison stripped all the way down. "OK, take it off. No prudes allowed on this beach!"

"What about them?" Temple pointed to a scattering of male forms in the distance.

"They're a mile away, and they're gay. So strip!"

Temple slipped out of her bikini and tossed it in a heap.

"Put on plenty of grease," Allison warned, spreading sunscreen across her stomach. As an Italian I'm half olive oil so I really don't need any." She rooted her tummy into the towel and closed her eyes. "The sun feels so good on my butt! Oh, Temple, no talk of dance today. Let's enjoy our freedom."

"Sure, but I got a hot piece of gossip."

"OK, let's hear it." Allison replied wearily, her mouth muffled by the blanket.

"No, you're not interested. It can wait. But it's about Victoria and Juri."

"What? Let's hear it."

"I'll tell you after tonight's performance."

"You let it out now, or I'll kick sand in your face."

Temple grinned wickedly, knowing her interest in the subject. "Well, they're having marital problems...Juri doesn't do it with Victoria anymore."

"How come?"

"Rumor is Victoria took on all the straight guys of the Royal Toronto Ballet!"

"That must be one guy."

"It was actually two. Anyway, they're an inch away from divorce!"

Strangely, what she supposed Temple regarded as choice gossip didn't interest Allison very much. What had happened to her because of Juri and Victoria seemed a century old. Allison looked at Temple, as lovely as ever with her fine, translucent skin, not a blemish—even a freckle, and thought, "She's perfect, like a mirage. A man would really enjoy making love to Temple."

"Temple, I can't believe you haven't bitched about not getting opening night. You're a Soloist! You should have been chosen ahead of me."

"Nonsense! Beckett picked you, that's all. But Roberto and I shared last night's performance with you. When you breathed, we breathed. We partnered you on every step. We were happy for you and so proud of you."

Allison reached across the blanket and squeezed her hand. "Thanks. Sometimes I really love you, Temple. I've never had a better friend."

Temple leaned over and kissed Allison on the cheek. "And you're my best friend."

"Allison," Temple dug her toes into the white, warm sand. "Are you still taking those pills?"

"God, Temple, once in a while I take one to relax."

"What about the coke?"

"I haven't done that since…Atlantic City."

"You're sure."

"I'm not a drug addict." Allison snapped.

"OK, just checking. I worry about you."

Allison put her arms underneath her head. "Don't worry about me," Allison thought, but there was something else she could worry about, if only she knew.

Temple grabbed Allison by the hand and pulled her off the blanket, "Come on, let's get our toes wet before the sun sets."

The girls walked along the shore, Temple in as deep as her thighs.

Temple looked at Allison with her hair matted with oil and sand, as she skimmed the shore no deeper than her toes. "You look like…a nymph, with long disheveled hair, dancing on sands, and yet no footing seen."

"I didn't realized you were a poet."

"Not me. It's something I had to memorize in school. Shakespeare I think."

"Ugh, I could never understand any of that."

"That's because you think with your feet."

Allison kicked water over Temple. "Think about that."

Temple ducked and scooted back to the safety of the sand. "No splashing!"

Allison smiled. "OK. I'll let you live."

The sun did its cruise across the hot sky and a final dip into the Pacific in a classic orange-ball glow. They caught the sudden, bright red flash as it went under, standing up holding hands like twin figures of Venus emerging from the sea.

Under the shower, in a hurry for the last ballet that began at 9:30, the needle-like jets suddenly stung Allison.

"Ouch!"

She turned off the water and looked in the mirror. She was bright red from head to toe. She dialed Temple.

"Temple, I'm as red a boiled lobster. I'm cooked. Gregorov will know I played hooky—he'll kill me!"

"I thought you were half olive oil. OK, take some aspirin, and layer on the Noxzema. I'll camouflage you with make-up at the theatre."

The make-up worked, at least as far as her appearance was concerned. But nothing lessened the torture of the tutu. The bodice felt like a suite of armor around her swollen torso, and its stiff net tulle skirt cut short with jagged edges, sliced into her arms like a hacksaw every time she moved them below her hips. She danced horribly, her worst performance of the tour, a performance of *Raymonda Variations* she would never forget.

Curtain down, she was painfully edging herself out of costume when the stage manager called that Gregorov wanted to see her after performance in his room.

"Oh, Christ! He noticed. Or else…God, I hope not. If he touches me, I'll both get sick and puke, or my skin will pop. Either way, I'm in trouble!"

Gregorov opened the door in his black Chinese robe. "The executioner's costume again." She thought.

"Have a seat, my dear. Care for glass of wine?"

"Thank you, Mr. Gregorov."

"Have you seen the evening papers?"

"Here it comes. Bad reviews. A glass of wine and then chop off her head, she thought. "Why, no."

Gregorov chuckled. "How nonchalant! When I was young I stayed awake all night to grab first edition of the newspaper! Young people so different today. Well, the critic called you a new Pavlova, the reincarnation of Margot Fonteyn."

"I'm shocked. I mean, for such a simple piece."

"Sometimes a simple piece shows one to more advantage than a difficult work. So what do we do? We should make you Soloist, of course."

Allison froze, startled. She had not expected this, at least, not this fast!

Gregorov lifted her out of the chair as though she were the ballerina doll in Petrouchka. "Tomorrow we give you new contract. Minimum Soloist salary, of course."

Allison floated back to her hotel room two feet above the carpet. Her mother cried when she called her.

"I've prayed for this every night since you were little, Allison."

"I know, Mother. Thank you for everything…"

In the morning Allison went to the theatre, so early a guard had to unlock the door. She snapped on a light, and surveyed the corps dressing room for the last time. A concrete gray room with rows of long black tables attached to mirrors with make-up lights, cluttered in a chaos of wigs, pancake make-up, eyebrow pencils, soaps, baby oil, cotton balls, and tissue boxes. Her nostrils filled with the familiar stale odor of dried make-up, the scents of heavy perfumes, hair sprays, and sweaty costumes airing on hangers.

She found an empty cardboard box and swept make-up, sprays and bottles into it, then breezed out without turning around. "Never again will I set foot in a corps dressing room, never!"

A withered white-haired guard with a ring of keys waited to lock the door. Allison asked if he would open the soloist dressing room.

"Moving up?" The guard asked.

"Yes, I've been promoted to Soloist."

"Good for you." He slowly moved down the dim concrete corridor. "I've been promised Sergeant next year. I'm seventy years old, so I hope to live long enough to make it."

They reached the door. "Call me when you're ready to leave." He shuffled to a wooden chair near the stage door to continue his nap.

Allison unloaded her belongings on a table near Temple's. She examined her new residence with satisfaction. Plush deep red carpets, almond colored painted walls and private showers. Allison counted the make-up tables, and determined she was the eighth soloist. All the soloist's tables were coordinated in one color, a Center Ballet tradition. Delphine was hot red, Kathy was sunshine yellow, Nadine was forest green, Cori was steel gray, Kira was sky blue, Michelle was pink, and Temple was white. Allison had to pick her own color, and there wasn't much left to choose. There was purple, ghastly, Allison thought; and there was brown—which Allison rejected as too dull, and there were off colors like mauve or orange; but Allison rationalized that one of the dancers would get jealous since it was too close to their own color. There was one color nobody had picked. It was daring and dramatic! Black!

She darted past the security guard, "I'll be back in an hour," and hopped in a cab for the nearest department store. The first purchase was a set of black towels, then make-up jars, bottles, make-up brushes and hair brushes' she had no trouble finding everything in black, even an entire collection of Lazlo skin care products—including black soap. The cost didn't bother her; she would make it back in one month from the difference in the raise from a soloist salary. In the dressing room she unpacked the purchases on her table, promising to be neater as a soloist. She meticulously arranged her new toiletries, then looked in the mirror and found a luminous smile on her face.

"How foolish to think dreams don't come true. Everything is going my way. I have everything now...except...him...and how do I get him?" The mirror did not have an answer. "Zhandra loves Beckett...but I could love him more!" Her eyebrow raised in the mirror, "What would Victoria do? Not just moan and groan." Allison rested her head on her hand. "If God is good, he'll find me a way."

CHAPTER 27

Allison met Temple and Roberto for breakfast. It was hot outside the smog-blurred hotel windows; inside blurry-eyed businessmen perked up over coffee. "Freshly-shaved chipmunks," Roberto called them, twirling a packet of instant protein powder into his orange juice.

"Chamacas," he proceeded, "LA's a drag. For almost a month my eyes have been like a goddamned red eyed rabbit from this smog. I can't even get up for gossip anymore."

"Roberto," Temple gave her best fake whine, "How are we going to know who's screwing who if we don't get it from you?"

"Believe me, darlings, I am too busy with my own affairs to trifle with such carnal matters."

Allison was thinking how boring she found all this at times. "Didn't you get laid last night?"

"If I don't get laid it's because I didn't wanna get laid! I tell all the pretty boys not to bother me."

"Roberto, don't you ever worry about Aids?"

"Now why would I worry about that? Just because half of my friends have died is that anything to worry about?"

"OK, sorry." Allison did not appreciate his sarcasm so early in the morning. "So what do you do about it?"

"I have charms from the *santeros*."

"That's it?"

"I use protection, of course. Why? Do I look like an idiot, Allison?"

Allison decided not to answer, "I'll be sorry when we leave LA." Allison commented. "I got a performance of *Preludes*, good reviews, the weather is perfect, and there were lots of good parties…remember the night Pearl Jam and the Backstreet Boys showed up at the same party, and the time Pacino sat on one side of us and Mick on the other?"

"Big whoop!" Roberto snorted, sipping his juice. "Pacino sat there like a statue, and Mick only grunted. Mick's getting old, you know? Nobody wrinkles as fast as Englishmen. Now, you want to hear something really interesting?" Roberto's smile was as wide as the Cheshire cat. "Georginna is doing Gregorov."

"No!" Temple almost choked on her orange juice.

"Good!" Allison figured now Gregorov would leave her alone for sure.

"Allison, don't be naive, you of all people! Why do you think she doing it?

"Why?

"She wants opening night of *Preludes* in New York."

Allison's cheeks flushed red. "She can't get away with it! Casting is up to Ashley."

"For the premiere only, dear. After that, it's up to Gregorov—he's company director, remember."

"The little bitch!" Allison stamped her foot so hard the table shook and everything on it. Two chipmunks peered between glasses-on-fore-heads and newspapers at Allison's table. Roberto, ever appreciative of even the smallest audience, threw one of them a sweet, toothy smile. One of the chipmunks quickly lowered his eyes into his paper.

"What's worse, Zhandra is pitching for Georginna. Every time she gets a chance, she's slipping little things into Gregorov's ear."

Allison's Los Angeles euphoria was disappearing like rain into a sewer. Did Zhandra suspect her and Christopher?

"Roberto, why would Zhandra do that?"

He stared at her, disbelieving. "Pendejo, because you got better reviews than she did for *Preludes*."

"But that's more reason to keep me in for the opening in New York."

"For God's sake, Allison!" Temple hissed. "You're a threat to Zhandra. Since you got promoted you're a threat to everybody. Zhandra doesn't give a damn you're a soloist, but she does care you got better reviews than she did."

"It's only natural." Roberto swigged down the last of his juice, and stared glassily out the window. He'd had his share of the undercuts rooted in jealousy.

Allison did understand. Her jaw tightened as she remembered the sharp nails of Victoria dragging a bloody path across her cheek.

"Not again—not this time!" She stood up abruptly, dropped a few dollar bills on the table and ran to her room.

"Think, Allison, think! There's not much time before the opening in New York!" She made her fingers into a fist and squeezed, trembling with rage.

The last party for the Los Angeles engagement was held at The Roxy. Grateful to be nearing the end of a month-long engagement under the knives of LA critics, the dancers relaxed as they hadn't been able to since the beginning of the tour. The pulsating barrage of lights and the hypnotic spell of the heavy, steady rhythm washed the last trace of tension from their coiled limbs and limber brains.

Roberto on the dance floor was swinging his ass and jerking his head like a jackhammer. His partner was a burly guy with tattoos on heavily muscled arms in tight jeans and an artfully torn shirt. The girls could tell he was the one Roberto would decide on that night by the sly, toothy grins he was giving him as he spun around and threw his arms from side to side.

"Roberto's a beauty," Temple commented.

Suddenly Beckett was on the floor. He was in a crisp, white suit. The spots bounced and glistened off his magnificent body, his hair. He danced alone. Roberto and the Tattoo left the floor—they had to. Beckett used it all and established his claim by making a wide swing with his leg extended. Beckett's ballet control and grace were gone. Allison was mesmerized, her knuckles went white gripping the edge of the bar.

When it was over, Allison was exhausted. He had possessed her as he had that night in Atlanta. Any resolve she might once have had to forget him fell away like molted feathers. Her determination to have him at whatever cost congealed, as hard and solid as the center of an iceberg.

Allison grabbed Temple's hand and pulled her into the ladies room. They sat on a dark red velvet bench before the mirror. Allison opened her purse.

"I got a treat." Allison shook some cocaine on the glass table. "Hurry before someone walks in." Allison inhaled the line of white powder by snorting through a dollar bill.

"I thought you were done with that?" Temple admonished.

"I said I hadn't done it since Atlantic City. But tonight is kick back."

"Where did you get it?"

"A friend of Roberto. Go on, take a hit."

"Why are you trying to push me."

"If you don't want it, fine, there's more for me."

"Well…all right." Temple inhaled a line and then passed the bill back to Allison.

"The prescription that never fails to solve your problems." Allison took another snort.

Temple looked into the mirror. "Look at us. A couple of addicts!"

"God, you're priceless! One snort and she's an addict!" Allison quickly finished another line. "You need to take the edge off, Temple. With our schedule, we'll fry if we don't. Dancers don't know how to relax because they're so perverted."

"Perverted?"

"Yeah, perverted. You have to be perverse to submit to the physical and mental torture dancers endure."

Temple nodded in recognition of the truth. "When I was a student I had this teacher, Mr. Dubinski, an old Russian bull. He used to carry a cane and a large white kerchief, which was always soaking wet, because he sweated like a pig. One class I did a step looking at the floor. He rolled his kerchief and whipped it across my leg, 'Never eyes on the floor,' he shouted. He hit me so hard he opened up a gash on my knee." Temple raised her skirt and showed Allison.

Allison remembered seeing it before when they were nude on the beach.

"I finished class with blood streaming down my leg. But I didn't cry. After class, you know what Dubinski said to me? 'I am proud of you, little one,' Temple mimicked a Russian accent. 'You finish class. You will be professional dancer one day, you have right attitude.' I had to have stitches. I went home and cried all night...not because I hurt. I cried because it was the best compliment I ever had. I was so proud of the scar at night I would kiss it before I went to sleep. It was a perverse pride. Face it, Allison, there has to be something wrong here," she tapped her head, "...to be a dancer. We're like Kamikaze pilots."

Allison thought of the white rose. "Kamikazes in tutus!" She proposed a toast: "To dancers!"

Delphine swayed in the ladies room. "Hey girls, what'cha all doing?"

"Girl talk," Temple answered.

"Oh God, how boring. Men talk is so much better. Can I borrow a brush?"

Temple handed her a hairbrush.

Delphine perched on the bench. "Thanks."

"Allison, have you ever seen new Delphine's ring?" Temple asked.

Delphine extended a hand with a large diamond ring.

"It's beautiful."

"Zhandra has her eye on that ring," Temple added.

"She'll have to do with the one she already has," Delphine snapped.

"Girls, it's time to dance."

"But there's no men out there," Temple moaned.

"So we dance together. Come on. Let's dance the night away." Delphine dragged the two girls to the dance floor. They danced together holding hands; Allison felt the sharp edges of Delphine's ring. Cocaine and music worked through Allison's veins. Delphine was surprised how wild and free Allison danced, and how friendly she was towards her. And there was something in Allison's eye—a devilish gleam. Almost as if Allison was seeing into the future.

Before the performance that night the Soloist dressing room buzzed with exaggerated stories of meetings and bedding of famous movie celebrities. Allison, at her table carefully lined her eyes with thick black mascara; through the mirror she saw Delphine. She watched Delphine slip off her diamond ring and place it in a red and black lacquered box. Jewelry on stage could easily cut a partner's flesh or costume; and it was a strict company policy not to wear it.

The intercom signaled "Places, Act I, Coppelia." Soloists filed out of the dressing room like soldiers to a bugle call. Allison followed at the rear, but let the door swing close after the last girl. She ran to Delphine's table, hesitating only a moment above the ordered rows of make-up and beauty tools. She picked up the lacquered box and ran her fingers over the slick enamel finish.

"Last call, Places, Coppelia, Act I." She looked quickly around the room. She plucked out the ring and tucked it inside the fabric of her belt, putting the box back on the table.

She stopped at the door. Her heart pounded. Fear rushed through her. She had never done anything like this before. She put her back against the door. For a full ten seconds she stood, hardly breathing, listening to the room. She had never heard it so quiet. Something made her stop, hesitate, something inside told her to put it back. But some other voice commanded her to go on. She closed her eyes, took a deep breath. She would not turn back.

She hurried to the stage and began warming her leg muscles in a quick jog step in a dark part of the wings. She cracked her neck, rolling her head from side to side. Some dancers did Yoga breathing exercises, twisting their arms at the same time, or other combinations of spasms and contortions they had developed to give them the last burst of energy, the last off-stage elasticity they needed to push them blooming on stage. It was a scene an uninitiated public would expect to see before a track and field events rather than before a romantic ballet performance.

Allison felt dizzy, what she had done weighted heavy on her conscious and twisted her stomach into a tight knot. She couldn't go through with it; she had to put it back! But when she started for the dressing room, Temple grabbed her arm. "Allison, where're you going? We're on!"

As the curtain opened, she propelled herself on stage to a din of applause, a din behind the buzz of the music. She'd never been so 'off' it was going to be a dreadful performance unless she could pull herself together. The stage smile, the one a professional dancer pastes on as easily as smearing lipstick, wouldn't form on her wooden jaw. The lights blinded her eyes as she wondered where to direct them. She tried to remember if she had ever stolen anything before, and couldn't.

On the last note of music of Act 1, she darted off the stage to be first in the dressing room. Flinging open the door, she saw Delphine brushing her hair before the mirror, the lacquered box in front of her.

"The tempo was too fast." Delphine shouted, trying to catch her breath.

"Yes." Allison toweled sweat from her face. Delphine was not due on stage until the middle of Act 2, and Allison had a variation at the beginning; the dressing room would not be clear again until the end of Act 2. Allison sat through the fifteen-minute intermission, like a French queen waiting for the guillotine to slice off her neck, but Delphine never opened the box.

In the wings before Act 2, she dug her foot into the rosin box as Zhandra Amaya dipped hers on the other side.

"Don't think you can get away with it, Allison."

"What?" Allison's heart stopped.

"A poor performance like your first Act. They'll boo you off the stage in New York."

Allison excused herself. "Oh, I'm not feeling well."

"Then you shouldn't be on stage." Zhandra crisply walked away.

Allison felt like kicking Zhandra's departing behind with her pointe shoe. She was finished being victimized by the stinging remarks and attacks from Principal dancers. Anger oozed from her stomach, bile-flavored, and she forgot to be afraid. Zhandra had finally done it. Allison now had the strength to go forward with the plan.

"I must not let the diamond be found on me! But where..." She quickly went over to the stage manager's desk, pulled out a lower drawer and fitted the diamond into a dark recess. She would retrieve it after performance, or perhaps the next day."

For the next two acts she danced on automatic pilot, hoping Gregorov was watching someone else. In spite of the weakness of her individual performance the company bowed to a thunderous ovation.

Dressing room chatter enveloped her as she slipped out of costume and wiped off her make-up, waiting.

"My ring! It's gone!" Delphine shrieked.

The girls stopped dead, then rushed over to Delphine's table and helped her turn everything upside down looking for the diamond.

"I always keep it here during performance...always..." her words trailed off.

Temple took her hand. "Are you sure?"

"Yes, yes!" She looked wildly about the room, as though her diamond might be swinging on a ribbon from the ceiling. Allison joined the search, and Kira called Gregorov. He hurried into the room the girls rushed to cover themselves. Allison was nude and threw on a robe.

"Mr. Gregorov." Delphine's tears streamed down in mascara rivulets.

"What happened, child?"

Delphine could only babble; Temple explained.

"Anyone see stranger on this floor tonight?" Gregorov asked. All girls shook their heads. "Stagehands?" No one saw anyone. "Who else is on this floor?"

"Dressers are on this floor," Allison proffered. "How many?"

"Two for the soloists. And there are three Principal dancers on the floor with their own dressers."

Gregorov nodded. "Temple, ask them to come to this room." Temple was back within minutes with the five dressers. Gregorov addressed them, "Ladies, we have had a theft of a diamond ring. Do any of you know about it?" One plump lady and her four thin friends looked blank. "Did you see anyone in this area you did not recognize?"

"No men, on this floor, that's for sure, mister." The plump Mexican woman with curly black hair spoke.

"So, it had to be someone on this floor." Gregorov looked at her.

The woman realized she inadvertently cast suspicion upon herself and her comrades. "Hey, mister," she barked, "I work this theatre for nine years. No thefts, ever. Me and the ladies not gonna start now."

"Madam, I am not accusing any of you. I am trying to find out what happened."

"Then play Sherlock Holmes by yourself, not with us." The woman folded her arms over her ample breasts.

"I'm afraid you all have to submit to a search. Kira, please call security on intercom," Gregorov ordered.

Allison asked, "Are you going to search the Principals too?"

Gregorov looked at her surprised; his nose twitched. "I see no reason for that. There's Carlotta Gray, Georginna Haviland and…Zhandra Amaya. They would not do anything like this."

"And a Soloist would!" Allison asked.

"Of course not; this is where it was taken—it is where we have to start."

A security team of two men arrived. "Are there no women on force?" Gregorov questioned.

"Their shift is over at eight." A ruddy-faced policeman answered. Gregorov had the bewildered look of a little boy lost in the deep Russian woods.

The Mexican spoke again. "You better talk to the Union Steward before you touch us, mister! Our unions will be on your ass if you try."

Gregorov looked helplessly at the security team awaiting further instructions. "It looks as if there is nothing we can do." He touched Delphine on the shoulder. "I'm sorry." He walked briskly out of the room. It was a rare moment in Gregorov's life when he did not get exactly what he wanted.

There was an uncomfortable silence once again in the dressing room. Everyone dressed hurriedly and the girls filed out, leaving Delphine confused and in tears, pawing through her make-up collection as though the ring still might be found.

Roberto in black harem pants; hooked his legs around a barstool and stirred a rum swizzle. "It's her own fault for wearing a diamond ring around the theatre. Did you hear where she got it?"

Allison and Temple were all ears.

"She met this Arab at our first party in LA. Greasy as an oil well…Kira said he smelled like a camel, in spite of his Hugo Boss cologne. Dear little Delphine got visions of a mansion in Beverly Hills so she wore herself out on him. Could hardly dance for a week! And he had some unusual tastes. Let me tell you she earned that ring. Beauty sold for an Arab's gold."

Temple sipped her drink. Roberto grabbed Temple's drink. "Lemmee have some of that drink. I'm dying of thirst and I'm broke."

"Can you find a new friend?"

"Everybody's turned straight all of a sudden."

Allison was already lost in her drink. "It was a beautiful ring. I remember Delphine saying how much Zhandra liked it."

"Yes!" Temple perked up. "I remember too. You don't think—?"

"Don't be ridiculous, Temple." Allison chided.

"Don't be so sure, Allison. Zhandra can be very sneaky. I wouldn't put anything past her." Roberto warned.

"Well, whatever you do Roberto, don't spread any rumors." Alison demanded.

"Que me crees, chismoso? On my honor I wouldn't say a word."

Chapter 28

"Chicago is crap." Roberto sulked in the plane, watching the Great Plains roll by out the window, an undulating green and gold carpet of corn and wheat.

"I thought you couldn't wait to get out of LA. "Temple, who had been trying to nap, opened an unsympathetic eye.

"Yeah, but LA is better than a meat freezer like Chicago."

"Look at all there is to do in Chicago! We can go shopping at Marshall Fields."

Roberto shrugged. "I can't go shopping. I spent all my money in LA."

"We can go to the museums."

"I saw them all last year."

"Bull, Roberto, you've never been to one! Roberto pushed the button for the stewardess "I need a blanket. My feet are already numb from the cold."

"You are a pain in the butt! Or is that cold too?"

"I require a perfect environment. Some of us are orchids, and some of you are weeds."

"Then sit by yourself, orchid boy." Temple started to unbuckle herself. "And I'll go sit with the weeds."

Usually she laughed off Roberto's whining, but like everyone else in the company, she was infected with a mid-tour malaise. First, there was the tour itself with its incessant routine, the daily pressure of keeping in shape, and the strain of rehearsals and performances. There were the late nights, the booze, the rumors, the backstabbing; the paranoia of losing roles and worrying about the possibility. Hearing the same old complaints; looking at the same faces day after day trapped with them in the plane; the dressing room and the studio didn't help. And now here was a new demon, a thief. It had to be somebody within the company! Temple still sat there, too depressed to move.

"It will be beautiful if it snows over Christmas." She tried to cheer herself up.

"And cold as my butt!"

"Oh, shut up! I've had enough," she hissed at him, finally propelled enough by his acidity to get up and walk down the aisle. She found Allison at the front of coach section absent-mindedly flipping through a new dance magazine.

"Hi," plopping down.

"Hi."

"Allison, I got some news about Zhandra."

"Shhh! She's sitting right there!" Allison put her hand over Temple's mouth and pointed to Beckett and Zhandra in the last seat of first class.

Temple whispered in Allison's ear, "Zhandra's leaving for a guest appearance in Rio."

"Really? And why are you telling me this?"

"Because if she leaves the tour then I'll get a chance to dance *Preludes.*" Temple beamed.

"Oh, yes, sure, of course."

"You sound so defensive."

"Sorry, it's just the tour."

"Yeah, I have a touch of tour fever also."

"So when does she leave?" Allison squelched a smile. "After the first week in Chicago. She'll be gone past New Year's."

Suddenly warning chimes sounded and the "Fasten Seat Belts" sign flashed on. The captain's voice boomed over the P.A. system.

"Ladies and Gentlemen, may I have your attention please. We will be experiencing some turbulence in the next few minutes. We have been in contact with ground control at O'Hara Airport and they informed us that they have a six-inch base of new snow, with more on the way. We request that you return to your seats and fasten your seat belts. We will keep you informed of the latest developments."

The dancers were sprawled about the plane. Some perched on the arms of the seats; a few slept across three seats, heads in willing laps, shoes and boots off. Immediately everyone took their places and followed instructions. Again the captain's voice resounded through the plane. "We have just received a report that snow is accumulating fast. They are having trouble keeping the runways clear. We will go to into a circling pattern and hold until we get clearance to land. If we are unable to land, we will proceed to the nearest airport with favorable weather."

"Make it Puerto Rico!" yelled Roberto.

But nobody laughed. The mood was fear! Georginna doubled over, clutching her stomach and grabbing Gregorov's arm.

The captain continued, "There is no need to panic. We ask you to stay calm and return to your seat, and keep you seat belts fastened."

"I'd better go." Temple returned to her seat.

From the front of the plane, a thin voice could be heard sobbing; it was Georginna. She ran down the aisle to sit next to Allison. "I need more of those pills?"

"Sure." Allison discreetly fished out a bottle from her purse, and put some pills in Georginna's hand.

Georginna swallowed. "Will that be enough?"

"Sure, ah…" Allison looked at Georginna's fragile face and envisioned her taking away Allison's role in *Preludes,* "maybe a few more wouldn't hurt." Tears streamed over the cheeks of the child dancer. She trembled, and Allison stroked her hair. "Are we going to crash, Allison?"

"No, no, this happens all the time. Everything's going to be all right. You had better go back to your seat now."

Zhandra watched coolly, as Georginna walked down the aisle. She turned to Christopher. "Georginna should be in a mental ward or a kindergarten."

Beckett frowned at his wife. "Have some compassion. Some people are terrified of flying."

"I'm scared too, but I control myself. How can they call her a ballerina? Look at the clothes she wears! Have you seen her in anything but those disgusting ripped jeans since the tour began? She looks like a bag lady. Pigtails, with little bows! I mean, you must admit, Christopher, she's a bit bizarre even for a Prima Ballerina!"

Beckett shrugged. He had more sympathy for the female dancers than his wife, for obvious reason: he knew them better than she did. "So she's a little eccentric."

"Eccentric? You call wearing leg warmers on her arms in rehearsal just eccentric?"

Beckett cut her short. "Darling, do you think we could talk about something else? Particularly since we might be about to crash?"

"Sorry." She stroked his neck. "At least you can be proud of your wife. If I die, I die well dressed. Remember the poem that says 'dying is an art'?"

"Yes, dear, but so is living."

The stewardesses were passing out Scotch. The Captain's voice came on again.

"Ladies and gentlemen, we received word that a runway has been cleared, and we will be starting our descent. We ask you stay in your seats and keep your seat belts fastened. The landing may be rough. In case of a severe jolt, bend your heads as close to your laps as possible. Hang on, everybody!"

The plane descended in a frightening, rapid drop. The dancers felt their stomachs leave them fifty feet above. The plane filled with moans and screams. Dancers huddled together, holding each other's head in their arms. Suddenly the wheels touched ground; the plane bounced up and down in convulsions, then skidded. Rigid with fear, they felt the huge machine sliding, totally out of control. There was an abrupt, terrifying lurch as the wheels snapped off. Objects flew about the cabin. Then came another jolt and a final lunge. The plane skidded off the runway and lurched into a ditch. A wing was severed off by the strain, with a grating metallic screech. The plane then dropped sharply on its right side, as though in a terminal spasm, hung perilously over the ditch and then heaved and fell to rest in the snow-covered, muddy field. There was complete silence on board as they waited for an explosion, but it didn't come.

One by one the dancers raised their heads and looked at the chaos inside the cabin. Trays, plastic drinking cups, blankets, pillows and books were strewn in the aisles. But everyone was alive!

Sobs, chatter and hugs erupted throughout. Amazingly, no one seemed to have been hurt. There would be a few swans with ruffled feathers, make-up covered bruises and rubbery legs during that night's performance of Swan Lake, but the damage was minimal in human terms for the force of the crash. But all had not escaped unharmed. There was a frantic commotion taking place at the front of the plane, and someone screamed for an ambulance. The cabin door sprung open, letting a gust of chilling air surge through.

Temple squeezed her way down the aisle to Allison. They looked out the window, but could not distinguish the cause of the ruckus, but they saw a stretcher being carried onto the plane from an ambulance out the window. The stretcher was lowered from the emergency ramp after it picked up its victim, but the swirling snow made it impossible to see who it was. Then, through a momentary gust of clearing wind, Allison made out a pair of frayed jeans covered with blood, glistening red in the flashing lights of the ambulance.

Temple squinted, "I think it's Georginna. But I can't be sure, there's so much blood!"

"Oh, God, pray for her!" She crossed herself, the automatic reflex of a Catholic from childhood.

Word traveled quickly through the company; indeed, the figure on the stretcher was Georginna. She had unfastened her seat belt prior to landing and stood up. Gregorov had tried to pull her down, but she struggled free of his grip. When the plane landed, she was bounced and flung around the cabin like a snowflake in the storm.

A bus pulled up at the side of the disabled plane. The dancers slid down portable ramps and climbed aboard for the ride to the Hotel Webster in downtown Chicago. Time was running short for the evening performance. They would have only thirty minutes to check into the hotel, drop their bags in their rooms, pick out a pair of tights, and be back on the bus for the trip to the theatre.

Within ninety minutes of the crash, the company was on stage. Barres and ladders had been set up, and the dancers waited for the company class to begin. They had finished the warm-up exercises when Gregorov entered and walked to Center Stage. Total silence greeted his solemn face.

"I just returned from the hospital. Georginna is in coma. She suffered a severe concussion, and fractured her left leg. But the doctors believe…she has also damaged a nerve in her vertebrae. If true, it is possible that she will be paralyzed from the waist down. I repeat, this is only a possibility…there is still hope."

The company stood numb. He resumed, distractedly. "Of course, it is tragedy when a dancer is unable to dance, but crueler if she is not able to walk." Almost inaudibly, the words drifted onto the stage, setting on each dancer like a shroud. Every dancer knew His personal story. His first wife, the beautiful, world-renowned ballerina, Ari Asseyevna, had been paralyzed in a car accident the first year of their marriage and died a painful, lingering death. "Let us pray that God grant her the ability to walk." He bowed his white head and clasped his hands, at that moment not the master of the greatest American troupe, but a humble man of faith, from an ancient country, Russia, which in his youth had been a deeply religious place.

The dancers stood still, harshly reminded of their own fragile mortality and the daily vulnerability of their magnificent bodies, their exposure to disaster. The firmness returned to Gregorov's voice. "We will post Georginna's room number on the call board. When she regains consciousness, she will need help and support from all of us. Now, it has been a bad day, and we are all shaky. But the only thing to do is go on…to dance. To forget our tragedies in the glory of our great profession. So, let me have the first line of girls. This is the combination…"

He demonstrated steps, and the dancers followed like mindless zombies, gradually getting into it and forgetting, as he knew they would, their tragedies. Thus it was, thus it would always be, every time these perfectly trained athletes gave themselves over to the magic of dance, and particularly to dancing on stage with lights and music and thousands of eyes upon them. They were creatures of magic, and not only to the audiences they thrilled.

In the great scheme of things, in the confused, turbulent twenty-first century world they graced, they were dancers, little else—or else the rest was insignificant. And nobody knew it better than Gregorov. The difference between him and the dancers in his charge was that he had learned to manipulate the circumstances, and now circumstances were beyond control.

The first Chicago performance flew by in a blur. Allison came back to consciousness taking a headpiece of swan feathers out of her hair at the make-up table. Temple leaned against the table, dressed in a white swan tutu.

"Allison, we were like barnyard ducks out there tonight! How do you feel?"

"Rotten! How do you feel?"

"Rotten! Allison, I saw you giving Georginna a pill, what was it?"

"Oh, it was just an aspirin, she had a headache.

The next morning they only had time for a cup of coffee before leaving for class. Gregorov reported Georginna was out of the coma and asked them to visit her at 4 p.m., the only free time during the heavy schedule of rehearsals for *Nutcracker*, to be performed on Christmas Eve.

A chartered bus took them to St. Luke's Hospital. Georginna was in a private room, her face greenish under bandages that left only her nose and eyes showing. Her body was criss-crossed with tubes. Machines blinked red lights and green spectrographs indicating vital functions. Since there were almost a hundred in the company, each member had only a few seconds to spend at her bed. It was like reviewing at a funeral parlor, as each dancer knelt down, touched her, said a few words and moved on.

It was a bleak afternoon for the company, not only the sight of one of their ballerinas, one of the best, in a situation hardly preferable to death. Foremost in the minds of many, back on the bus rumbling through the bleak, steel gray streets, was the thought that it could have been any one of them.

Temple and Allison slipped into the booth of a late night coffee shop.

"There, but by the grace of God..." Temple shuddered.

Allison confessed, "I feel worse than anyone seeing her like that."

"Why?" Temple asked her, knitting her brow.

"I hoped that something bad would happen so she wouldn't take my role."

"That's only natural. Everyone secretly hopes something bad would happen to another...either for revenge or jealousy."

"But it happened."

"Allison, don't get creepy on me! You had nothing to do with Georginna's standing up in that plane!

"Temple, I shouldn't say this, but I hoped something bad would happen to Zhandra as well..." she ran her fingernail around the rim of her mug.

Temple rubbed her usually bright blue eyes, at the late hour red and puffy.

"Don't be silly! Come on, it's one-thirty in the morning, let's get back to the hotel." She took Allison's hand and led her away from the table. "I don't want to hear any more about your guilty, super-natural powers! Nobody can cause accidents by wishing them!"

"Yes," thought Allison to herself, "It does take more than just wishing…" as she tossed a tip on the table and followed Temple out into the street twinkling with the red and green lights of Christmas.

Only the mood of the company was more depressing than the weather those two long weeks in Chicago. No one had laughed since the plane crash; since the surgeon's last report they even avoided each other's eyes. Georginna's paralysis was permanent…one of the youngest and loveliest stars on the stage of American dance would never walk again.

Gregorov located Georginna's father. Four months prior to her accident he had been committed to a state mental institution and was not expected to recover from his increasingly dangerous psychosis. Georginna's mother had left the family ten years before, and there was not a trace of her. Georginna's only sister, Christina, was a dancer with the Brazilian Ballet Company. She was sent a telegram about the tragedy, and she wrote back: "Sorry I am unable to visit now as I am premiering two roles during our current season. We will tour the United States during the summer. I will see Georginna then."

The waif with the coal black, bright button eyes, so recently reviewed by raving critics, would have visitors while the company was in town. After that, she would spend the rest of her life alone. All the major newspapers ran short pieces about her; the last time her name would ever appear in print except for historical references in some dance publications.

Temple perched on Allison's make-up table. "Try this," as she opened a container of eye shadow. "The color you're using doesn't bring out your eyes enough. A darker shade will do it better." She rubbed the color on Allison's lids. "And one more surprise." Temple stood up. "Close your eyes and don't move!" She produced a box wrapped in silver foil, placing it in front of Allison. "Merry Christmas."

"Temple, you shouldn't have!" Allison tore the paper off and lifted the lid. Inside was a handsome, antique, black silk robe, with *Allison* monogrammed on the pocket."

"It's beautiful, I don't know what to say! Now you sit down and close your eyes!"

She reached into her ballet bag and took out a square box in red and gold paper and ribbons. Temple peeled off the wrappings and squealed as she pulled out a pair of red wool leg warmers, a red sweatshirt and a red, terry-cloth bandanna.

Temple chortled, "So you noticed the holes in my tattered old leg warmers. And red! The perfect color for Christmas." Temple hugged Allison, "Merry Christmas."

There was to be one more Christmas present for Temple.

Allison and Temple stood in the hotel lobby waiting for the bus that would take them to the theatre. Allison saw Gregorov coming out of the hotel's magazine shop. "Well, God has left Olympus to mix with us mortals."

Gregorov walked to the girls. "Good morning, ladies. Temple, do you know Aurora's role in *Sleeping Beauty*?"

"I did the pas de deux once in a high school Christmas show."

"Good. I want you to do the closing night performance."

"That's in four days."

"Five. Georginna was scheduled, of course, but...and Carlotta Gray leaves for tour in a few days. Zhandra does the matinee so I can't ask her to do two *Sleeping Beauties* in one day."

"Mr. Gregorov, I would be honored, but I have rehearsals for—"

"I'll clear your schedule so all you will have will be *Beauty* rehearsals. And I'll assign Steven Simon as your partner to rehearse you. And, of course, the performance will be with Christopher Beckett."

Temple stood stunned not sure what to say. Allison stood mute, hoping Temple would turn down the opportunity.

"Well?" Gregorov waited impatiently.

"Why…yes. I'll do my best."

"Good. You'll need to see Madame Tulliers for a costume fitting as soon as possible."

Gregorov walked out of the lobby and hopped into his limo for the ride to the theatre.

"Temple, Are you nuts? What took you so long? Any dancer in the country would kill to do *Beauty* with Christopher Beckett!"

"But there's so little rehearsal time, I could fall on my face."

"Or it could make you a star."

"I hope you're right."

"Ay, cararumba! Anyway let's get you to wardrobe as soon as we get to the theatre."

At the theatre Temple and Allison went to the wardrobe room where a cheerfully plump French woman was stitching a costume.

"Madame Tulliers?"

"*Bonjour*, ladies." Madame Tulliers took off her reading glasses and looked Temple over. "Yes, you are quite right for the role. Very delicate and pretty." She pulled out a tape measure. "Now let's get you fitted, *cherie*." She pulled the tape around Temple's waist. "Such a tiny waist, a man could put his hands around you and touch his fingers…I once had a waist like that, but then…age takes it toll…ah, c'est dommage!" Miss Tulliers lifted the tape to Temple's breasts. "And you are as flat as a boy." Temple blushed. "Oh, but you are lucky, *cherie*, Gregorov will cast you in the modern ballets."

Miss Tulliers measured Temple head for a tiara. "And a nice small head. You would be surprised how big some girl's heads get when they get to dance the lead in *Sleeping Beauty*." Temple laughed. "All right, you are finished."

Allison hovered over a glass case that housed the companies more valuable tiaras. "These are so beautiful."

"Ah, yes, they are the ones with the real stones, diamonds, rubies, sapphires, opals. They are for the Principal dancers, but for now…" Miss Tulliers placed a rhinestone tiara on Temple's head. "You will have to wear rhinestones like the other soloists. But your day will come. You are both destined to be *etoiles*. You speak French, no?"

"No." Temple admitted, "a little Louisiana patois"

"Ah, that's not real French, but a sort of gumbo. When I was a girl, everyone spoke French, of course, I lived in France."

They all laughed. "An *'etoile'* is a star, and only a star can design her own tiara. And if you have admirers, as I'm sure you will, they will give you diamonds to adorn your tiara."

Allison asked. "Miss Tulliers, would it be all right, if I…"

"I would be disappointed if you didn't ask." Miss Tulliers took out her keys and opened the cabinet." Madame Tulliers took out a tiara and placed it on Allison's head.

Allison's face became instantly radiant. "It's beautiful. Whose is it?"

"Regina Christian. The ruby was given to her by…well…an admirer."

Temple and Allison exchanged glances. There was a quick understanding of who gave it to her.

Temple looked in the mirror at the rhinestone tiara on her head. "Madame Tulliers, if I gave you a diamond could you fit it into this Tiara."

Madame Tulliers scolded, "Only for Principals." Madame Tulliers looked at the disappointed look on Temple's face and smiled. "But since you are doing a Principal role I see no reason why not."

Temple reached into her purse, and took out the ring given to her by Billy on the backwaters of the Bayou. Allison's eyes grew large. Temple handed the ring to Madame Tuillers.

"I'll have it ready by the end of the week. Now…don't you girls have rehearsals!"

"God, yes." Temple quickly kissed Madame on the cheek, "Thanks."

Allison started to follow Temple when Madame Tuelliers called. "Allison!"

"Yes?"

"The tiara."

Allison's hand reached up to her head, and she unpinned the crown. "Sorry, I forgot."

"It is hard to go back to being a peasant, yes." Madame smiled.

"Yes." Allison placed the tiara back in the glass case. "Yes, it is."

Temple spent the next five days frantically rehearsing against the clock! She thought enviously of the Russian system where dancers are nourished, like Maya Plisetskaya, the Prima Ballerina, who was meticulously trained for five years in the role of Juliet. But this was American style and Temple had only five days to learn one of the most important roles in ballet.

She learned dancing behind Zhandra, who carried on like a pampered brat. If the pianist slowed the tempo, she stamped her foot. If he played too fast she stomped out of the room. If she fell out of a pirouette, she flung herself to the floor, threatening suicide. She cried at the slightest provocation. A delivery boy brought her a bacon, lettuce and tomato sandwich with mayonnaise. She screamed that she had ordered no mayonnaise. Gregorov had to stop rehearsals for fifteen minutes to console her.

Allison's partner, Steve Simon, was little help as he was ruffled about having to run Temple through *Sleeping Beauty*.

The final rehearsal for *Sleeping Beauty* was a full dress rehearsal with the entire company. Zhandra and Christopher would dance in front and Temple and Steve would dance behind them. During the Rose Adagio section a line of boys have their backs turned away from the ballerina, and as she leaps into space they turn and catch her at the last possible moment. Terry Wilson, a new member of the company, was the last boy in the row. Across the stage Alison distracted him by a seductive wink.

Zhandra leapt into Terry's arm, but he was a split second late, and he fumbled her like a football and she crashed to the floor. Her screams were heard as far as the dressing rooms. Gregorov and a crowd of dancers and stagehands surrounded her.

"It's my ankle. God damn it!"

"Get a cold compress." Gregorov ordered the stage manager. "Quick."

The compress was applied and Zhandra was laid on a blanket, her head propped up by a ballet bag, and her foot raised on a chair.

Temple watched as precious seconds ticked off from the rehearsal. She wanted to suggest that they take her off the stage and continue the rehearsal, but she had not climbed the pecking order far enough to open her mouth.

A half-hour went by as attention was continually bestowed on Zhandra. Gregorov quietly asked her if she felt she could perform in tomorrow's matinee.

"I don't know, Mr. Gregorov."

Gregorov looked at his company. "Does anyone know the role of Aurora?"

From out of her mouth and without a second's hesitation Allison spoke. "I do."

"Good. You and Temple are about the same size you can wear Temple's tutu for the matinee"

Gregorov finally requested that Zhandra be carried off stage, and that Allison would dance behind Temple.

As Allison stood behind Temple the realization hit her that she had stuck her toe shoe in her mouth. She had never danced the lead role in *Sleeping Beauty*, except in her bedroom where she danced to the music a million times. But this was real time in the big leagues.

Christopher came from the wings and stood beside Allison. It was too late to retract her offer. She would prefer to fall on her face during the performance then to make an idiot of herself in front of Christopher. Besides even if she flopped badly she had a perfect built-in excuse. All dancers marshaled excuses as insurance against a bad performance: a slippery floor, a stage too narrow or too wide, bad tempo, a bright spotlight. But the best excuse was inadequate rehearsal time, the perfect excuse for anything that didn't go perfectly.

In her dressing room Allison couldn't stop her heart from beating. She reminding herself it was just a matinee. There would be no critics; the change in schedule was so sudden that there was no time to notify the press. But despite her rationalizations her heart would not stop racing. Allison looked in her purse; maybe a half a pill would take the edge off a little. She took tweezers and cut the pill, swallowing it with a warm coke. It would kick in before her first entrance.

She started to relax as she felt more confident. This was an opportunity that couldn't be passed up, dancing a lead role with Christopher Beckett would provide an arsenal of ammunition to argue for a Principal contract next year.

Minutes before the matinee Allison walked into the wings, readying herself to go on when she saw Zhandra on stage with Beckett. Allison was shocked. Nothing seemed wrong with her. Allison didn't know whether to be sorry or rejoice. Zhandra saw Allison, and flashed a smile. Was it stage-smile, or was Zhandra rubbing it in? Zhandra was shattering her dream of dancing *Sleeping Beauty* with Christopher, and she was relishing it.

Allison ran to the dressing room to change into her corps de ballet costume. Other dancers huddled around her, inquiring what happened. Allison shrugged and laughed, but she felt humiliated. When she was alone Allison blotted a tiny tear with her finger. Zhandra would pay for that tear. She would pay dearly.

Allison unpinned the new tiara she borrowed from Temple.

The intercom blared. "Places, *Sleeping Beauty*, Act I."

Allison spotted Kira putting on her headpiece and heading for the door. "Kira! Wait!"

"What, Allison?"

"I have something I want you to put in safe-keeping for me." Since he theft of Delphine's ring, the girls had designated Kira to keep their valuable during performance.

"Damn, Allison, I just put everything away!"

"Kira, please I just got knocked out of the lead role. Give me a break."

"Sorry, kid, I'm just in a hurry. Give it to me."

Allison handed Kira the tiara. "For god's sake, it's just a rhinestone tiara."

"No, Temple had a real diamond put into the center. She let me borrow it."

"OK, OK, give it to me."

Allison went back to her table. She watched Kira's reflection in the mirror as she stood on top of a chair and placed the tiara on top a heating duct, pushing it back out of sight. Kira jumped off the chair and rushed out, hardly noticing Allison was still there.

The intercom called, "Last call, places Act I."

Allison joined Kira in the wings.

"It's really too bad you couldn't do this performance" Kira commiserated, "It doesn't seem fair."

"And who said ballet was fair," Allison replied curtly as she watched Zhandra holding hands with Christopher.

After performance Kira distributed the valuables to the other soloists. Allison asked for the tiara.

"Oh, I must have pushed it back further." Kira stood on the chair, scraping her hands around the top of the heating duct, but found nothing but air. "Allison, it's not here."

"What?"

"I was so rushed I just hid it on top of a heating duct. It must have fallen. Maybe it was kicked under a table." Kira hollered for attention. "Girls, Temple's tiara has been misplaced, it has to be somewhere in the room. Help us look?"

The girls threw themselves into the search hoping to contradict the belief in the bottom of their hearts that there was another theft.

No tiara was found. Gregorov was called. Allison explained it was a valuable tiara with a diamond stone.

Gregorov shrugged. "I'm regret there's nothing can be done. But the company has insurance; we'll get this reimbursed."

"It's not the money. It was Temple's good luck piece, hand-made for her. And now it's gone. Temple will never speak to me again." Allison sobbed into her hands.

Gregorov embraced her. "I know how much personal mementos mean. But you are not to blame; you gave it for safekeeping. Temple will not blame you."

"And I lost the chance of doing *Sleeping Beauty*."

"Don't worry, we'll make that up to you. You will do *Beauty* when we get back to New York." Gregorov held her in his arms.

The other soloists in the room were stunned by Gregorov's promise that Allison would perform the coveted lead role on the New York stage. Girls who moments ago felt compassion now stiffened at the news. Allison's eyes, barely above Gregorov's shoulder, saw Delphine seething. Allison smiled to herself as she nestled on Gregorov's shoulder.

Later that evening Temple faced the mirror. She put on a new emergency tiara that Madame had made for Temple during the break between performance. She placed clusters of rhinestones on the side frames, but on the front had used simulated diamonds. They were molded carefully into graceful loops and arcs. Allison came in the soloist's dressing room and presented Temple with a *merde* gift, a tiny troll in a ballet costume and wearing a tiara through its fuzzy orange hair. Temple laughed, "It looks how I feel."

"You'll be great, you were born to play this role."

"Allison, I'm so sorry about what happened to you today. I feel somehow responsible."

"It wasn't your fault."

"Still—"

"Allison, forget about it!"

"Well, *merde.*" Allison spit through her two fingers at Temple's cheeks, another superstitious good luck tradition between dancers.

Temple glided on stage in an ethereal pink and white tulle costume, looking every bit an angel. She had the fragility of fine translucent porcelain china. She danced with Christopher in a dream.

But in the middle of the pas de deux when Temple looked in his eyes she realized the secret that she had been hiding in the deepest recesses of her heart. Temple was in love, hopelessly in love with Christopher Beckett.

She thought he must have sensed it in the one second their eyes locked on stage. Of course, they were supposed to look at each other as if they are in love, but this more than just acting. It made her dance with even more radiance than she had ever danced before.

It was a performance no one would forget. Her love gave her not only strength, but daring as well. She pulled off triple pirouettes where a single turn was required; and balanced in arabesque as if her foot was cemented to the stage. At the curtain calls she glowed as Christopher presented her to the audience for wild applause. A new star was born!

The performance was scintillating for everyone, one of the rare occasions when everything clicked into place. Suddenly everything looked rosy; the road tour was winding down, and only one more stop before the New York season, which now promised to be a great success. Even Gregorov smiled for the first time in days as he announced a cut of one hour of rehearsal daily. A necessary kindness to ease the pressure.

But the festive mood evaporated in an instant, as Temple stood in the middle of the soloist dressing room with the contents of her ballet bag emptied on the floor.

"My new leg warmers are gone!"

Kira volunteered an explanation. "Maybe you left them on stage."

Two girls went to search the stage while other looked in the green room and the ladies. The leg warmer were not to be located.

Temple eyes watered as she held back her tears. "First my tiara, now this, a Christmas present from Allison. God, who's doing this."

"Someone's obviously jealous." Allison could only answer.

"Or very sick." Kira added.

This time the dancers were more angry than bewildered. It was now certain that the thief was one of them. They demanded an investigation. Gregorov scheduled a full company meeting before warm-up the next day.

The stage was cold and drafty. Dancers wore extra sweaters to keep their bodies warm. The company was a powder keg ready to explode, ready to detonate at any incendiary word. Kira whispered loud enough for everyone on stage to hear, "Where's Zhandra?"

"Flying off to Rio," Roberto replied, "And how convenient. Wasn't she in the theatre every time there was a theft?" Everyone recalled the first theft when the two Principal dancers were excused from the meeting, the other Principal was now in a hospital bed.

Allison leaned against a portable barre and whispered back to Roberto, Kira and Delphine. "Roberto, I told you before just because she said she wanted Delphine's ring doesn't mean she would steal it. And it's just a coincidence Zhandra was present for each theft. "

Kira put her hand over her mouth. "My God, that's right, I forgot. Zhandra made a big deal about how much she wanted Delphine's ring."

The wheels in Delphine's brain slowly began turning. "I thought she was just hinting to get Christopher to buy her a ring."

"One would have though that." Kira chimed in.

"But certainly she has the money to buy a pair of leg warmers." Allison protested.

"One would have though that." Kira repeated.

"And what would she do with another tiara? She has a dozen of her own." Delphine questioned.

"Maybe she a kleptomaniac."

Allison coming to Zhandra's rescue, scolded him, "Roberto, we don't know for sure it's her."

"What more do we need?" Roberto snapped.

"Roberto, I asked you before not to talk about this among the company." Alison reminded.

"It's about time we did talk about it." Roberto countered.

Gregorov appeared, and sat on a chair downstage. The dancers stood at attention. "Whoever is responsible for these thefts, please step forward. There will be no penalties if you admit it now."

All stood immobile; eyes darting back and forth; waiting for someone to speak, to move. No one did.

Gregorov's mouth tightened at the disregard of his authority and generosity. "Step forward now!"

The dancers shifted on their feet, but no one stepped forward. Gregorov squinted, his nose twitching in exasperation. "I will not tolerate this. We are artists, not gypsies, thieves. Step forward now, or there will be severe consequences."

Still no one moved.

"So be it! The thief will be fired and never dance in this or any other company. That is my vow!" He ran his fingers through his hair. "I am in no mood today to teach class. Do your own warm-up. Rehearsal in one hour." And with that he thrust his fists into the pockets of his jacket and left the stage.

The dancers offered Temple condolences. Delphine loaned her a pair of leg warmers. Beckett, at far stage right, watched Allison on the floor, with her legs split in a stretching exercise. He moved next to her.

"Hi."

"Hi." She stretched her back and touched her head on the tip of her pointe shoe.

"We haven't talked for some time."

Allison wanted to make a sarcastic comment about it, but kept her cool, concentrating on the exercises. Across the stage Temple worked on *tendus* at a portable barre across the floor, watching Allison and Christopher out of the corner of her eye. A suspicion drifted into Temple's thoughts. Was there something going on between Allison and Christopher? No, that was absurd. Except for a ride on the Circle Line Temple was a goody-goody. And certainly Temple has not forgotten Allison's disaster with a married man at the National Ballet.

"Do you have any plans for New Year?" Christopher whispered to Allison.

What could she say? She had arranged to go out with Temple, but— she shook her head.

"Good, I know some hot spots."

"Isn't this awfully sudden? I haven't existed in your life for weeks, and all at once…"

He interrupted her, sure of his track. "I thought you understood. If Zhandra had even a suspicion she would made hell for you."

Allison lowered her eyes. "You could have paid me a little attention."

"Darling, it broke my heart not to speak to you." His eyes blared concern and sincerity, as clear and guileless as the sky.

Allison looked into his eyes, and fell for it. "Really?"

"Of course." He grazed the back of his hand across her thigh. "I'd better move, or tongues will wag. We'll discuss it over dinner."

"OK." Her heart beat like a homing pigeon let out of a cage.

She wandered through the evening performance in a daze. Afterwards while she was cleaning off her make-up, Temple came up behind her.

"What did Beckett want?" she asked to the reflection in the mirror.

"You saw me talking to him?"

"Everybody did. Well?"

"Oh, nothing."

"Nothing. I see." Temple put up her foot on the table and started untying a shoe.

"OK, he asked me out for New Year's Eve."

"And you accepted?"

"Yes, Temple, I accepted. We're friends, all right?"

"I thought *we* were friends. Didn't we make an arrangement to go for New Years?"

"Is this the third degree or what, damn it!"

Temple's eyes narrowed. "You fool! You think he loves you? After he's done screwing you, he'll drop you."

Temple walked away, madder at herself then at Allison. Temple was also a fool, an idiot, and a total blockhead sinking like a rock into quick-sand over a desperate love with a man she could never have, a married man. And she was angry for realizing a new sensation that was flowing through her veins—jealousy!

Allison looked suspiciously at Temple as she stormed out of the dressing room. Could it be? Could it be Temple also had feelings for Christopher? But it didn't matter. Christopher did not love Temple or Zhandra. So what did it matter?

But that night Allison did not find sleep easy. So if Temple was jealous, too bad for Temple. She would not give up Christopher. How could she? Certainly it was unthinkable to turn him down for New Year's. She would be a fool not to accept. So would any girl in the company. Temple Drake didn't matter! What did matter was Christopher's wife! However, she had a plan to end that problem. Zhandra would be part of his past, but Allison would be his future!

It was three in the morning and she had to get some sleep, taking a pill from the bottle that never left her bedside would resolve that, she swallowed them and was soon asleep.

Next evening she met Christopher at Chicago's famous Palmer House. Champagne was opened with a ceremonious pop; bubbles foamed and spilled to the floor. Christopher proposed a toast.

"May we never have less than what we want!"

Allison thought how perfectly it expressed his philosophy of life; Allison thought it as profound and clever a toast as she had ever heard, inasmuch as it also reflected hers. His second toast was to gluttony.

"Tonight we gorge on life...no diets. We surrender to the best the Palmer House can supply." He clapped his hands for the waiter. "Caviar to start."

Over appetizers he made his excuses, weak ones except to a willing listener.

"Zhandra is Latin so, of course, she's possessive. If she senses my interest in another woman she...turns to the bottle."

"She an alcoholic?" Allison was stunned.

"You're the only one who knows this. Please keep this a secret."

"Of course. What are you going to do? Have you thought about divorce?" The words slipped out, Allison wished she could jam them back in her mouth.

"Divorce? Why no. She's my wife. I wouldn't abandon her—it would destroy her completely."

"Have you suggested professional help?"

"She won't hear of it."

"Then you've done all you can do. She's on her own."

"Allison when I married I made a commitment. I can't walk away when she needs me. Would you think me noble if I did."

He had her there, all right. His nobility was at the core of her hero-worshiping for him, and well he knew it. Allison stared at the armature of his magnificent neck and shoulders supporting the elegant head and visor-like jaw. His eyes held hers, languid but hypnotic. Sure his prey was in the net, he took her hands and kissed them, palms up, Russian style.

"You deserved an honest explanation. I know a side-line affair isn't what you want, but it's all I can offer."

Innocent, naive Allison! Allison, of no memory, led by the oozing warmth between her legs. He almost laughed at her next question.

"What if Zhandra were to leave *you*?"

Christopher smiled in arrogance and amusement. "She would never do that."

"But *suppose* she did?"

He shrugged; it was after all only hypothetical. "Then I would be free."

That, for the moment, was enough. Whatever crumb he flung her, she would eat it—and more. The future would unfold as she planned.

"Come, Christopher, it's almost time." She took his hand and led him to the dance floor. He put his hands around her waist and pulled her close, and she encircled his neck with her arms. She whispered passionately into his ear. "I'm yours Christopher. I love you so much."

At midnight the sirens, whistles, and horns blared the promises and hopes of a New Year; confetti, sparklers and streamers fell from the ceiling, covering them like falling snow.

"Do you love me, Christopher?

"What?" Christopher yelled over the din.

"Do you love me?" Temple shouted, almost desperate.

"I'm here with you, aren't I?" Christopher kissed her tenderly on the lips.

"Do you love me more than Zhandra?"

"Allison, love is not a contest."

"Then what do I mean do you?"

Christopher smiled at her over the sirens of the New Year. "You are my enchantress, my angel of the night, my midnight dancer." He whirled her around the floor as the confetti rained down on them.

CHAPTER 29

The next few days were a revel of bliss for Allison. She danced like an angel and spent the hours between midnight and eight in Christopher's bed. How well he knew to play her moods to achieve his pleasure. She would start out a grateful Cinderella, entering the door as though she were about to courtesy. He would pull her brusquely out of her clothes, throw her on the bed on her stomach. She would become so exited she trembled and did everything he requested. He caressed her like a favorite childhood toy until she relaxed and then started all over. He was not unlike a bull elephant; it seemed he could go on for days if necessary. The emotional and physical roller coaster kept Allison's head spinning, while her groin lay back as battered and relaxed and peaceful as an ancient Pacific beach.

But the bliss had to end. The company would move to Washington, D.C., the last city before going home to New York for the rest of the year. Zhandra would rejoin the company in Washington.

Allison and Temple sat apart on the plane. Temple exhausted and drowsy but happy to be bound for Washington. Not that the nation's capital was a citadel of earthly pleasures, but it was an escape from the Arctic climate of Chicago and one city closer to home in New York.

On the plane Roberto ran back and forth between Allison and Temple relating details of his New Year's Eve at the bathhouse, a revel of lust and invention Caligula would have envied. Suddenly he switched to an expression of pity for Georginna. Knowing the dark side of life as well as he did, he was very affected by her tragedy. Then someone called him for a game of "Botticelli", and he was gone.

The aircraft descended for Washington International, a wave of nerves electrifying the company. The landing was perfect, and the dancers cheered "bravos" to a surprised pilot carrying out a routine landing.

Of the several choices of hotels near the Kennedy Center, some dancers opted for the less expensive Holiday Inn; others chose the Watergate, not unreasonably priced at group rates and a favorite of principal dancers who needed the pampering of a health club: saunas, whirlpools and masseurs. Other dancers chose the Intrigue Hotel across the street from the Watergate, its rooms furnished in a decor reminiscent of New York apartments. Temple and Allison made reservations at the Watergate, but not together. After unpacking, Temple called Allison.

"Listen, I can't take the stress of not talking to you anymore. Are we friends or not?"

"Just because we both love the same man doesn't mean we can't be friends."

"Allison, I do not *love* Christopher." Temple sat up indignantly.

"All right, lust after him. It's all right, any woman would."

"Can we talk about something else. I need a sauna and a massage. Interested?"

"God, yes, I'm stiff as a board! I'll call the Health Club and make an appointment."

Fortunately, two masseuses were available. The girls chatted as they lay on the tables.

"Are you going to dinner with Beckett?"

"I don't know."

"You know Zhandra is due back today."

"Oh, my God, that's right!" Allison nodded to the masseuse that she was done. "I gotta run."

Allison dressed hurriedly, ran to the hotel corridor and called Christopher's room. No answer; the coast was clear. Probably he was at the airport to meet Zhandra. If he forgot he had packed Allison's things, Zhandra might find them! She had to get into Christopher's room.

At the hotel desk she asked for the key.

"We were expecting you later. Welcome to the Watergate. It is an honor to have such a great artist at our hotel."

Allison felt her face redden. Obviously she could not pose as Zhandra. She leaned across the desk.

"I'm not Mrs. Beckett. I'm a very close friend of Christopher Beckett, and there are some things I have to get out of his room before Mrs. Beckett arrives. You understand?"

"In that case I really can't give you…"

"You'll be doing *everybody* a great favor, believe me!" She gave him her best fluttering of the lashes treatment and the sweetest of smiles. He gave her the key.

Inside the room, she spotted Christopher's bag in a corner. Pulling out her belongings, she notices some of Zhandra's things: pink tights, shoe ribbons and a black silk scarf. The letter "Z" was monogrammed at one margin. Allison held it admiringly. She realized that Beckett and Zhandra might come into the door momentarily…she had to decide right away…stuffing the scarf into her ballet bag, she darted out of the room.

She jogged the two blocks to the Kennedy Center, barely in time to get to the theatre for the start of rehearsal. Roberto was huddled in a corner of the wings sucking at a box of fried chicken. He told her that Zhandra was in the theatre. Allison took the elevator to the third floor, the Principal dressing area. She knocked on Zhandra's door.

The door opened and Toni, the portly wardrobe assistant, walked past her holding a tutu. Zhandra sat at her make-up table. "What can I do for you?"

"I have something that belongs to you." Allison extended the black scarf.

"My scarf! Where did you find it?"

"Oh, I don't remember."

"How long have you had it?"

"A couple of days."

"That's strange! I haven't worn it since the beginning of tour." Zhandra took the scarf and looked suspiciously at Allison.

"Where did you get this?"

"I really can't say." Allison started to leave, but Zhandra grabbed her arm.

"What's going on?"

"Please don't ask any questions."

Zhandra blocked Allison's exit, noticeably upset. "Are you seeing Christopher, my husband?"

"Would I return your scarf if I was?"

"Then how did you get it?" Zhandra paused. "Of course...your friend, Temple! I should have suspected her...the sweet ones are the always the ones you have to worry about...it is Temple, isn't it?"

"I have to go." Allison reached for the door. Zhandra gripped her arm.

"Is it Temple, tell me!"

"Do you think I would tell if it were?"

"The fact that you're not saying proves it!" Zhandra locked the door, putting the key in the pocket of her robe. "You're not leaving until you tell me how you got this."

Allison feared that Zhandra would strike her.

"Please, don't tell anyone! Temple and I were rooming together in Chicago. I saw the scarf on the floor in the bedroom."

Zhandra fell back against the door, and tears rushed from her eyes. She smacked her head back against the door. Allison was afraid that she was going to crack her head. She clutched Zhandra's head in her hands to stop her from banging it again.

"Zhandra, stop!"

But Zhandra's head rolled back and forth. Allison tried to hold her still, but her body jerked as if she had received an electric shock. She screamed, and someone pounded on the door.

Allison opened it a crack. It was the wardrobe mistress. "Anything wrong?"

"No." Allison took the tutu out of Toni's hands. "Just a tantrum. But there is something you can do: get the Gucci ballet bag from the Soloist dressing room, it's mine. Please hurry!"

In a few minutes the woman returned. Allison searched her ballet bag for the pills. She held Zhandra in her arms. "Here. Take two of these."

Zhandra shook her head wildly. "No, no."

"You think you can dance the way you are? Take them!"

Zhandra swallowed the pills; Allison helped her to the sofa; sat besides her, stroking her hair. "They'll work in a few minutes."

"Will I be able to dance?"

"Yes. Just don't fall asleep in the dressing room."

"Stay with me so I don't, please."

"I have to get dressed. Would you like me to send for Christopher?"

"No!" Zhandra sprang up, her dark hair flying in all directions. "I don't want him to see me like this!"

"All right, I'll dress here. I'll get my costume and make-up. Back in a minute, okay?"

When Allison returned, she was surprised to see Zhandra doing *plies* and *releves,* using the make-up table as a barre. "I thought this would keep me awake," she said.

"Don't worry. You'll get through the performance."

Zhandra became calm as she put on her make-up and took Allison by the hand. "I want to thank you, Allison. Most girls would love to see me miss a performance. The pills are working; I feel much better."

"I'll get more for you tonight."

Zhandra kissed Allison on the cheek and left for the stage.

That night there was a command performance for the President of the United States and his guest, the President of Mexico. The importance of the occasion helped pump adrenaline through Zhandra, counteracting the drowsing effect of the pills. Although shaky in spots and less than dazzling on the whole, she managed to dance with her usual ethereal delicacy. The President could only stay a half-hour after performance, so the eception had to begin fifteen minutes after the curtain came down. Dancers scurried through the halls, and the girls helped each other undo ostumes under the amused and curious gaze of the Secret Service. A ecret Service agent escorted each group of ten dancers. The dancers complaining that the plastic security badges clipped to their clothes uined their outfits. The agents turned a deaf ear.

The President, the First Lady and the President of Mexico and his wife stood in a reception line flanked by more Secret Service men. Gregorov was the first to meet the President. He bowed and spoke in a ow voice. The President smiled, shook Gregorov's hand and promised hat he would nudge the National Endowment for the Arts to be more generous to his ballet company.

Gregorov moved to the President of Mexico and spoke a few words of impeccable Spanish. He only nodded to the President's wife, who had frizzed-out black hair, heavily painted eyes and was as over-tinseled as a Christmas tree. The Principals were next on line, then the Soloists and he Corps. Men bowed and the women curtsied in the old-world formality reserved for such events. The President and his guests obviously njoyed meeting the performers who had touched their hearts only minutes before. The President thanked the Center Ballet for the performance and mentioned the possibility of a special performance at the White House, to appropriate murmurs from the dancers, and then a spirited cheer.

A security man motioned, and the four dignitaries were escorted out. Zhandra turned to Christopher. "Will you answer a question?"

"Of course, dear." He bent his ear down to her lips.

"Are you having an affair?"

The cheeriness drained from Beckett's face. "This is not the time for this conversation."

"I feel like discussing it now."

"We are expected to join the party!" He started to walk away, but Zhandra held his arm. He swung around and stared at her in disbelief.

"I want to know, or I'm leaving!" Her look was hysterical.

"Suit yourself!"

He flicked his arm from her grasp and walked out of the room. Zhandra felt the nerves of shock running through her body again, the inside layer of her skin crawling. Allison had been watching. She moved over to Zhandra and handed her a bottle of pills. "Take as many as you need."

Zhandra nodded, her eyes glazed, and drifted out of the party.

The next morning Roberto observed Allison intently as she sat down for breakfast. "Did you sleep well, or did you sleep at all?"

Allison was riled by his less-than-subtle suggestion but ignored it. "Hmmm, let me see what I should order." She covered her face with the menu. Roberto tipped the menu down to look at her.

"*Amiga,* word is out. Delphine saw Christopher leaving your room."

Allison put the menu down, her appetite gone.

"She's telling everybody she couldn't sleep because of the noise in your room, and she's going to ask Christopher to put a muzzle on you."

"Bitch!" Allison slapped the table.

"Calm down, *querida.* Everyone in the restaurant is watching you."

"Does Gregorov know?"

"If he doesn't, he soon will."

"Christ!" Allison put her hand over her forehead. Roberto poured coffee.

"I've done it again! I've screwed myself right out of the company!"

"Not necessarily." Roberto slid the Washington Post across the table to her. Allison read a review of Zhandra's performance of the night before. The critic called her "proficient" but "lacking the fire we have come to expect."

Roberto leaned toward her. "You or Temple could be Gregorov's next choice for Principal. But your problem now is how to survive the fall-ut when Zhandra drops the bomb on your affair."

"What are you talking about?"

"You should know Roberto knows all"

"She doesn't suspect me."

Roberto froze, coffee cup suspended between lips and saucer. "Maybe ot, but it's not going to be a secret forever."

Allison's eyes took on a distant look. "Then I have time."

"Time for what?" Roberto wanted to know.

She didn't answer and hurried out of the restaurant.

At the theatre early, Allison planted herself on a chair in the dressing oom corridor and sewed ribbons on her toe shoes. Half an hour passed before she saw Zhandra leave her dressing room. It had to be now; the hance might not come again! Allison picked up her ballet bag and ran o Zhandra's door. Like a cat on a prowl, she slipped into the room and quickly transferred Delphine's diamond ring, Temple's leg warmers, nd Temple's tiara into Zhandra's bag. Once outside the corridor, she walked nonchalantly to the Soloist dressing room.

The loudspeaker blasted: "Dancers on stage for Company Class." All he Soloists, including Temple, Kira and Delphine sauntered out. Allison lagged behind with the excuse of having to finish sewing her ribbons, and was the last to arrive on stage. Gregorov clapped his hands t her.

"Hurry, Allison, you're late!"

Apologizing, she spotted Zhandra's ballet bag in its usual privileged place, center stage behind Gregorov's chair.

Allison continued apologizing as she circled Gregorov's chair owards her place at the barre. Walking sideways she kept the corner of her eye focused on Zhandra's bag, as clumsily as she could to make it ook like an accident, she tripped over Zhandra's bag, spewing the contents over the stage floor.

"My God, I am sorry. I didn't see the bag." Allison gasped.

Dancers tried to stifle laughter at such a graceful creature caught in an awkward moment; but giggles broke, and spread until the entire company was laughing. Even Gregorov smiled. Allison dropped to her knees to pick up the contents of Zhandra's bag. She held up the first item, "Why, it's Delphine's ring!"

Delphine sprinted from the barre, and examined the ring. "It is mine!"

The company was silent.

Allison picked up a pair of red woolen leg warmers. "The leg warmers I gave to Temple." Allison caught a sparkle from Zhandra's bag; she pulled out the item. "And this tiara! It looks like the one that was made for..."

She raised it above her head for the company to see.

"That's my tiara, my diamond." Temple screamed.

It was at that moment that the powers of Heaven marked the end of innocence of Allison Fain. As she lifted the tiara aloft she was converted into the creature that Gregorov had promised: Odile, the Queen of Darkness who would steal another woman's lover, Odile, the Black Swan. So convinced was Allison of the practical necessity of her act, its logic and correctness under circumstances out of her control—in the world of ballet where the political system was not of her design—that to conquer love and achieve success, she committed an act of horrendous destruction. But there was no one in the company who noticed the black wings flapping around Allison's frame, no one that heard Odile's mocking laughter.

All eyes turned to Zhandra, who was mystified. She retrieved her bag, and turned to Gregorov.

"I don't know how those things got there." Gregorov squinted at her. "You don't think I would take those things?"

Delphine spoke first. "You always wanted my ring."

"I could buy a ring ten times bigger, you idiot." Zhandra lashed back

"Then explain why all these things were stolen on the same nights ou were in the theatre, never on any other night?" Delphine hissed.

"That's not true!" Zhandra shook her head.

"It is true. You're a thief!" Delphine screamed.

"Liar!" Zhandra shouted, her fists clenched, she swung at Delphine.

Delphine ducked and missed the punch by inches. Delphine grabbed Zhandra by the hair, off balance, together they sprawled on the floor.

"Ladies!" Gregorov separated the two. "Zhandra, you had better go to our dressing room. Later we talk." Zhandra slung her ballet bag over her shoulder and stomped off.

The company was shaken. Some so upset they had to leave the stage, others stood immobile. Beckett started to leave for Zhandra's room. Gregorov called,"Christopher, you have a performance. I will talk to Zhandra."

Christopher resumed his place at the barre. Gregorov continued, "All of you, forget this! We have performance tonight. We must go on."

Dancers at the barre strained to concentrate, but no one could clear their mind of the startling scene. After class, the Company's Union Representatives called an emergency meeting. It was noted that Gregorov had sworn dismissal for the thief. The call was for equal justice, for Principals as well as corps. The majority voted to instruct Management to immediately fire Zhandra, or incur a walkout by the company. It was a drastic motion, and some dancers feared reprisals when the company returned to New York.

After performance Christopher raced to Zhandra's dressing room; her door was open, but she was gone.

Beckett changed out of his costume quickly, not bothering to wash off his make-up. He ran to the Watergate Hotel, knocked on Zhandra's door, then louder, and then furiously; but there was no response. He brought a security guard to open the door, but Zhandra had deadbolted the door from inside. Beckett pleaded for ten minutes, but it was futile, obviously she would not talk to him tonight. He went down to the lobby and saw Allison, who had just returned from the theatre.

He told her, "I'm worried. She's never done anything like this before."

"Why don't you come to my room and call her from there?"

Christopher tried several times, but no answer. He sat on her bed, "I can't believe she would steal those things. She could have had anything she wanted."

"Sssh," Allison put her fingers on his lips, "no more talk. You need to relax." She dried tiny beads of sweat from his forehead with a handkerchief.

"Allison, we can't go on having this affair." Allison stiffened. "It's not right." He stood. "I have to see Zhandra."

"She's probably asleep. Allison massaged his shoulders. "Relax, Christopher. Please. No more talk." She unbuttoned his shirt. "Tomorrow everything will be all right."

Allison took off his shirt, then slipped off his slacks.

She knelt down before him. "I love you, Christopher." She touched his face but said nothing.

There was nothing more to say.

CHAPTER 30

"Your call, sir. Seven o'clock," a digital voice announced.

Christopher quietly nestled the phone on the cradle so as not to wake Allison. But she was already awake behind the closed eyelids. She listened to him stumble in the dark trying to find the bathroom door, heard it click and then the muffled sound of water splashing in the shower. She smiled, thinking of the many wonderful mornings she would have with him. The shower stopped. A shaft of yellow light pierced the bedroom. Christopher whispered through the door, "Allison, are you awake? I need a razor."

"In my ballet bag on top of the bureau."

Wrapped loosely in a towel, he rummaged through her bag. "Would you like me to call room service?" she inquired.

"No time. The TV interview's at eight."

He finished dressing and sat down next to Allison on the bed, his strong profile like a Rodin sculpture in the slanting, abrupt light from the bathroom. He pulled the blanket up to her chin.

"Stay in bed. The company doesn't leave for New York until noon."

Allison's eyes were moist. "What happens when we get back to New York?"

Christopher shook his head. "I don't know."

"What about Zhandra?"

"She must feel very alone. I should have gone to her last night."

Allison felt a sudden jolt of emptiness in her stomach.

"If Gregorov doesn't take her back, would you leave with her for another company?"

"No, I told you that once before!"

Allison clutched his hand, desperation electrifying even the tips of her fingers. "I love you, Christopher, more than anything." Tenderly he kissed her palms.

"I'm flattered."

He rose and left her in the dark.

Allison sorted thoughts in her head. Of course, he had to go to Zhandra; she expected that; it was his first noble reaction. But in time he would surely be hers! She stretched out her body and felt vibrant, young and graceful. She threw open the drapes to the early morning sun, which crashed wildly through the room. It was a brilliant day! Catching her image in the mirror, she lifted her breasts and looked at the tiny scars from her operation. It seemed strange that in all of their lovemaking, Christopher never noticed the scars. She shooed away the thought as irrelevant and leapt back into bed. A whole sunny Sunday was before her with nothing to do, and everything was going perfectly according to plan.

In her mind she replayed the previous night's performance. At first the audience booed at the announcement that the famous Zhandra Amaya would be replaced by an unknown dancer; but Allison danced so charged with current, with such excitement, that the audience forgot Zhandra and rewarded her with a long, well-deserved curtain call. She wondered what the reviews were like. She had to see the morning paper! Springing out of bed, she splattered water on her face, dabbed on make-up, dressed and went down to the hotel lobby for a paper.

The review was an absolute rave! One paragraph in particular caught her eye: "Allison Fain is the most ravishing ballerina to come along in many years. It was initially a disappointment not to see Zhandra Amaya, but Miss Fain performed the role with such youthful zest, she won the hearts of the public. And made us forget all other ballerinas."

Allison glowed. How lovely! She would read the entire review more carefully over coffee. It was eight o'clock, too early for the company to e down for breakfast; and so, Allison, the adulteress, would not have o endure their ogling. But once the company read the review the nasty talk would stop. As a ballerina they would have to respect her. She realized now what Christopher meant by "Artistic License." Arrogance flowed through her veins, making her feel like she could get away with anything.

Allison walked through the hotel lobby towards the breakfast room. As she passed the elevator, the doors opened. Two men in rumpled, green hospital uniforms wheeled out a stretcher with a body covered in a white sheet. Allison stepped back. Fear rushed through her as the stretcher was lifted into the ambulance. She raced to the hotel desk to confirm her suspicion. It was the same man who gave Allison the keys to Zhandra's room. Allison did not have to ask, the question was in her eyes.

"I'm sorry about your friend. A tragic loss." Allison's head shook in disbelief at his words.

"How?"

"Suicide. They found an empty bottle of pills beside her."

"Does anyone else know?"

"Mr. Gregorov found the body. He tried to reach Miss Amaya all night and this morning. Finally a security guard broke down the door. I'm sorry."

Allison ran for the elevator. She had to find Temple! Running to her room, she pounded on the door. Temple opened it in the midst of tying a belt around a pink satin robe.

"Allison? It's only eight o'clock!"

"Where's Roberto?"

"Out with a trick, I suppose." She saw the horror and the alarm in Allison's face. "What's wrong?"

"Zhandra is dead...!"

"What?"

Temple sat on the edge of the sofa as Allison collapsed on the sofa. She was not sure Allison's words were not part of some ridiculous nightmare.

She hoped when she reopened her eyes that Allison and her words would be gone. "How?"

"Overdose of sleeping pills. I saw her body wheeled out."

Allison put her hand in front of her mouth as though to stifle a scream. "It was ghastly! Why would she do that?"

"Why? Because she had nothing left…no career, friends and finally …no husband! He wasn't with her when she needed him the most, he was with—" Temple stopped.

"With me!"

"Yes…but Christopher is as much to blame."

Allison pulled away from the accusation in Temple's eyes.

"I should feel guilty because I slept with Beckett the night his wife committed suicide? Well, I don't feel guilty! I had nothing to do with I didn't force Beckett to sleep with me! I didn't force those pills down Zhandra's throat!"

Temple was surprised at Allison's defensiveness. "What pills?"

"What?

"You said she had taken some pills."

"Maybe, I don't know. Why are you asking me? I didn't do anything."

"Then nobody will blame you, but you will have to live with some responsibility."

"What responsibility?"

The fact is that Christopher was sleeping with you when it happened. Both of you have to live with that. Christopher may never be able to forgive himself, or you!"

"Not forgive me!" Allison was enraged. "How absurd! Christopher loves me."

Temple frowned, "You silly child. Do you think you're the first girl he's picked up for a screw?"

"It's different—we love each other."

"You may love Christopher, but he doesn't love you."

"He does love me!" Allison's voice was rising.

"If you believe that I feel sorry for you."

Allison was distraught. "Sorry for me! We'll see!"

"So sure of yourself, Allison?"

"I feel sorry for you. When the New York season is over I'll be a principal and you will only be a soloist. Here." Allison flung the morning paper at her. "Read the review; it's a rave! They said I was ravishing, even better than Zhandra."

Temple's eyes turned flinty. "It's not hard being better than a dead dancer."

Allison's hand smacked Temple's face. The force of the blow, knocking her backwards onto the sofa. Allison stepped back, not believing what she had done. She wanted to say she was sorry, but the words choked in her throat. The horrid red mark on Temple's cheek mesmerized her. Temple averted her eyes and just lay there. There was nothing to be said, no purpose in retaliation.

"Get out!" Temple's voice quivered as she struggled to keep under control.

Allison retreated, wanting to apologize, but knowing it would have been useless. Their friendship was over. Once outside she thought, "Just as well! Victoria Bennett would not have apologized!"

The company bus began its pick-up at noon, stopping first at Howard Johnson's, then the Intrigue and finally the Watergate. Allison stood in front of the lobby surrounded by dancers and mountains of suitcases. She assumed Christopher would not be there, assuming he had been told about Zhandra at the TV studio. He would be involved with details of handling the body. She guessed that Zhandra would be buried in New York, with services at St. Patrick's Cathedral. The church was large enough to accommodate Zhandra's many fans and large family. Allison winced at the thought of the funeral. It would be a particularly unpleasant experience to have to go through. Beckett was not the only dancer missing on the bus. Temple was absent as well, and Roberto.

Allison remembered that one of Roberto's lovers had driven down from New York, and probably Temple had gone back with them. The bus ride to the train terminal took fifteen minutes, and there the dancers were directed to private train cars. Fortunately, Allison found a seat to herself, where she would not have to talk to anyone. After such a long tour, the last ride home was usually a miniature Mardi Gras, but festivities that morning were totally inappropriate. All in the company shared a sense of guilt about Zhandra's suicide. It was, after all, a unanimous vote to dismiss her. Allison listened to conversations of dancers who had despised Zhandra. They were calling her their friend, and a 'living legend.' Her death even made them forget the tragedy of Georginna Haviland, left crippled in Chicago. If she had continued in dance, she would have indeed become a legend, joining the ranks of such as Pavlova and Makarova. It was the most traumatic tour of most of their professional careers.

Also sitting alone was Gregorov. In one winter he had lost his two Principal dancers, two fine young ballerinas! The final entry on the tour sheet was Zhandra's death. He clenched his hands in his lap, for once no arrogance or severity visible in his manner. The old man thought of the cruelty of his profession, its rugged hostilities, the presence of death behind the marvelous facade of lights, music and beautiful costumes. He forced himself not to remember the other dancers he had lost, including his beautiful wife.

On the train Gregorov gazed dumbly at the rushing scenery: the stark telephone poles, dreary factories and slums separated by ugly patches of brown grass and black mud. It was like a journey that he had made many years before with his mother, on a train between Leningrad and Moscow.

A wave of nausea came over him, strong enough to make him suppress retching up his breakfast by slapping his hand over his mouth and lying back against the reclining seat. The smell, the terrible smell! The mell of death, of living cells withering under the onslaught of cancer. He also was approaching death and perhaps like Zola's famous prostitute, Nana, rotting away. Still he did not see the Black Swan in the figure of his beautiful new star except in the literal sense, on stage in costume. If only he could hear the terrible wings swirling in the air about him.

"Is there anything crueler than ballet?" he thought. Now he had to find the strength to plan his next moves to bring his company out of the despair it was in.

Allison rode the train tormented by guilt and visions of Zhandra on stage, dazzling yet ethereal. She was terribly afraid, although no one could blame her openly. Was she afraid of losing Christopher? Temple had scared her. She thought of Temple's tale of being whipped across the knee in ballet class when she was a little girl. Now she understood the old Russian teacher who had done it. It was his warning that Ballet was war, complete with spies, counter-intelligence, sneak attacks and blind-side maneuvers. Everything was permitted to further your career, if one was not found out; all tactics were fair. Tour was simply part of the battle, and when it was over, the company counted casualties and went on.

Allison had won; she would celebrate her victory somehow, although it had to be in private. Adrift in a collision of images of Zhandra, Christopher and Temple she was startled when Gregorov sat down next to her.

"Such a useless death! I tried to reach her to tell her I would not dismiss her. The company would soon forget such a silly incident! A tragedy! To be a famous ballerina and then be disgraced as a thief. What pain she must have suffered!"

Allison flushed. She wanted to sob, but she couldn't allow herself to lose control. Gregorov reached into the pocket of his coat and unfolded a piece of hotel stationery. "I show you something." He put the paper in Allison's hand. It read:

Christopher, my love:

I have tried to understand why you would want another, but I could not, I have forgiven you; but I cannot give you up. I cannot. I take you with me. With my last breath I will whisper "I love you" and your love will be mine forever.

Zhandra

Gregorov retrieved the note from Allison's trembling hand. "I will not show Beckett. It is better he does not see. He made a mistake, and he will suffer for it the rest of his life. Why should he suffer more by reading this? I show you because I know you and Beckett see each other, yes? You understand he will always associate you with the death of Zhandra. I have heavy heart for Christopher. I know the pain of losing a wife." Gregorov was speaking of his own second wife, the Ballerina Nina Voljsky, who died slowly and ingloriously of cancer over a period of three years. "But Allison," Mr. Gregorov patted her on the thigh like a father, "we must put it behind us, and go on! You must give your heart and your love to the stage; dedicate yourself only to the dance. Become real when you are on stage. The rest of life makes only an interlude between performances then you will not feel the pain. Do you understand?"

"I think so, Mr. Gregorov."

"Tomorrow, Zhandra was to open at the Met. We must do another program, unless you can do Swan Lake lead?"

Allison did not hesitate, "Yes, I can do it."

"Brava! Tomorrow morning, you have photos taken at Dutton's studio; wardrobe will meet you and refit you into the costume. Charles will call and give you specifics." Allison remembered Charles, the publicity man she met on her first day at the ballet center. She wondered what his reaction would be to the girl who he thought had come to the studio for the housewife's class.

Gregorov continued. "Tomorrow afternoon we present you at Press Conference." Allison looked at him, puzzlement in her eyes. There was o reason to call a press conference for a change in casting. Announcement will be made that you and Temple Drake will be promoted to Principal dancers of New York Center Ballet."

"Mr. Gregorov!" Allison shouted. A few heads twisted in the seats in ront of them. Allison whispered, "Thank you." She pecked a kiss on is cheek.

Allison was grateful but she also understood that there was no madless to the promotion. The company simply did not have a ballerina on land. There was no way the box office could endure the first week of a Jew York season without a name; and so they would push Allison and 'emple with an instant media blitz with the hopes that the public would ine up to see the new ballerina babies. The opening night performance t the Metropolitan Opera House would be a baptism of fire, but so vhat—she had already gone through a tour of Hell.

"Will I do *Swan* with Christopher?" she wanted to know.

Gregorov shrugged. "If he is able to perform. But rehearse with iteven Simon in case." Allison nodded. He patted her for the last time ind stood up. "Remember…make the stage real, let everything else be nake-believe."

The train chugged into the dark tunnel of Penn Station on time. Dutside it was pouring. Allison hauled her bags to the street, and :ursed; she knew it would be nearly impossible to get a taxi in this iunday deluge. She tried hailing a few cabs and was ready to give up and vait out the storm when incredibly a cab pulled up in front of her. She dropped her suitcases on the seat.

"One Sherwood Plaza, please."

"Right." The cabby looked through the rear view mirror. "Hey, you're the dancer I took three blocks to Lincoln Center a few months ago?"

Allison remembered him. "Yes."

"I saw one of 'dem ballets because of you."

"Oh, yes." Allison flashed a pleased smile.

"Yeah, I hated it."

Allison unlocked the door of her apartment. She picked up the telegram that has been slipped underneath her door, hoping it was not more bad news. It was from her parents welcoming her home, and informing her that they would be at the Opening Night. They would have a little shock when they saw Allison performing the lead as a principal dancer.

Allison hardly recognized her apartment, which was understandable since she had spent only a few weeks there before leaving for tour; but she was amazed to realize she had forgotten what the furniture looked like, the colors of the carpet, or the decorations on the wall. She even forgot the direction to the bedroom. It was not that anything had changed except for a layer of dust that covered everything; she had simply forgotten what home was like. Allison threw her suitcase on the bed, screwing up her nose when she saw the dust fly. She would change the sheets and in the morning advertise for a maid, now affordable on her Principal's salary.

That night she couldn't sleep. And she could not shut off the visions. More visions of Zhandra tormented her: phantasms of Zhandra dancing, holding hands with Christopher wrapped in a white shroud. Would Christopher blame her for Zhandra's death? And there were more images of Temple: of the time they made love, of Temple's red face after she slapped it. There were too many thoughts, images, and horrors. She turned on a light and found a bottle of sleeping pills. She would take just one, which would be enough to push her into a deep sleep. It was two AM; one pill usually made her sleep for six hours and groggy for another four, but she would not have to rehearse in the morning because of the photo session, costume fitting and the press conference. Probably it wouldn't hurt to be somewhat numb for those activities! One pill would erase the apparitions and prevent the nightmares. And a

ottle of pills could erase her life and wash away everything that she has
done. How easy it would be. No! She threw the bottle across the room.
No, she would not give up the fight now. She was not one of the weak
ones. She was so close to having everything she always wanted. She
would not be defeated by the demon visions whirling in her head. She
would win. And in the future, she resolved to stop taking pills.

Charles called at eight and detailed the schedule: wardrobe would
meet her at the Dutton studio at 9:30. The press conference was 12:00
in the Crystal Room of the Regency. Immediately after an interview
with *Dance Magazine*, then a photo shoot for the cover of *Pointe
Magazine*. Rehearsal for *Swan Lake* was 2:00 to 4:00. A dinner interview
at 5:00. Charles tentatively had arranged an interview with Lester
Richmond of the Times, who wanted an exclusive for next Sunday's
front page of the "Arts and Leisure" section. Would she mind doing it?
Allison, of course, agreed.

She took not a breath all day; and found it terribly exciting except for a
trivial faux pas. At the Opera House Allison, without thinking, entered
the soloist dressing room, and then realized she no longer belonged there,
but Kira and Delphine saw her. Allison, not wanting to admit her mistake,
covered. "I just stopped by to see if you girls can exist without me."

Delphine not knowing if an insult had been intended flicked a quick
retort. "As happy as if you were not here, Allison."

Allison retreated, and searched through the labyrinth of corridors for
her dressing room. She passed doors, scanning the names of Regina
Christian, Carlotta Gray, and Christopher Beckett…oh, Christopher!
He had not been in rehearsal, but was still scheduled for the opening
performance. Allison assumed he would not partner her tonight. At the
end of the corridor, she found her name. It was Victoria Bennett's old
dressing room! Alison smiled. If only Victoria knew! As Allison opened
the dressing room door, the elevator opened in the corridor, she turned
to see Christopher and Temple exited, holding hands.

Allison dropped her bag on the dressing room table, and sat before the mirror. Were her eyes lying? It couldn't be! Temple and Christopher were good friends, but that was all. Allison did not have time to think about it now. She had the major performance of her career.

Every important critic in the country was in the audience, seeing her for the first time. She stood, balanced herself by holding onto the chair with one hand, and started her first *plie*. She watched her long legs come perfectly to an arch as the legs began to bend and straighten. And then *tendu*, shiny satin slippers snapped at the heels, "*Tendu* front and one, and two, and three and four, and repeat. Concentrate! You are a ballerina! You are a ballerina!"

After warm-up she tried on the headpiece she would wear in Act I as the White Swan, her eyes shone more brightly. She was ready. She called in her new personal dresser, and was hooked into her costume. By the time she reached the stage, Beckett was already at center stage practicing. She stood directly in front of him, The Prince and the Swan.

"Christopher! How are you?"

Christopher closed his eyes, squeezing back a rush of tears. Zhandra had been buried that morning, from St. Patrick's cathedral on Fifth Avenue. She had never looked more beautiful than in her casket, her marble skin so white in contrast to her black hair, as dignified an artist in death as she could have wished. This fiery, vibrant and talented young woman who had loved him so, and whom he had loved more than anyone in his life, as much as his selfish nature had ever permitted him to love anyone. As the priests prayed and swung the incense, as Beckett fixed his eyes on the cold, perfect form and avoided the stares of her black-clad family, the hundreds of fans, the television cameras, the cameras flash. The furrows in his cheeks were as still and deep as granite fissures, and he came as close to regret and repentance as he ever had in his self-centered life.

"Zhandra was buried this morning."

"I'm so sorry." Allison repeated.

The performance was far from Beckett's finest, but the audience understood; news of the suicide had been splashed over the front pages and television. Allison, on the other hand, gave a brilliant performance. She was the vision of frail femininity, the archetype of the White Swan. At the end of Act I, Allison performed a series of *bourees* suggesting the Swan must forever abandon the man she loves. Allison's arms fluttered, her head flailed in despair as she looked upon her Beckett, her Prince, for the last time. It was a portrayal that was so real that the audience thought they could see Allison's heart break.

Then in a dramatic reversal in Act II, the audience watched in amazement as Allison transformed herself into the negative image of the Black Swan. She became a vulgar seductress, Odile, a vile creature of treachery and intrigue, a phantasm of the Underworld. It was the role that would catapult Allison into the ranks of legendary ballerinas. Later critics would write of their fascination how one dancer could possess two such opposite souls.

The audience was emotionally drained, divided between awe of Beckett's courage and adulation of Allison's bravura. They lavished praise on both. Bouquets of flowers were carried on stage; but the flowers hurled on stage from the audience outnumbered the audience. Programs were ripped into tiny pieces and flung from the balconies, and showered the couple in confetti. No one counted curtain calls. Applause and screaming would have lasted all night, but the stage manager had to close the performance before musicians and stagehands went on overtime. Allison stood with Christopher as the curtain closed.

"Christopher, what happens to us now?"

She did not get an answer before fans engulfed them, separating them into two camps. Allison was carried by well wishers as if she were caught in the rapids of a river. She somehow found herself rescued and deposited in her dressing room. Inside her room Allison had brief sanctuary, but only for a moment. A guard opened the door a crack and announced a visitor.

"Mother!" Allison yelled like an Apache. She clasped her arms around her mother, and found emotions that had welled up inside of her let go, at first a few tears, and then the damn broke loose.

"Allison, you were wonderful." Her mother could not contain her tears. "Can you have lunch with us tomorrow?" Ruth asked.

"Love to. I'll ask to be scheduled out of rehearsal."

Ruth embraced her daughter. "Allison, you have made us so proud."

"It was all your doing."

"What about me?" Her father pressed through the crowd. "I had to drive you to all those damn dancing lessons."

"And I love you for it." Allison lavished a dozen kisses on her father.

"You have to get dressed. There's that mob outside, and you shouldn't disappoint your fans." Ruth sighed, "You're a Principal now, a ballerina."

Gregorov nudged through the door. "Babushka! You were magnificent!"

"Thank you. I would like you to meet my family. My mother, my father."

"*Enchante.*" Gregorov, the American citizen shook Domenic's hand, and the Russian gentleman kissed Ruth on both cheeks. "Mother, you taught our Allison well."

Ruth was speechless. The legendary Gregorov kissed her, the man whose choreography Ruth had admired for so many years had actually kissed her hand! Ruth had never been this close to the upper echelon of the professional ballet world. "You trained a great dancer."

Allison had never seen Ruth at a loss for words, worse, Allison thought, she looked like she was about to faint.

Gregorov turned to Allison. "Tonight you became a ballerina. Tomorrow the critics will proclaim the night of a new star."

"Thank you, Vaslov." Allison instantly realized she had called him by his first name. Nobody did that, but Gregorov did not seem to notice.

"Our star must change. She is guest of honor at a reception. Come, come, we all go." Gregorov ushered out the clan. Domenic gave Allison one last bear hug. It felt so good in his arms; she looked forward to seeing them tomorrow and telling them everything, or almost everything.

Allison heard the noise of the crowd outside. Where do all these people come from, she wondered as she began to wipe off her make-up.

Roberto wiggled in the room. "How's it feel to be on top?" Allison was not smiling. "What'za matter?"

"Roberto, is something going on with Christopher and Temple?"

"Christopher needs the comfort Temple can give. Besides I heard he's good in bed." Roberto lifted one eyebrow, "Of course, you would know that."

Allison blushed. Roberto knew, and if Roberto knew, the company knew. "So what," thought Allison, she would not be the first ballerina with a tainted past. "You are one son-of-a-bitch!" she cursed Roberto.

"That's why we get along so well. Birds of a feather."

Allison ignored his remark. "She's wasting her time. Christopher loves me!"

Roberto did not respond. The young Latin with the irrepressible grin was not smiling, his castanets mouth usually so quick with a joke or insult was sealed tight.

"He doesn't love Temple." Allison confirmed.

Roberto sat impassively as a sphinx, his eyes fixed on Allison, "He needs someone now, and—it's not you."

"No!" Allison stood, "You're wrong!" She darted out of the dressing room and through the corridors to Christopher's room. She opened the door and saw Christopher embracing Temple. They separated when they saw Allison, but continued to hold hands; both had tears in their eyes.

"How dare you do this behind my back." Allison was frantic. Christopher roughly grabbed her arm and brought her to the make-up table and picked up an empty bottle, and pushed it in front of Allison's face. "It was found next to Zhandra. Temple says it's yours. Is it true? Did you give it to her?"

"No." Allison's mouth went dry. "I mean, it wasn't like that. Zhandra asked for it."

"So you admit it?"

"I don't admit anything. I'm not on trial here. How would I know what she would do—"

Christopher gripped her arm tighter. "You knew she was an alcoholic! You knew how dangerous it is when these pills are mixed with alcohol."

"I didn't know, I swear to God! My mother gave me the pills to relax. I thought I was helping her."

Christopher unloosened the grip on her arm, and turned his back.

Allison looked at Temple who looked away, and then she swung Christopher around to confront him. "What makes you think you're so innocent. You're as much to blame as I am, you were with me when she died."

Christopher nodded. "Yes, and I will live with that the rest of my life. And so will you."

"No, Christopher we have our life ahead of us. I'm sorry about Zhandra, but isn't it what you wanted? Didn't you want to be free…and be with me?"

"No."

"That's a lie. That's not what you said in bed."

Christopher sighed, "Allison, I'm leaving the company."

"What?" Allison staggered back.

"There would be too many memories here. I've made arrangements to join the Royal Ballet."

"Then I'll go with you. We can both—"

"No." Christopher took Temple by the hand. "Arrangements have been made for Temple to join with me."

Allison and Temple looked at each other, and in that moment Allison realized she would never have Christopher. The battle was over. Her love vanished. Her friendship with Temple gone. Temple, the hick from the backwater, who just waited in the wings had won the grand prize. Allison retreated towards the door, then seized by a random thought, suddenly turned.

"I'm still in your ballet, right?"

"No. I am withdrawing *Preludes* from the company. It will never be
anced again." Christopher lowered his eyes, "Good-bye, Allison."
hristopher closed the door.

Outside in the hallway Allison promised a group of fans she would
gn programs after she had changed. In her dressing room Allison
ooked in the mirror, hoping the mirror would give her some reassur-
nce. She looked into her eyes and realized all was not a total loss.
emple had a certain victory, but it was a temporal victory. Temple was
teadfast and true, but in the end how far would that take her? The
oyal would not further her career. Allison could not think of one
merican dancer who had ever been promoted to a principal rank at
he Royal. And in time she would quit dancing to have Christopher's
aby. Allison, on the other hand, had perhaps soiled her soul, but she
ill have gained immortality. Her soul might sink to hell, but her name
ould ascend to the hallowed plateau of prima ballerina, she would be
nore than special, she would be a legend.

Roberto, strode in her dressing room, and stared at her as he came in.
So what happened?"

"Oh, nothing. I just told Christopher I didn't want to be in his ballet,
hat it would be better for my career if I concentrated on the classics." She
npinned her Tiara, and placed it carefully in front of her on the table.

"That's not what Christopher told me."

"Really Roberto, don't be so naïve. What else would he say? He's
bviously disappointed I left his little ballet. Well, anyway, it looks like
ou get to be my date for the reception tonight."

"Sorry, chiciquita, I may not be too choosy, but I don't stoop that low."

Allison turned quickly, "What do you mean by that remark?"

"You think you fooled everybody, even me? I might not have been
razy about Zhandra, but I like you even less. I don't know how, but
omehow I think you planned the whole thing."

Allison flushed white and stood abruptly, "How dare you! Get out of my dressing room!"

"Gladly." Roberto paused at the door. "You may be a star, but you will be a very lonely one." He walked out of the room.

"Well, screw him!" Allison muttered, "He's just a little corps de ballet boy. I'll have him fired at the next opportunity."

As the door closed Allison heard someone in the crowd ask "Is she coming out soon?"

Let the fans wait. There was no reason to hurry, and strangely nothing more to think about. Allison felt as vacant, abandoned and dark as a stage an hour after the curtain went down.

On the way to the limousine, Allison was swarmed by autograph seekers, mostly young girls. She dutifully signed a few programs; the fans respectfully cleared a path.

In the limousine Allison looked out the window as she passed the brightly-lit fountain of Lincoln Center; she remembered looking at the fountain, the night she vowed to become a star. And now she had made it—adoring fans, limousines, and flowers at her feet. She had everything…including those visions of Zhandra that haunted her, but that problem would have to wait for another day.

Alison picked a white rose from a bouquet she held in her arms; she brushed the rose lightly across her face and breathed in the seductive scent. Well, there was one thing missing –- but surely that would come in time.

She remembered hearing recent rumors that Vladamir Rudowski was coming over from the Bolshoi to guest with the company next year. He was one of the most handsome men in the world, often pictured on the cover of international glamour magazines. According to the gossip magazines he was involved with Yvonne Hart, a Hollywood movie starlet. "Good. That means he's straight," Alison thought. Allison glanced up at the marquee lights along Broadway. "The actress can be taken care of."

The sleek black limousine slithered through traffic as if there were no
ed lights to pause Allison from her destination. A slight drizzle began
o fall and raindrops glistened on the black windows like tiny dia-
nonds. A dense fog was stealing in from the Hudson River, mixing with
team rising from beneath the streets. Allison felt a chill and shut the
vindows and closed her eyes. The limousine glided through the heavy
nist like a celestial chariot floating over the starry lights of Broadway.